It was a town that nobody in Siskiyou County had ever heard of or would've cared about if they had. Except for Donnally.

The image of Livingston, California, stuck in Donnally's mind like a live moth on flypaper. In the late eighties, as a young officer working the SFPD fugitive detail, he'd driven down the heart of the state through fog yellowed by agricultural burning, breathing in smoke and diesel fumes, hunting for a wino who'd stabbed a postal worker in a skid-row hotel lobby. In morbid irony, the killer who'd been drunk on the fortified wine marketed to alcoholics that had made the Gallo brothers rich, had sought refuge at the Gallo labor camp.

For years, Donnally's memory of Livingston had been anchored in a single image: walking into the shed, finding the killer hanging from a rafter, his neck snapped, his dead body still rocking above an overturned crate. And by a single thought: that the last sounds the man had heard were Donnally's footsteps on the wooden porch and the squeak of the turning doorknob.

Now that memory had broken free and all Donnally saw when he imagined that place was a little girl molested by her father . . . a young Mauricio Quintero . . . and a gunshot.

Turn the page for praise for the previous novels of STEVEN GORE.

FINAL TARGET

"An action-packed debut thriller with a unique plot and vivid characters that gives readers a fascinating look into the world of international industrial espionage. I'm looking forward to [Gore's] next."

Phillip Margolin,
New York Times bestselling author of *Supreme Justice*

"Steven Gore bursts onto the international thriller scene with a captivating debut. . . . Lightning paced, deftly plotted, and compulsively readable. . . . We will be hearing much more from Steven Gore."

Sheldon Siegel,
New York Times bestselling author of *Judgment Day*

"With his command of storytelling and insider's knowledge, Gore can go up against Nelson DeMille and Daniel Silva and come out a contender."

Library Journal

"A smart, riveting, knock-your-socks-off debut thriller—James Bond for grownups."

Cornelia Read, author of *The Crazy School*

ABSOLUTE RISK

"*Absolute Risk* continues Gore's winning ways. . . .
A truly thrilling thriller."
San Jose Mercury News

"Masterful. . . . Sharp, smart writing and
convincing economic detail put this in the
front rank of genre fiction."
Publishers Weekly (*Starred Review*)

"Steven Gore, himself an international private
investigator before he turned to writing,
brings a credibility to his high-octaned action."
Washington Post (online)

"Gore stuffs a lot into his plot . . . but he
manages it well, with a winning protagonist
and a plausible premise."
Booklist

"Gore has effectively introduced the reader
to the world of the private investigator. . . .
[He] has crafted a solid thriller."
Salt Lake City Deseret News

"A brisk pace and an intriguing plot make
the pages turn themselves."
Richard North Patterson,
New York Times bestselling author of *Silent Witness*

By Steven Gore

ACT OF DECEIT
ABSOLUTE RISK
FINAL TARGET

ACT OF
DECEIT

A HARLAN DONNALLY NOVEL

STEVEN
GORE

HARPER

An Imprint of HarperCollinsPublishers

HARPER

An Imprint of HarperCollins*Publishers*
10 East 53rd Street
New York, New York 10022-5299

Copyright © 2011 by Steven Gore
ISBN 978-0-06-202506-7

First Harper premium printing: September 2011

HarperCollins® and Harper® are registered trademarks of HarperCollins Publishers.

Printed in the United States of America

Visit Harper paperbacks on the World Wide Web at
www.harpercollins.com

10 9 8 7 6 5 4 3 2 1

For Seth Norman, breaker of currents

CHAPTER 1 ═══════════

Harlan Donnally gazed down at the weathered Hispanic face framed by the white pillowcase, then reached out and gripped the little man's shoulder. Withered skin and fragile bone met his hand, a body thinned first by the creeping starvation of failed chemotherapy and now by the pneumonia that would kill him.

This wasn't the first time that Donnally had found himself standing at the precipice of death. Not only had he watched others die, but a decade earlier he'd looked up from a San Francisco sidewalk at paramedics fighting his descent into the void that would soon claim Mauricio Aguilera.

Despite the name on the signs he'd followed through the Northern California hospital, in Donnally's mind it wasn't really a hospice, a way station, for the man lying in the bed was neither a stranger in Mount Shasta nor passing through on a pilgrimage.

In truth, it was a dying room, a place of endings, not of passages, and of final conversations for those with the courage to have them.

Donnally had seen enough of death to know that for most visitors the rooms along the hallway were nothing more than temples of silent pretense, their fluorescent lights falling on pairs of cowboy boots shifting on linoleum, on wordless men in church shirts and pressed Levi's, on fidgeting hands of scrubbed children, and on women fretting over untucked sheets and unfluffed pillows.

But only one set of boots occupied the sand-colored floor of Mauricio's room.

"You got better things to do," Mauricio said in a whisper, looking up at Donnally, his thinning black hair matted against his head, his face lined like a parched desert lake. He coughed and wiped his mouth. "Than watch a man die."

Donnally pulled over a chair. He clenched his jaw as he sat down, anticipating the bite in his hip joint, trying not to let his face show the pain. It was a move he'd practiced for months during his rehab, hoping to deceive the San Francisco Police Department doctors who'd been determined to retire him out on disability.

But the move hadn't worked then, and didn't work now.

Mauricio glanced toward Donnally's hip. "Why don't you just get a new one?" He licked his lips and swallowed hard. "I heard the nurse talking about her father . . . titanium." He struggled to smile. "Like a golf club. He can square dance again . . ." He raised his eyebrows. "And everything."

Donnally shrugged. "I'm used to it."

Mauricio stared up at the ceiling fixture set into the sound-muting tiles, and then said, "You've got to let go of the past, Harlan."

Donnally knew Mauricio wasn't talking only

about the Mission District shootout that had ended his career ten years earlier, for there always had been a duality in their conversations, one that sometimes left Donnally stranded in the shadowed gap between Mauricio's words and his thoughts.

"Give me a good reason," Donnally said.

"I'll tell you what I figured out lying here all these weeks. If you're going to be dead to the present, you might as well not be alive at all."

Donnally slipped his .32 semiautomatic from the pocket of his jeans and extended it butt-first toward Mauricio.

"You want to shoot me and get it over with?" Donnally asked.

Mauricio waved it off. "Been there. Done that."

Donnally lowered the gun and squinted at Mauricio, trying to detect a killer behind the mask of the gentle man who fed stray dogs, freed kitchen spiders into his backyard, and gave shelter to the homeless passing through town.

"You what?" Donnally asked.

In a decade of running their businesses side by side, Donnally figured he'd heard all of Mauricio's stories. Knew each step in his migration from Guadalajara to Tijuana, to the pima cotton fields in Southern Arizona, to the California Central Valley, and then to Sacramento. Attending adult school at night, and then community college, working toward the American Dream. And finally moving north to Mount Shasta after he'd saved enough money to open his own business: an unnamed fix-it shop and junkyard next to Donnally's Lone Mountain Café.

Mauricio blinked, but didn't respond. Donnally

figured he was trying to decide what version of his past to tell, for he'd never told the same tale twice, or at least the same one twice in the same way.

Perched at Donnally's counter before daybreak, sipping black coffee, looking out through scratched eyeglasses, he'd talk about when he first met César Chávez outside the Gallo vineyard in Modesto—

Or was it during the pesticide protest in Delano?

Or maybe at the grape boycott march to the capitol?

For the first few months after Donnally moved up from San Francisco and bought the café, he'd look over at Mauricio and wonder what he was hiding. Back then, when Donnally was still steered by a detective's habit of mind, he plumbed for the big truth beneath the little lies. In the end, he came to view Mauricio less as fact than fiction, as a poet of his own life, sometimes just following his words to their own destination, with truth somehow nestled in the sounds and rhythms.

Listening to Mauricio day after day, watching him nurse his coffee, Donnally often wondered whether there was any real difference between Mauricio's poetic recreations of his past and his own father's evasions and self-deceptions—except for the rage it generated in him.

Donnally slipped the gun back into his pocket.

"What do you mean?" Donnally asked. "Been there, done that. You shot somebody?"

Mauricio still didn't answer. He just stared vacant-eyed at the ceiling as though his mind had moved on to something else.

Donnally settled back in his chair. There was no

reason to press the issue. Mauricio's kind of poetry couldn't be created on demand. And Mauricio knew better than Donnally how much time he had left to compose it.

"A priest came by last night," Mauricio finally said, his voice stronger. "A young guy. Skinny as a *calaveras*, a skeleton, and pale as fog." He smiled, then glanced toward the hallway. "Everybody around here thinks all Mexicans are Catholics waiting for the magical words to escort them to the afterlife." He laid his hand on his chest. "But the truth is that campesinos like me are Indian first and Mexican second, and the Day of the Dead is the only sacrament we need."

"You talk to him anyway?"

Mauricio shook his head. "I pretended I was asleep. He said some stuff in Latin. I think it made him feel better."

Donnally peered at Mauricio. "What about you?"

"I didn't get the sense he was doing it for me. It was more like he was getting extra credit on a take-home assignment."

That was the one thing he and Mauricio agreed on, but for different reasons. For Mauricio, religion was a straitjacket. For Donnally, it was an unknowable ocean.

"He the only one who's dropped in?" Donnally asked.

"The third. I feel like one of those guys at the county fair who sits on the little seat above the water and people throw softballs at the target." He smiled again. "Whichever child of the cloth dunks me wins a teddy bear and a place in heaven."

The window rattled as a logging truck passing by compression-braked its descent toward the center of town.

Mauricio waited for the clattering to fade, then said, "A Mormon lady dropped in, too. She told me that she'd be coming back to baptize me after I'm dead."

Donnally's eyebrows furrowed and he drew back. "Isn't that a little late? I thought the whole idea was that you needed the right state of mind to go to heaven. Seems to me that if you're dead you can't have any state of mind at all."

Mauricio looked out of the window at the snow-dusted pines surrounding the one-story hospital, then back at Donnally.

"I'm not so sure about that," Mauricio said. "What do you think? We go somewhere after we die?"

"Sure. In the ground or up in smoke."

"I mean after that."

Donnally leaned in toward Mauricio. "You worried about something?"

Mauricio shrugged. "Lying here I came up with an idea about why people need to believe in an afterlife. I don't know if it makes sense or if it's just the drugs talking. I've been thinking that only bad people need to believe in it. Good people got nothing to be afraid of and nothing to make up for, so oblivion is fine with them."

Mauricio picked up a plastic cup from the over-bed table and took a sip of water. Donnally pulled a tissue from a Kleenex box and wiped away a drop that slipped by Mauricio's mouth.

"There's something in there for you to read," Mauricio said, setting down the cup and tilting his head toward the side table.

Donnally reached toward the drawer, but Mauricio raised his palm, stopping him. "Afterwards. Everything is just like we talked about." He then looked toward the open door. "Except one thing."

CHAPTER 2 ═══════════

Harlan Donnally stared down at the headstone. It read "Mauricio Quintero," not "Mauricio Aguilera."

It bore no epitaph, nor age, nor dates of birth or death, for as Donnally now understood, any further inscription would've just compounded the lie that had been Mauricio's existence.

Right at the end, just before he died, Mauricio had said his true name was all he wanted on the marker. The only part of the Bible he'd acknowledged he believed in was the phrase "for dust thou art, and unto dust shalt thou return," and he didn't think there was any reason for people to come honor the fiction he'd created out of his life.

Donnally stood on the snow-covered ground next to the gravesite as the backhoe pushed the mound of dark soil over the coffin. In those few minutes, the mist slid in, bleaching out the brown and green of the pines and turning the red dirt gray. Only the granite headstones standing around him like lost souls seemed impervious to the whims of light and fog.

After watching the rusty John Deere grind its way back to the equipment barn, Donnally took a final look at the etched name, then walked over to his truck and climbed in. Lying on the passenger seat was Mauricio's last will, and the confession he had denied the priest.

January 23

Dear Harlan:

My real name is Mauricio Quintero.

On March 14, 1965, I shot and killed my father.

I came home from school and caught him molesting my sister in a migrant shack where we lived outside of Livingston in the Central Valley. I was fifteen. She was five.

I don't think she understood what he was doing to her. Maybe she just thought it was a weird game. Eventually she would've figured it out, because he wasn't going to stop.

It was up to me to put an end to it, and that meant putting an end to him. There was no one else because my mother had died giving birth to her.

The news article about my crime is in my safety deposit box at the Valley Bank. It's only a couple of lines. Mexicans didn't count for much back then.

My sister's name is Anna. I don't know what her last name is now.

I didn't know what to do, so I took her up to Berkeley one night and left her on the doorstep of New Sky, one of the communes they had there back then. (The address is in the box, too.) I hoped they'd do the right thing, but not call the police.

I went back there in 1974 and waited around the high school for a couple of days until I saw her walking toward the bus stop with some girls. I didn't try to talk to her and I never went back. She didn't need the burden of being the sister of a boy who killed his father. It would've cast a shadow over her whole life. It's one of those crimes that's like a genetic disease, only one that kills the spirit.

And I didn't want to lie to her. I thought that would've been even worse.

But lying here the last few weeks made me think differently. I figured out that everybody needs to be from somewhere, otherwise you're just kind of floating. Even though you hate where you come from, Harlan, at least you know where that is.

I realize now that I should've started thinking about death a lot sooner, but I guess I did too much pretending all my life. You're different. You stopped pretending about things when your brother got killed in the war. I hope you didn't stop forgiving back then, too, because I need some forgiveness now.

I didn't tell you before because you'd have turned me in. You wouldn't have wanted to, but you would've because there isn't a statute of limitations for what I did. I know that there are just certain things we have to do in order to live with ourselves. I've got mine and you've got yours. And one of yours would've sent me to prison.

I'd like you to find her. Use whatever money you need from selling my place and give the rest to her.

I'm sorry to dump this on you, but I just ran out of time and of life. Or maybe I was a coward all the way along.

If you want, show her this letter so she'll know I was thinking about her at the end.

And take care of Ruby, she's been a good dog to a bad man.

Mauricio

Donnally stared through his windshield at the snow now swirling around the cemetery. All these years he'd thought that Mauricio made up his life because the truth didn't mean anything to him. It was the opposite. The truth meant everything, but he'd just never known what to do with it.

And Donnally didn't know what to do with it either.

Find Anna and do what?

He folded the letter and slipped it into the inside pocket of his parka, then switched on his wipers against the obliterating flurry, the flakes growing larger and wetter and collecting on the mound of cold clay and scraps of dead grass and weeds now piled on top of Mauricio.

Find her and do what?

Donnally found himself gripping the steering wheel. His body telling him that anger was finally emerging from the grief.

Mauricio was right about himself and there was no maybe about it: He was a coward.

You don't leave it to other people to clean up after you. You're supposed to learn that as a child, when your father trips over one of your toys, or when you spill the milk, or when you've got to break up with a girl.

But Mauricio had just shrugged it off.

It was one thing to be the executor of someone's estate. That Donnally had been willing to do. It was another to be the executor of his life.

Anyway, Donnally thought, executors were supposed to follow instructions, not make them up as they went along.

Donnally lowered his hands and turned off the wipers. He poured himself a half cup of coffee from a thermos. Steam rose in the dead air of the cab, and the headstone disappeared behind the fogging windshield.

That slab of granite might as well not be there at all, Donnally said to himself. Might as well be a pauper's grave, or a John Doe's, for nobody in Mount Shasta knew who Mauricio really was.

Mauricio Aguilera had simply been a prism that had refracted away the truth of the who, and the what, and the where of Mauricio Quintero.

And the foundation on which his life had been built lay not in Mount Shasta, but in a Central Valley town that nobody in Siskiyou County had ever heard of or would've cared about if they had, except for Donnally.

The image of Livingston stuck in Donnally's mind like a live moth on flypaper. In the late eighties, as a young officer working the SFPD fugitive detail, he'd driven down the heart of the state through fog yellowed by agricultural burning, breathing in smoke and diesel fumes, hunting for a wino who'd stabbed a postal worker in a skid-row hotel lobby. In morbid irony, the killer, who'd been drunk on the fortified wine marketed to alcoholics that had made the Gallo brothers rich, had sought refuge at the Gallo labor camp.

For years Donnally's memory of Livingston had been anchored in a single image: walking into the shed, finding the killer hanging from a rafter, his neck snapped, his dead body still rocking above an overturned crate. And by a single thought: that the last sounds the man had heard were Donnally's footsteps on the wooden porch and the squeak of the turning doorknob.

Now that memory had broken free and all Donnally saw when he imagined that place was a little girl molested by her father . . . a young Mauricio . . . and a gunshot.

A snowdrift climbed up Donnally's windshield. He took a sip of coffee and wondered what it was about death that got your mind interlocking things, like putting a jigsaw puzzle together without having the picture to tell you what you're aiming for, and not even knowing whether all the pieces came from the same box.

What's the picture supposed to be? he asked himself as he rolled down his window and drained the cup on the ground. *And what am I supposed to say when I find her?*

Hi, Anna, my name is Harlan. Your father molested you as a kid. I thought you should know.

Hi, Anna, my name is Harlan. You used to have a brother. I thought you should know.

Hi, Anna, my name is Harlan. Your brother murdered your father. I thought you should know.

Donnally turned the ignition and flicked on the wipers. He stretched his arm along the top of the bench seat and looked through the rear cab window as he backed up between the pines and the rows of headstones until he reached the dirt road that bisected the cemetery. He then shifted into drive and headed toward Main Street.

Screw him. I ain't nobody's postman.

CHAPTER 3

Son of a bitch.

The words rushed through Donnally's mind even before he was awake, as though he was providing a voice-over for his own dream.

He saw himself in the mid–1970s standing across the street from Berkeley High School. He was wearing a serape and a soiled cap and holding a short-handled hoe. Hippies were flashing him two-fingered peace signs or raising clenched fists in claimed solidarity with farmworkers striking in the Central Valley.

Cops kept ordering him to move along, but he circled back hour after hour, day after day, until he spotted a Mexican girl walking toward the bus stop.

Son of a bitch.

Even after Donnally rolled over and looked at the glowing digital clock, the image stayed with him. He knew he was awake. No doubt about that. It was just that he was still dreaming.

Now the girl turned toward him and headed down the sidewalk, her hand jittering against the chain-link fence enclosing the basketball courts.

She stopped two feet away and said, "Everybody's got to be from somewhere, Harlan. Where am I from?"

A Buddhist monk in an orange robe walked up to them. Not a Hare Krishna chanting bullshit and beating drums, but a real one. Bald as citrus and skinny as a carrot.

They turned toward him.

Then a clash of cymbals.

Donnally reached for the telephone before he understood it was ringing.

"We're out of half-and-half," his waitress said, not giving him a chance to say hello.

He sat up on the edge of the bed. "Go get some from Mauricio's."

"I'm sure whatever he had is spoiled by now," she said. "Anyway, I don't have a key."

Donnally rubbed his temples to clear his mind.

"Yeah, that's right." *Mauricio's dead.* He looked again at the clock. Five A.M. The Food Mart wasn't open yet. "I've got some in the fridge. I'll bring it down."

He lowered the handset back into its cradle, wondering why he'd never before made the mistake of thinking someone was alive after they'd passed away.

Never once had he thought of picking up the phone and calling his grandmother after she died, even though he felt a connection to her that transcended her death. He'd heard about other people doing that, and other things, too. Looking for birthday cards after the birthdays had stopped. Worrying about whether their grandmother would fall and hurt herself. Wondering how white carnations would look on her dining table.

Except Donnally never forgot that his grandmother's table was out in his garage, disassembled and leaning against the wall, and her chairs were lined up by the café door for people to sit on while waiting for a table to open up.

It was only Mauricio who wouldn't go away.

He slipped on Levi's and a parka, retrieved a carton of half-and-half from the refrigerator, and drove it downtown. He parked behind the restaurant and entered through the back door because he wasn't in the mood to banter with the guys from the Caterpillar dealership, or from the Valley Bank, or from the feed store, or with the retired sheriff who planted himself at the counter each morning as if the red Naugahyde stool on which he sat was his throne.

Donnally knew that Mauricio was dead for them; it was only his possessions that were still alive. He'd already heard people talking about how Mauricio's house could be used as a real estate office and how his front yard would be perfect for displaying tractors or snowmobiles. Just about everybody in town had been driving by and wondering what was going to happen with the Aguilera place, and many were conniving about how they could get it cheap.

Donnally glanced toward the dining room and spotted ex-sheriff Wade Pipkins's waves of white hair mounding up beyond the pass-through counter from the kitchen. He suspected that Pipkins was going to miss Mauricio more than anyone else. Not miss Mauricio the person, just the idea of him. Miss the opportunity to opine about what was wrong with U.S. immigration policy loud enough for

Mauricio to hear. Miss giving Mauricio the stare he otherwise reserved for homeless people and suspects and Hispanic day laborers.

For Pipkins, all Hispanics were Mexicans. Even the Guatemalans, and Salvadorans, and Peruvians. He called them Pancho or Paco or Pedro. And when he looked at them, all he wanted to see was their hats off and their gazes lowered, especially when he was hiring them to clear brush on the dozens of properties he owned in the county.

The popping of bacon grease on the grill brought Donnally back to the present and to the cold half-and-half in his hand.

"Thanks, boss." Will, Donnally's cook, reached out a tattooed arm to take the carton. "The funeral go okay?"

Donnally shrugged. "What could go wrong?"

"I don't know." Will smiled, then pointed through the window toward the abandoned cars and rusting washing machines in Mauricio's side yard. "He never seemed to get around to finishing anything he started."

Will's smiled faded and he lowered his voice, as if not wanting to be overheard by Pipkins.

"What's this I hear about the name on the stone? Singleton came by. He said the name was Quintero or Quintana or something."

That was another reason not to bother with a headstone, Donnally thought. There would be less to explain.

Donnally responded with the lie he'd worked out as he'd driven back from the cemetery the day before.

"Mauricio always used his grandfather's last name out of respect," Donnally said, "on his mother's side."

"That the kind of thing Mexicans do?"

"Yeah," Donnally said, "lots of them."

Donnally looked around the kitchen, then glanced at his waitress standing behind the counter.

"Can you two handle things for a couple of days?" Donnally asked.

"Sure, boss. I'll even keep Ruby at my place if you want. Where're you going?"

Donnally thought for a moment. He wasn't sure of the where, or even the why. He finally settled on an answer that didn't even satisfy himself.

"Let's just say I'm going to deliver a letter."

CHAPTER 4

"Get off my property," a deep male voice yelled at Donnally through the closed front door of the West Berkeley cottage.

The smell of rot and mold infused Donnally's nostrils, seeping from the yard behind him that had long since gone native with generations of intermingled grasses and weeds: the green, the yellow, and the brown composted by rain and heat and trampling shoes. Even the house's blue paint seemed to have surrendered, fading into the gray of the bleached wood siding underneath.

"Subpoena me or leave me alone," the man said. "My lawyer told you assholes that already."

A gap appeared between the frame of the window on the right side of the door and the blue wool blanket that served as its curtain. Brown fingers gripped the material, the fingernails ragged and yellowed, and two eyes looked out from the shadowed interior.

Donnally took off his Giants cap as if disarming himself, then scratched his head and said, "I'm not here about anything that involves subpoenas."

A wry smile exposed tar-stained teeth. "But you're a cop, right?"

There was no point in pretending. Once you've got a cop's eyes, a cop's walk, and a cop's face, no one is going to mistake you for anything else.

"Once," Donnally said, "but not anymore." He then made a show of glancing back toward the sidewalk, where a handful of crack and marijuana dealers were waiting for the mid-afternoon rush, then side to side at the apartment buildings flanking the house and framing the yard like the walls of a box canyon. "You think a cop would've come here alone?"

The gap widened and the rest of the face appeared. Mid-sixties. Long, thin. The scleras of his jaundiced eyes were just a shade lighter than his skin, and there was too much of that, as though he'd suffered a sudden weight loss. The man pulled the curtain further aside, then looked to Donnally's left, checking for a second person.

Donnally spotted the man's right elbow extending from behind his body, but his hand was concealed. He couldn't stop his mind from transforming itself into a booking sheet. 12021 of the California Penal Code. Felon in possession of a firearm.

"What do you want?" the man said.

"I'm trying to get a hold of Willie Goldstine, the guy they used to call Sonny."

The man's face didn't change expression.

"How come?"

"About the New Sky Commune."

"Son of a bitch. Another asshole writing a book."

"That's not it," Donnally said. "I'm trying to locate a girl, I mean a woman. Her name is Anna. She was dropped off there by her brother in 1965."

The man's eyes flickered. Donnally couldn't tell whether it was recognition or calculation.

"What's it to you?"

"Somebody in her family left her some money."

"So you're a PI."

"Just playing the part to help a buddy."

"Maybe he should've come himself."

"He would've, but he's dead."

Donnally watched the man's smile fade.

"Then he should've come sooner."

"Look, man, I need to know if you're Sonny. If not, I've got to move along."

"How do I know you're not really here about Tsukamata?"

Donnally repeated the name, then said, "I don't even know what that is."

"It's not a that. It's a him. The cop who got killed." The man laughed. "You stupid or do you think I'm stupid?"

"Neither. I'm just not from around here." Donnally pointed north. "I'm from Shasta. I didn't even know a cop got killed. Haven't even read the paper since I arrived and didn't hear it on the radio driving down. When did it happen?"

"Nineteen seventy-five."

Donnally threw up his hands. "How am I supposed to know what happened over thirty years ago?"

"It's been on the news a lot lately."

"And it had something to do with you?"

The man shook his head.

"You lost me. Then why are we—" Donnally then understood the why. "I get it. Somebody's now saying you did it and you're thinking I'm somehow trying to box you in?"

The man flashed a smile. "If I was Sonny."

Donnally didn't smile back. "Yeah. If you were Sonny."

More of the picture came into focus.

"Let me guess," Donnally said. "People have been trying to break your alibi. And you're thinking I'm one of them . . . if you were Sonny."

"About every five years some retired cop gets a bug up his ass, wanting to be some kind of cold case hero. Get his face on *60 Minutes* or a cable TV crime show, then make a buck selling his memoirs."

Donnally folded his arms across his chest and exhaled. "How do we get around this roadblock? I really want to find this gal."

Sonny let go of the blanket. A moment later the door opened.

"Wait here," Sonny said. "I'm gonna call my lawyer. He's in the city."

"Who's that?"

Sonny narrowed his eyebrows. "I thought you wasn't from around here."

"I was a cop in San Francisco."

"Mark Hamlin."

Donnally felt his stomach tighten. Hamlin hated cops, loved money, and made every case into a political cause. Ten years earlier, he was on TV almost daily. Rimless glasses. Black hair slicked back like snake scales. Just an hour after the shootout that ended Donnally's career, Hamlin was on television claiming that the cops—Donnally and his police department conspirators—had instigated it in order to start a Mexican gang war.

"You don't need to call—"

But Sonny was already dialing.

Sonny glanced back and forth between a business card on the coffee table and the number pad on his cell phone, then waited as the call connected.

"It's Sonny . . . doin' okay . . . Look, a guy's here about the old days . . . no . . . New Sky . . . I don't know."

Sonny looked back toward the door. "What's your name?"

Donnally told him and Sonny repeated it. He listened for a moment, then handed over the phone. "He wants to talk to you."

Donnally put it to his ear. "This is Donnally."

"How you doing, man?"

Donnally recognized the nasal whine, but not the tone. Hamlin sounded like he meant it.

"I felt really bad about you getting shot," Hamlin said. "What do you want with my client?"

Donnally said as much as he'd already told Sonny.

"How'd you end up knocking on his door?" Hamlin asked.

"I found a bunch of names in an old book about Berkeley communes and he's the first one I got a lead on who wasn't dead, drugged, or deranged."

The old Hamlin voice returned. Half question. Half accusation. "Is this for real?"

"Yeah. But I don't know how to prove it." Donnally looked over at Sonny. He could see the outline of a small revolver in his front pants pocket. "Wait. Maybe I can." He held his palm up toward

Sonny, telling him not to panic. "I checked over at the courthouse. Sonny's got two felony convictions, and he's got a gun on him. The feds could lock him up in Leavenworth for twenty years."

Sonny glared at Donnally, clenching his fists.

Donnally kept his hand up. "But I'm not interested in hurting the guy."

"Shit," Hamlin said. "I told him to get rid of that thing. One of these days his door's gonna get kicked in. They won't even need to convict him on the murder. At his age, twenty years on a federal gun beef would be a life sentence." Hamlin fell silent for a moment. "I've got an idea. How about you work for me?"

"I thought you hated—"

"Just so you can't use anything he tells you to hurt him. Attorney-client privilege. You had a reputation as a straight shooter. I'll trust you in this."

"But if he killed a cop—"

"He didn't kill Tsukamata. Back then Sonny was so doped up he'd fall over trying to pull on his pants. He could barely hit a vein with a needle much less shoot a cop in the head from two hundred yards away. Give him the phone."

Donnally extended it toward Sonny, who reached back as though he expected handcuffs to emerge and snap around his wrist.

Sonny took the phone into the kitchen. He returned a couple of minutes later, then walked over to the dining table and removed a dollar from his wallet. He was nodding as he crossed the room and handed it to Donnally. "I gave him the money . . . yeah, I'll talk to you later."

Sonny disconnected and looked up at Donnally, who was still standing in the doorway.

"She's dead. Murdered in nineteen eighty-six."

"What?" Donnally felt himself flush. "Then why'd we do this stupid dance? Why didn't you just tell me that in the first place?"

Sonny backed up a step.

"Take it easy, man. Not because of her. Because of her mother. I mean the woman who got her, Trudy Keenan. She's alive. And the police have been trying to find her since the seventies because she . . . uh . . . did some stuff."

Sonny again looked past Donnally toward the street, then tilted his head toward his living room.

"You're not gonna like what you're gonna hear, especially if whoever sent you was a pal, but maybe you better step inside and hear it anyway."

CHAPTER 5

Donnally glared down at the Alameda County prosecutor.

"Are you telling me that the crook who murdered Anna Keenan hasn't been examined for competency in twenty years?"

"That nut was never going be competent to stand trial. Charles Brown was crazy *and* retarded." Chief Assistant District Attorney Thomas Blaine tossed his pen on his desk and grinned. "Sorry, mentally ill and developmentally disabled." His grin faded and his face hardened. "It was a waste of taxpayers' money to keep bringing him back to court."

Donnally hadn't bothered to sit down. He'd marched from the Criminal Clerk's Office into the elevator, then ridden up the nine floors to the Office of the District Attorney. Blaine, who'd been the prosecutor in the case, had agreed to see him because twelve years earlier they'd served together on a Bay Area gang task force.

Looking at Blaine now, from a distance of years and experience, Donnally saw that the prosecutor's ambition had so melded with his duty that his aging frat-boy face had come to display the same cunning and self-righteous rectitude as the preachers who ran the annual tent revivals in Mount Shasta.

"So he got away with it?" Donnally said.

Blaine shrugged. "If you want to put it that way."

"Can you think of another way?"

"I don't make the laws," Blaine said. "Anyway, things have to come to an end someday."

An image of Mauricio's now maggot-ridden body flashed in Donnally's mind. He shook it off.

"Where's Brown now?" Donnally asked.

Blaine shrugged again. "How should I know? Napa State Hospital. Atascadero. Some loony bin where—"

"Where he can prey on women just a little bit crazier than he is because nobody ever bothered to bring him back to court and send him to prison where he belongs?"

The prosecutor's face went sunburn red. "I mean . . . I assume . . . Look. We've had thousands of murders in this county since then. We can't track every—"

Donnally's gesture of disgust cut the prosecutor short.

Blaine reached for the telephone resting on the desk that had been used by Earl Warren during the 1920s when he was the Alameda County district attorney. Donnally remembered once looking at it during their task force years and imagining a Senator Lloyd Bentsen–type figure telling Blaine, a Dan Quayle stand-in: "I knew Earl Warren. Earl Warren was a friend of mine. Blaine, you're no Earl Warren."

"Send an inspector up here," Blaine said into the telephone. "I don't care which one. Anybody who's sitting there with his thumb up his ass and nothing to do."

Donnally cringed. Blaine hadn't changed, and he was sure that the rest of the pretty-boy prosecutors in the office hadn't either. They all still thought that jousting with defense lawyers in court was fighting the real war and that cops and DA inspectors were just stable boys.

Blaine set the phone into its cradle. "We'll know where he's at in a couple of hours." He then leaned back in his chair, a satisfied look of command on his face. "Why the interest in a decades-old murder?"

"I'm not sure that has anything to do with why you let this guy get away with it."

"Don't go Lone Ranger on me, Harlan. Everybody's got an angle. Even you."

Blaine walked Donnally to the kitchen after the inspector came by to receive his assignment.

"I guess I shouldn't have sounded so cavalier about it," Blaine said, pouring Donnally a cup of coffee. "I sure as hell didn't feel that way at the time. That's why I still remember Brown after all these years."

Blaine paused with the pot still in his hand. His eyes went blank for a moment as though he was trying to stare into the past.

"Berkeley was a swamp back then," Blaine finally said. "One lunatic after another coming through the court system. We didn't know what to do with them. There wasn't enough room in the locked wards, so unless the defendant started beating on the bailiff right in the courtroom, we just kicked them back out on the street. The whole city was littered with them. One more or less didn't seem to make a difference, it was like just another drop of water in the bay."

Blaine pointed down the hallway toward his office, then led the way.

"What about Brown?" Donnally asked, dropping into one of the two wooden chairs facing Blaine's desk.

"He came through half a dozen times during the first year I was assigned to Berkeley. They kept sending him over to the county hospital on forty-eight-hour psych holds. But they never kept him. The diagnosis was always the same: crazy and retarded. We didn't bother sending him back after that. The judge just told him to go see his shrink at the city mental health clinic and to take his meds."

Blaine paused for a moment. "I mean, it wasn't like he was committing serious crimes. We may have charged him with burglaries a couple of times, but they were just aggravated trespassing. Breaking into businesses, usually corner markets, for a place to sleep and something to eat. County jail was no deterrent to loonies like him. And he'd get violent if he was locked up, like a caged animal. The Sheriff's Department couldn't protect him or protect other inmates from him, so the court kept putting him on probation. Then, when he stopped taking his meds and started acting out again, the cops up on Telegraph Avenue or at People's Park would tie him up and haul him to the county shrink in Oakland to get dosed. It would take him a couple of days to find his way back to Berkeley."

Donnally followed Blaine's eyes as he gazed out of his window toward Lake Merritt on the north side of the courthouse, grayed by winter fog, its surface ruffled by the gusting wind, the broad boulevard encircling it crowded with soundless traffic.

"Damn." Blaine sighed. "Anna Keenan was a sweetheart. Not one of those tie-died Berkeley do-gooders. She was something special. The kind of teacher every parent wants their kid to have." Blaine's eyes went blank for a moment. "And to die like that, looking up into the face of the maniac who killed her." He looked back at Donnally. "It was the first homicide I ever got called out on. I swaggered in like an old pro, then about cried when I saw who it was." He paused, reliving the moment. "You remember Eddie Washington?"

"Got killed executing a search warrant in nineteen-ninetysomething."

"Ninety-eight. He was in homicide back when Brown murdered Anna. Eddie's daughter was in her third grade class. He used to drop her by Anna's house on Saturday mornings for tutoring. She wouldn't take any money for it. Not a nickel. Once she let him change the oil in her car, but that's all she ever let him do." Blaine closed his eyes and rubbed his forehead. "You should've seen Washington's face when he looked at her body. Hurt and fury like I'd never seen on a man before or since."

"So he went on a mission."

Blaine looked back at Donnally and nodded. "Like a linebacker. And it only took him an hour to link the homicide to Brown. Anna had let him sleep in her shed so he wouldn't keep getting arrested. He'd been there a few months, off and on. He'd help her in the garden and in her greenhouse. Neighbors heard some kind of yelp or scream, then saw Brown escaping over her back fence. We found his fingerprints on the sill of the window where he climbed out and let himself down into the backyard. His hand size matched the bruises on her neck. We snagged him four days later hiding out in an encampment by the marina. He'd slipped into some hippie girl's tent and she shrieked like hell. A bunch of Dead Heads corralled him."

"Did he make a statement about killing Anna? I didn't see one in the court file."

"Unintelligible. He acted like he was caught by his parents after killing the family cat. And by the time the hospital got him on his meds, the public defender was representing him so we couldn't talk to him anymore."

The court file had told Donnally how it ended. "Then he was found incompetent to stand trial."

Blaine shrugged. "We fought like hell. We had an informant in the county jail telling us that Brown was faking and that he had a fantasy that Anna wanted him to come into her bedroom to have sex with her. He strangled her when she refused."

"That would've made it a capital case."

Blaine smirked. "Not in California and not in Alameda County. No way a jury here would sentence a lunatic to death. Anyway, there wasn't any forensic evidence of an attempted rape, no semen, no vaginal bruising."

"Maybe Brown just didn't get very far before she started resisting."

"That was our theory. If he'd gone to trial we probably could've gotten the attempted rape in through the informant, but that didn't happen. We lost the competency hearing. Brown came back three years later with reports that he was still incompetent so he got transferred into the civil commitment system—"

"And no one ever bothered to evaluate him again."

Blaine reddened again. "That's the way the system works."

"That's the way the system doesn't work."

Donnally set his coffee cup on the desk, then rose and walked to the window. He looked out over Oakland, from the hills to the bay, and north toward Berkeley.

"And how many are there out there?" Donnally said without turning around. "Commit a murder, get declared incompetent, get sent off to some institution and forgotten." He turned back toward Blaine. "What's your guess? How many?"

Blaine swallowed hard. "I . . . I don't have the slightest idea." He reached again for his telephone and punched in two numbers. "Is he in? . . . I need to see him." Blaine looked at Donnally. "You want to come with me to see the boss?"

Donnally shook his head. "Just call me when you find out where Brown is." He then turned and walked from the office.

As he rode the elevator down, Donnally was overcome with an amorphous rage that tried to focus on Brown, then on Blaine, and then on the court system itself. Instead it locked on a thought: if only—and painted crosshairs on Mauricio's face.

If only Mauricio hadn't taken Anna to Berkeley, if only he hadn't left her at New Sky, if only he'd gone back to get her . . . she'd still be alive.

The chain of causes and effects snapped tight.

If . . . only.

And Mauricio's "I had no choice" just wasn't good enough.

But as Donnally started down the steps of the courthouse, a wind whipped his face and ripped at the web of blame his mind had constructed.

Mauricio had been a fifteen-year-old kid who'd done the best he could, but had not only been too young to decide to take a life, but too young to take his own and his sister's lives into his hands. And that single act had dispossessed him of his family, tormented his heart, and deprived him of the good death he deserved.

Donnally stopped on the sidewalk and stared at the lake. He tried to imagine what Anna must have looked like as Mauricio walked her past their dead father's body and out the door and toward the highway heading north. He struggled to force his mind to compose a picture of a tiny girl with brown skin and round cheeks and black hair and dark eyes, but all that appeared was the mournful face of his own older brother, fair and angular and framed by his marine dress blue tunic and cover, who'd been killed in Vietnam when Donnally was eight years old.

And surging outward from that image came the

molten terror of his childhood, of loss and helpless-
ness in a world spun out of control.

An hour later, Donnally's cell phone rang as he
pulled into the driveway of his ex-fiancée's house in
San Francisco.

"I need your promise you won't go to the media
with this," Blaine said.

"With what?"

"I need to hear you say the words."

"Okay. No press."

"Sorry, man. Brown's out."

CHAPTER 6

The dull glaze of the owner's eyes didn't sharpen after Donnally spoke the name: Charles Brown.

Lumps of skin oozed from the sleeves of the flowered shift encasing her body. The smell of coffee and urine wafted past her from inside the East Oakland group home and swirled around the porch. Cigarette butts littered the concrete landing of the three-story converted house. Two vacant-eyed men with nicotine-stained fingers sat in white plastic chairs and stared at the street, oblivious to the tension building in the doorway.

Elsa Coady squinted toward the setting sun, then repeated: "Charles Brown . . . Charles Brown . . ."

"The Fresno Developmental Center sent him here six years ago."

Her difficulty in placing the name assured Donnally that the prosecutor, busy putting together a task force to identify and hunt down all the lost defendants, hadn't yet sent out a posse to round up Brown.

And that was fine with Donnally. He didn't want to give Blaine a chance to screw it up again.

She shrugged her shoulders. "He's not here. He walked away." She glanced at the two men as if they were living repositories of the history of the house. "About five years ago."

"Didn't you notify anyone?"

"Who's there to notify? If he's the one I'm thinking of, there wasn't nobody. He wasn't on no probation or parole."

"Didn't you know he still had a homicide case pending?"

Elsa's blotchy face darkened.

"This isn't a jail and I'm not a jailer." Her voice hardened as she spoke. "A roof over their heads, three meals, and their meds. That's all we do. People want to walk away, they can walk away."

The two sentences had a practiced feel, sounding to Donnally like she'd given that same answer many times before.

"You still have his file?"

"Sure. We have to keep that stuff. But I can't show it to you." A smirk emerged on her thin lips. "Confidentiality and all that."

Donnally folded his arms across his chest, then lowered his head and looked hard into her eyes.

"Let me tell you what my concern is," Donnally said. "In a couple of days, the press will be looking for someone to blame for Brown slipping away. It can be the court system, some weak-kneed judge, the county, the California mental health system, the Fresno Developmental Center, or it can be Elsa's Home for Men."

He made a show of inspecting the weathered wooden windows, the cracked and faded pink stucco, and the two men wearing grimy surplus overcoats that looked like they hadn't been washed since summer.

"Who do you think all these folks are going to gang up on? You're damn lucky I got here first."

Elsa bit her cheek for a moment, and then said, "I sure hope you know what you're doing."

CHAPTER 7

Donnally separated the damp pages and hung them on a clothesline in Janie Nguyen's unfinished basement. Some were moldy. Some were unreadable. Others were only readable against the light. It seemed to Donnally that the file, sent along with Charles Brown from the developmental center, had been stored in Elsa's often flooded garage for the purpose of letting it dissolve into a past that no one wanted to think about.

He called it Janie's basement even though he still owned the house and rented it to her for just enough money to cover the mortgage, taxes, and insurance. He came down every few months to make repairs, but otherwise treated the place as hers.

And not out of guilt. Or, at least, not out of guilt in an ordinary sense.

He and Janie were simply permanent features of each other's landscapes, like California place names weighted with history: Meeting of Two Springs. Creek of Sorrows. Canyon of Hunger. They both knew they wouldn't grow old without each other, but also not quite together.

The grinding of the garage door opener broke Donnally's concentration, and a minute later he heard her footfalls on the wooden stairway. He glanced up at her bare calves coming into view and imagined them already wrapped around him. A few more steps and her skirt came into view and he forced his mind to change the subject.

"You find him?" Janie asked, as she took the turn onto the concrete floor.

"He's in the wind."

Janie smiled. "More likely the bushes."

She held her nose when the odor of the moldy pages reached her.

"Jeez, those stink. Why don't you let some air in?"

She walked over to the workbench and pushed open the window set into the cripple wall between the foundation and the first floor of the two-story house. She turned back and pointed at the hanging sheets.

"What's that?"

"Charles Brown's file from the group home."

"You're not supposed to have those." Janie knew the rules. She was a psychiatrist at the VA hospital at Fort Miley, a half mile north. "You didn't steal it, did you?"

"The owner gave them to me."

She gave him an up-from-under look.

"It's true," Donnally said. "Turns out I was the least of many other evils."

A gusting Pacific wind that had skimmed the beach a few blocks away, now pushed in through the window and rocked the pages on the line.

Donnally glanced in the direction of the basement door. "You better close that or the house is going to get a dose."

Janie nodded, then headed toward the stairs. "Are you going to want to have dinner?" She looked back over her shoulder and winked. "Or just dessert?"

Donnally turned back to the file. The smile that Janie left him with died when he read through the fragments of Brown's diagnosis not obliterated by mold: bipolar . . . psychotic episodes . . . homicidal and sexual ideations.

He held the handwritten log up to the overhead fluorescent light. The chronology showed that Brown had been sent first to Atascadero State Hospital, then on to Napa five years later, when he was considered less dangerous. Ten years after that, the doctors got his mental illness under control and sent him to the Stockton Developmental Center, hoping that despite his mental limitations, he could be trained to control his violence. But he started assaulting female patients, so they moved him on to the more secure Fresno center.

Brown's violent outbursts lessened until he had two consecutive trouble-free years and the Fresno Superior Court released him to a local group home. He stayed there until he got caught fondling a sometimes delusional female resident. The local DA declined to prosecute, arguing that unless the staff could prove she didn't consent, there wasn't a crime. He recommended justice-by-bus-ticket and Brown was sent to Elsa's men-only home in East Oakland.

Donnally squinted at the faded handwriting on the original intake sheet from the late 1980s and made out the name of Brown's next of kin: Katrisha Brown, but the relationship field was blank.

And whoever she was—sister, mother, wife, aunt, or grandmother—over a decade working the San Francisco projects had taught Donnally that she wouldn't be pleased to find him knocking on her door.

CHAPTER 8 =========

"Retarded, my ass."

Katrisha Brown sneered as she gripped the paper coffee cup in one hand and an unfiltered Camel cigarette in the other.

"He's no more retarded than I am."

Katrisha and Donnally stood side-by-side in front of the blue metal railing facing Fisherman's Terminal marina along Salmon Bay, just east of Seattle's Puget Sound. Donnally had found something engaging in the athletic stride that had brought her toward him from the parking lot and in her alert eyes and the braids tied back from her mahogany skin.

Donnally turned away from watching the commercial fishing boats rocking in their slips and flashed Katrisha a playful grin.

She shrugged her shoulders. "So SF State ain't Harvard, but it's not Podunk Community College either."

"Is that where you met Charles?"

"Freshman year, 1981. We got married in '82." She took a long drag on her cigarette. "It was the lisp, wasn't it? That's what made them think he was retarded."

"What lisp?"

"He does this lisp thing. It's brilliant. He started using the gimmick after he got busted for groping a girl on a trolley car." She tapped the ash off her cigarette; it fragmented, then swirled in the wind. "You know San Francisco?"

Donnally nodded. "Used to live there."

"It was on the J-Church Metro Line, right along Market Street. That's where he did it. A couple of months after he dropped out of school. The cops arrested him, but cited him out and gave him a court date. By the time he showed up for his arraignment he almost had the lisp perfected."

"Are you telling me the whole thing is an act?"

"No, he's bonkers all right. He had a psychotic break when he was twenty-one, but that never kept him from working the system."

"What about violence?"

Katrisha glanced around, unzipped her windbreaker, then unbuttoned her blouse. She pulled down the top edge of her bra. Donnally could see a three-inch keloid scar across the top of her left breast.

"Why'd he do that?"

"Fuck if I know." She rebuttoned her blouse and zipped up her jacket. "I'm not sure he even realized he had a steak knife in his hand when he lost control. He was way out there that night. Way out. Usually he just punched the walls until his hands bled." She shuddered. "That night he started flailing."

"He get jail time?"

"He lisped his way through a two-day competency hearing and they sent him to Napa. A couple of years later he showed up on my doorstep. I hardly recognized him. He looked like some homeless veteran begging for spare change. A complete fruit-cake and scary as hell. I wasn't going to risk my neck trying to help him again. I put him in my car, drove him to that old Dead Head tent city on the Berkeley waterfront, then went home and packed up everything I owned and moved up here."

"But you kept his name."

"That's not it. I kept *my* name. I was born with the name Brown. Coincidence. I think there's a lesson there. It's like marrying your first cousin. Nothing good can come of it."

"Does he have family left?"

She shrugged. "No idea. His mother took off when he was six. I think she had some kind of breakdown, too. I never found out what happened to her. He was raised by his grandmother in San Jose, but she's long dead. I heard his father died of AIDS about ten years ago."

Donnally stared out at the afternoon rush hour traffic creeping along the bridge crossing Salmon Bay, each driver heading toward a known desti-nation. Finding Charles Brown would be just the opposite. He'd only know he'd arrived after he'd gotten there.

He looked back at Katrisha. "How did you hear about the murder in Berkeley?"

"The DA. He left a message at my mother's asking me to come testify that Charles was compe-tent to stand trial." She took a sip of coffee. "How was I supposed to know? I hadn't seen him for years. And there was no way I was gonna let Charles find out where I moved. I knew the DA would have to give my address to Charles's public defender if I even let him interview me."

"Has Charles contacted you since then?"

"I didn't think they let the patients make long-distance calls."

"He's not a patient."

Katrisha's body spun toward Donnally. Coffee exploded from the top of her cup, splashing her Levi's and Nikes.

"What?" She tossed her cigarette into the bay, then shook the hot liquid from her hand. "How the fuck did he get out?"

"Some judge in Fresno decided he wasn't dangerous anymore."

"He beat the system. That nut beat the system." Katrisha shook her head in disgust, her mouth tight. "He did better than that. Putting him in with mentally ill and retarded women. Talk about the briar patch. Then, when everybody forgot why he was locked up in the first place, they showed him the door."

"I want to find him and bring him back."

Katrisha turned away and scanned the horizon, as if hoping an image of where he was hiding would appear. "He could be anywhere."

"But he isn't. He's somewhere."

Donnally glanced down at Katrisha's coffee-splattered jeans, then pointed his thumb over his shoulder toward the terminal.

"Let's go inside and wash that off."

She shrugged. "Wet is wet."

She pulled another cigarette from the pack in her

jacket pocket, then lit it with a worn stainless steel Zippo.

Donnally pointed at the lighter. "Your father in the service?"

"No. Me. I joined the navy after college. I wanted the Pacific Ocean between me and Charles. I did twenty-plus years and got out last May."

"What are you doing now?"

"You mean besides looking over my shoulder?"

Donnally nodded.

"I teach industrial diving, training technicians to do underwater repairs on ships and oil rigs. Mostly welding."

"You get married again?"

"No point. I spent a lot of time at sea. After a while I realized I didn't need the baggage." She winked at Donnally. "I could get laid anytime I wanted."

"And now that you're on land?"

Katrisha's eyebrows went up, exposing twinkling eyes. "You interested?"

"I've kinda got a girlfriend."

"Kinda? How kinda?"

"I'm still trying to figure that out."

She leaned over the railing and stared down toward the water lapping against the pilings.

"I've been a kinda girlfriend a few times myself. Spent a lot of time sitting by a phone that rarely rang."

"It's more complicated than that."

She looked over. "That's what they all said, meanwhile they were screwing everything that moved." She caught herself. "Sorry. That's was out of line. I don't know you."

"It's okay. I've been prying into your life. It's only fair."

She smiled. "Keep my number, just in case kinda turns into used to be."

Donnally patted his jacket pocket where he stored his cell phone. "Got it."

Katrisha took a drag on her cigarette. "And make sure I'm the first one you call if he turns up."

"Any idea where he'd go?"

"You sure he's not in jail?"

"Not that we know of."

"Maybe he's six feet under."

"No evidence of that either."

She tapped her cigarette on the edge of the railing and stared down at the water.

"I'm thinking he'd be in some kind of homeless encampment. His lisp made other people want to adopt him." She thought for a moment. "Does People's Park still exist in Berkeley?"

"From what I hear nobody sleeps there anymore."

"Anybody camp out in Golden Gate Park?"

Donnally nodded.

"Lots of bushes. That's where I'd start."

"Would you recognize him if you saw him?"

She stared at him for a moment, then said, "There's no way I'm going to help you find him."

Donnally offered a half smile. "I had to try."

"But I'll tell you something that may help. He liked to be called Rover, like a dog. You might have better luck asking for him by that name instead of Charles. At first I thought it was kind of cute, but then one evening he started humping my leg at the dinner table, and the charm wore off."

CHAPTER 9

Donnally sat in his truck parked along the Embarcadero and watched the last of his digital photos download onto his laptop computer. In the previous two weeks he'd photographed nearly every homeless black male in San Francisco. He'd started at Golden Gate Park, then the skid-row, hotel-lined Tenderloin, and finally now along the waterfront. He'd attached them to e-mails and sent them on to Katrisha. She always responded within a couple of hours, and always in two words: "Not him."

He was starting to think it would've been simpler just to put out some dog food and start calling out, "Rover. Here, Rover."

And it pissed him off that Blaine hadn't put much effort into finding Brown, and had stopped returning his calls even sooner than Donnally had expected. The final one, spoken with the bureaucratic authority that Donnally had learned to despise when he was at SFPD, was abrupt:

"We've devoted all of the resources we can to this matter. It's time to move on."

Donnally had always wondered why careerists like Blaine were always ready to move on when it came to others' suffering, but displayed the mechanical compulsiveness of psychotic hamsters when it came to their tennis forehand or their putting game. Perfecting those was worth a thousand frustrating weekends, while the Anna Keenans of the world weren't worth even one.

Donnally watched a gray-suited man walk from the Ferry Building, stop at a sidewalk news rack, drop in a couple of quarters, and pull out a newspaper. His mouth formed into a predatory grin as he skimmed the business headlines, as though he'd discovered that he'd just profited from someone else's loss. He then turned and headed up Market Street toward the financial district. A homeless woman stared up at him from the curb, her expression saying that she had lots of better uses for his change.

The escape of Charles Brown still hadn't hit the papers, and Donnally was sure it wouldn't because everyone had an interest in making sure it didn't. The Alameda County district attorney's half-hearted, failed effort was the perfect solution to the public relations problem that was Charles Brown. Why call attention to the crack in the criminal justice system that Brown and perhaps countless other murderers had slithered through?

And Donnally couldn't go to the press, because he knew that even a rabid dog fears the cage, and Brown would go even further underground once his name hit the *Chronicle* or his face appeared on the local news.

Blaine's "It's time to move on" had told Donnally that he was now on his own.

But every attempt to find Brown had died in failure.

SFPD patrol officers had only shrugged their shoulders when Donnally stopped them on the street.

Detectives had leaned back in their desk chairs, offering war stories as substitutes for the information they didn't have.

All anyone possessed were vague memories of someone who sort of looked like Brown who'd been around the park years ago.

Donnally stared out at the ferry dock, wondering whether Katrisha had been right. Maybe Brown was dead, his bones long scavenged by rats in a ravine up in Marin County or down the Peninsula, with nothing but a rusting shopping cart filled with recyclable cans and bottles marking the spot.

He heard a foghorn blow, then a red and white tugboat glided into view, guiding a container ship through the swirling mist toward the Port of Oakland and leaving a black plume of diesel exhaust in its wake. He could just make out the captain standing at the controls inside the upper bridge of the rusting craft and the yellow-slickered crewman poised at the bow.

Donnally then felt his mind sweep upward and he imagined himself looking down at a nautical chart of the bay with its contours of land, depths of water, edges of coastline, tidal currents, and sunken hazards: all the details needed for navigation, except for a marked route, much less an inland passage leading to whatever bush Charles Brown was living, or had died, under.

Turning the ignition, Donnally realized that the mental map was missing something else: his point of departure. He was already at sea and wasn't sure where he'd started from. He didn't even feel as if he'd pushed off from solid ground, rather he'd just found himself in motion. He couldn't even say it had been the flesh and blood of Mauricio, for the truth of his crime had acted as a solvent, somehow dissolving him, leaving only a stain behind.

And he knew that's exactly what Mauricio would've called it.

Donnally checked his side mirror and pulled into traffic, the acceleration feeling for a moment like a rush of relief, for it carried with it the realization that with the death of Anna, the stain that Mauricio left had been washed away into the nothingness of the past.

But only for a moment, for he felt the vertigo of a waxing and waning tide swaying him first forward toward an unknown shore and then backward toward the depths of his own motives.

CHAPTER 10

"Your father called," Janie Nguyen said, looking over from the pillow next to Donnally's, her head backlit by the light on the nightstand. The smell of sweat and perfume and sex infused the upstairs bedroom air like wilting gardenias, overripe and cloying.

He glanced over at the bedside clock: 10:30 P.M.

"How come you didn't tell me before we got into bed?"

Janie grinned. "You really want me to answer that?"

He didn't.

"What did he have to say?" Donnally asked.

Janie giggled. "He asked me if I wanted to play an Asian madam in the new movie he's planning to shoot. No lines. I just lounge around in my underwear for a couple of days. He said he was looking for the classical Vietnamese look." She lowered the sheet, exposing her breasts. "I'm not sure he had these in mind or my face."

Donnally knew he meant both, because his father had insinuated a hundred times that Janie reminded him of the elegant prostitutes he'd met at the Autumn Cloud Hotel in Saigon during the war, the nouveau riche "dollar queens" who wore silk in the daytime and shopped in the officers' PX, and who were beyond the reach of the enlisted men, forcing them to settle on bar girls.

His father's almost incestuous sexual interest in Janie made Donnally nauseated and angry. He realized that his fury showed on his face when Janie pulled away and covered herself again, as if for protection.

"What?" she asked.

Donnally shrugged. "It's nothing."

"If it was nothing, your jaw wouldn't be clenched like that."

He stared up at the ceiling, deciding how much to say and whether to risk the sort of all-night conversations that had led to their last breakup by ranging into borderlands where neither wanted to go. He felt an internal shrug of resignation, of inevitability.

"He thought it would be funny to call you a prostitute," Donnally said. "And see how you would react."

She reddened. "He said he wanted me to play one, not be one."

"There's no difference in his mind, because what thrills him is the effect his words have, not the reality behind them. He knows that if you yell fire in a theater, everybody's going run for it, whether there really is one or not."

Janie rolled over on her back. "So offering me the job was him yelling fire in your theater."

"For the thousandth time."

She sighed, leaned back, and folded her arms over her breasts.

"Now I really do feel like a prostitute."

⎯⎯⎯⎯⎯

"Where's the director?" Donnally asked his mother as he walked into her third-floor bedroom in the Hollywood Hills mansion late the following morning.

She looked up from her book lying on the table in front of her and rolled her eyes.

"You mean your father?"

"He tried out for the part a couple of times," Donnally said as he approached where she sat in a recliner by the open window, "but couldn't carry it off."

"Maybe you should give him a new audition."

"I'll check the sign-in sheet and see if he's applied."

Donnally watched disappointment flood his mother's face. He kissed her forehead, smoothed a few gray hairs that had been disturbed by the breeze, then sat down in a matching chair and took her hands trembling with Parkinson's into his.

"Sorry," he said, "I didn't mean for things to start out this way. I really just came to see how you're doing." He glanced out the window, over the circular drive and toward Hollywood and downtown Los Angeles. "Where is he, really?"

She tilted her head in the opposite direction. "He needed a hilltop sunset for his new movie, so he went out early to meet a crew at Rattlesnake Mountain to shoot the dawn."

Donnally tensed. That was typical of his father, filming a sunrise and running it backward just for the pleasure of deceiving the audience. He couldn't hear the phrase without thinking of his father's most famous war movie, *Shooting the Dawn*, hailed as an existential masterpiece by academic critics who misunderstood the sarcasm of the title, believing that the message was that one's fate cannot be changed any more than "shooting *at* the dawn" can stop the sunrise.

For reasons it took Donnally years to grasp, this had been the theme of all his father's movies, and his method of delivery had always been the same: Take some massacre that haunted the public conscience, like My Lai or Wounded Knee or Hue, change the location, give it a new name, blame it on human nature or the nature of war or on Asian or Indian enemies who not only killed indiscriminately, but murdered the spirit and corrupted the soul and drove anonymous soldiers into berserk orgies of revenge.

Donnally had no doubt that the dawn rising over the landscape of his father's new movie would illuminate the same thing: men wearing army green or Union blue or Confederate gray portrayed somehow as the true victims of the massacres they themselves committed, as if the forces that drove them to violence were as irresistible as gravitation, as if no willful general in Washington or Richmond or Hanoi or Saigon had ordered them to march into villages and no sergeant had ordered them to fire on the old and the weak, children and infants, cows and pigs and goats, or had ordered the houses or teepees or thatched huts burned and the survivors concentrated in camps.

And as if they hadn't obeyed by their own will and hadn't pulled the trigger with intent.

It was just man's fate to do evil, that was his father's repeated claim. It was as natural as the sunrise. No other explanations need be given, no justifications need be offered, and no excuses need be made.

"If he's still shooting the dawn," Donnally said, "then I guess I don't need to check the sign-in sheet."

His mother cast him a fond and forgiving smile. "I think this was purely an economic decision," she said. "Not an existential one."

"Why? Did he put his own money into it?"

"Actually, he did. He even reduced costs by shooting some of the jungle scenes in Mexico instead of doing them all in Southeast Asia."

"Why? The Pentagon's movie budget got cut, so he found a way to get the Mexican taxpayer to foot the bill?"

Before she could answer, a light knock on the door drew their attention to Julia, his mother's nurse and companion, entering with a tray of tea and medications. Donnally rose as she set it down and then gave her a hug.

"I didn't bother asking her," Donnally said, gesturing toward his mother, "because she won't tell me the truth. So I'll ask—"

"The doctor said that nothing has changed," his mother said, then she looked up at Julia. "Isn't that right?"

Donnally held his palm down toward his mother, but kept his eyes fixed on Julia. "Well?"

"I better seek refuge in my constitutional right to remain silent," Julia said.

"Then I've got my answer."

"She's been dreaming a lot about your brother," Julia told Donnally as they stood next to his rental car in the driveway.

"Probably because Donnie's birthday is coming up."

Donnally looked up at his mother's window. He watched the breeze ruffle the sheer curtains next to the bed where she lay asleep.

"I wonder how she sees Donnie in her mind," Donnally said. "As twenty years old or as the fifty-seven he'd be now?"

Donnally felt a wave of sadness, imagining that his mother saw not how Donnie really would have looked, but as his father had looked at that age.

"Why don't you ask her?" Julia asked.

"Because we'd get lost in a circular conversation since she's not willing to admit to herself that if my father hadn't sold his soul to the Pentagon, Donnie would still be alive."

"You're wrong. She admitted that years ago. She's just unwilling to make the choice you want her to make between your brother and your father."

Julia paused, then frowned and lowered her gaze.

"No," she finally said, looking back up at him. "that's not really it. I think I've been framing it wrong. The choice you want her to make is between you and your father, between how you see the world and how he does, how you imagine the past and how he does."

"There's no choice. The world is the way it is and the past was the way it was."

Neither of them had to say what that past was, for

it lived in the present like an unhealed wound: advertising genius Captain Donald Harlan conducting a Saigon briefing, selling the war to the press, and to his elder son.

Donnie had been so moved by his father's story of Buddhist monks murdered by the North Vietnamese that he had enlisted in the marines, only to learn the truth eight months later when he talked to villagers near the DMZ: The monks had been executed by U.S. Korean allies.

He went AWOL and traveled to Saigon to confront his father, who claimed to have been deceived by the South Vietnamese military. Donnie returned to his unit and was killed in what the Silver Star commendation described as "a heroic battle in which he had engaged the enemy on all sides."

It wasn't until Donnally read the Pentagon Papers as part of a high school civics class that he discovered that Captain Donald Harlan had himself composed the lie, justifying it as having been told in the service of a greater good. He also learned that "engaging the enemy on all sides" meant in armyspeak that his brother had been ambushed, led into a trap by those he believed he was fighting for.

Coming home from school that day, staggered by betrayal and quavering with rage, Donnally had resolved to make his father the model for everything he wouldn't be.

The next day he moved out the house and got a job.

On his eighteenth birthday he went to court and switched his first name for his last.

And on the day he graduated from UCLA, he

drove north and swore his oath as a San Francisco police officer.

Donnally looked past Julia in the direction of the distant mountains, imagining his father's satisfaction as he wrapped up the shoot.

"My father still deludes himself that his fictions can be truer than the truth, when they're just lies he tells himself." He reached into his pocket for his car keys. "He'll never change."

CHAPTER 11

Just after dark, Donnally parked a battered Caprice station wagon along the tree-lined southern edge of Golden Gate Park. He shrugged a surplus navy peacoat over his work shirt and put on a tattered Oakland A's cap to give him the appearance of a man just a couple of missed paychecks into homelessness.

He slumped his shoulders in feigned defeat as he walked across the amber-lit street and passed by a collection of homeless men and lurking parolees. He entered the corner liquor store and bought two pints of E&J Brandy as bribes to make friends in the park with people who might know Charles Brown, and slid them into his coat pockets.

Two tattooed skinheads bracketed Donnally as he stepped back onto the shadowed sidewalk, as though they were cowboys cutting a cow out of a herd for branding. The shorter of the men kept his hand inside his unzipped jacket. The taller gripped Donnally by the left elbow and leaned into him, urging him down the sidewalk.

"Stay cool, man," the short one said, without looking up. "It'll be over in a minute and you can walk away."

Donnally slumped even lower as they pushed

him into a driveway leading toward the closed underground garage of a two-story Victorian.

"Just don't hurt me." Donnally said, as they descended. "I got kids."

Donnally stopped halfway down and looked at the taller of the robbers, then tilted his head toward his front right pocket.

"Take the wallet, man. It's everything I got."

The two skinheads glanced backward. Donnally followed their eyes. A homeless sixty-year-old Asian man was watching them from behind an overstuffed grocery cart parked on the sidewalk across the street.

The shorter man pulled a Buck knife from his jacket and pressed it against Donnally's side while the taller reached into Donnally's front pocket and worked the wallet out. He thumbed through the two hundred dollars, then smiled at his partner as he took out the cash.

He turned back to Donnally. "Where's your ID?"

"Hidden in the park. I got warrants. I don't want to make it easy for the cops."

"For what?"

Donnally shrugged.

The shorter skinhead snapped the Buck knife closed, slid it into his back pocket.

"No hard feelings, man. Just business."

"I know," Donnally said, as the skinheads strolled back up the driveway. "Dog eat dog."

As the two turned the corner back onto the sidewalk, Donnally heard the taller one laugh and say, "That asshole sure ain't gonna call the cops. Last thing he wants is to share a cell with us."

Donnally reached into his sock, pulled out his cell phone, and called his old partner at SFPD. He described the two and said, "Swing by and see if you can ID the guys and get some photos, but don't arrest them for a couple of days. I'm working on something in Golden Gate Park and don't want to get burned. I'll explain everything later."

Once he was certain that they'd returned to their posts by the liquor store, he walked back up the driveway and across the street toward the homeless man, now standing next to the station wagon.

The man lowered the hood of his grimy green parka, slicked down his black hair, and then looked up as Donnally approached.

"Tough break," the man said.

Donnally saw that he meant it. He nodded, and then leaned against his car.

"It's all I had," Donnally said.

The man peered up into Donnally's eyes. "When you lose your job?"

"About eighteen months ago. Baker's Yeast over in Oakland. Unemployment ran out last summer."

The man smiled. "Mine ran out five years ago. I learned to live without it. You got a name?"

"They call me D." Donnally stuck out his hand. "You?"

The man pulled off his knitted glove and held up his right hand; two fingers were missing.

"Saam Ji. Three Fingers."

Donnally shook the remnants of Saam Ji's hand, then reached into his coat pocket and withdrew one of the bottles of brandy.

"Want some?"

Saam waved it off. "Got a meeting with my probation officer early tomorrow. He's got a nose like a bloodhound."

Donnally unscrewed the cap and took a sip.

"Saam Ji. That Cantonese?"

"Good guess."

"How come you've got a Chinese nickname, but you don't have an accent?"

Saam Ji squinted up at Donnally. "You a cop or something?"

"I used to be a janitor over there at Gordon Lau Elementary in Chinatown until—" Donnally held up the bottle and shrugged. "Until this got in the way."

Saam Ji offered a weak smile of sympathy. "Yeah. I know how that goes. I'm not fresh off the boat. I was born in Cleveland."

Donnally pointed at Saam Ji's hand. "How'd that happen?"

"Let's say I lost them gambling."

"Loan sharks?"

"Over at Lucky Chances in Colma ten years ago. I was a pai gow dealer. Gambled in my free time. After I got in too deep, some gangsters took me across the road into Home of Peace Cemetery. Beat the crap out of me and stomped my hands." Saam Ji sneered. "Home of Peace, my ass." He held up his three fingers. "I wasn't much good without all ten, so I couldn't get hired anywhere else."

Donnally searched his jeans pockets and pulled out a balled-up five-dollar bill. He unfolded it and inspected it under the streetlight, then looked up and down the street. "There a McDonald's around here?"

Saam Ji pointed east. "In the Haight."

"Show me the way and we'll share whatever ninety-nine-cent stuff they got on special."

Saam Ji smiled. "Thanks. I haven't had a burger in months."

Donnally made a show of inspecting the bill and smiled back.

"Let's call it my last supper."

A half hour later, Donnally and Saam Ji were sitting at a metal table outside the McDonald's across the street bordering the east end of the park. Saam Ji's grocery cart was parked on the sidewalk ten feet away under a streetlamp.

The teenager behind the counter had packed their orders for takeout without their asking.

The five dollars and another fifty cents Donnally pulled from his coat pocket went further than he expected. Four burgers and a small bag of French fries.

"Why'd you come to the park?" Saam Ji asked, sticking a fry in his mouth. "You got a car. You can stay wherever you want. Police are always hassling us around here. You go into the bushes to take a shit and when you come back, a city crew has hauled your stuff away."

"I was staying over in Berkeley by the marina for the last month," Donnally said, "but there are too many psychos around."

Saam Ji grinned. "You mean worse than the guys that robbed you?"

"Not worse. Just unpredictable. Hard to get a good night's sleep. And I used to know a guy who lived up in the Frontier." Donnally pointed toward the most isolated and jungled area of the park where the hard-core homeless lived.

"I thought maybe I'd look him up." Donnally smiled. "He's a little unpredictable, too, but I'm friends with his brother."

"What's his name?"

"Charles, but people used to call him Rover."

"Rover . . . Rover . . ." Saam Ji squinted into the distance, then looked back at Donnally. "A black guy?"

"Yeah. About six feet. Fifty years old or so."

"I think I know who he is but he hasn't been around for at least a year, maybe two." Saam Ji smiled, his teeth yellowed and caked with French fry residue. "It's hard to tell time when you're not punching a clock."

"Any idea where he went?"

Saam Ji wiped his mouth with the sleeve of his jacket.

"He couldn't make it in the Frontier. Couldn't stand being alone. He was always looking for attention." Saam Ji's eyes narrowed, then he squeezed them shut. "Let me think . . . let me think . . ." He opened his eyes again. "Noe Valley. That's it. Noe Valley. I saw him over on Twenty-fourth Street by the bakery. Must've been a couple of months ago."

"Expensive territory." Donnally chuckled. "He come into an inheritance?"

Saam Ji shook his head. "He's what they call a mascot around here. A guy yuppie people in the neighborhood feel sorry for. They give him money and food." Saam Ji's face turned grim. "I couldn't live like that. It's humiliating, and you always have to be ready to fight anybody who tries to move in on your block."

"Was he doing okay?"

"Hard to tell. You know he's crazy, right?"

"Off and on."

"He's mostly on. If you catch up with him, look at his hands. He punches things. Trees. Newspaper racks. All scarred and scabbed up. And paranoid as shit." Saam Ji laughed. "I think that's why all them white women are always giving him things. He acts like a scared puppy."

Saam Ji looked around, then stood up.

"Thanks for the dinner. I better get to my spot in the park before somebody else moves in."

"I'll walk back with you."

"Better not. It's not good to be seen in the park with a cop."

"Cop?"

"Or something like it." Saam Ji winked. "You could've taken those two skinheads in a heartbeat."

"Then why'd you talk to me?"

"First just to see what you were up to. And now that I know it's about Rover, I'm glad I did. He's really gonna hurt somebody someday. Probably a woman. It's just a matter of time. And it's not because he's crazy." Saam Ji gestured toward the park. "Lots of crazy people out there. Almost all of them are harmless. But Rover sometimes looks at women a certain way. Gives me the willies. I was glad when he left the park 'cause I would've felt guilty if he did something. Shit, if I wanted to be responsible for other people, I wouldn't be living on the street."

"Has he done anything so far?"

"I seen him in the bushes with some women, ones like him, but I never saw him hurt anybody." Saam Ji shrugged. "I figured if they're all crazy, it's kinda no harm, no foul."

CHAPTER 12 ═══════════

Donnally looked over at San Francisco Homicide Lieutenant Ramon Navarro sitting in the driver's seat of the Mercury Marquis. They had been parked for a couple of hours in front of Jules' Jewels at Twenty-fourth Street and Castro, surveilling the Noe Valley Bakery across the street and watching the Saturday morning breakfast crowd lining up for sugar and caffeine.

"You're starting to look like a Mexican Buddha," Donnally said, pointing at Navarro's stomach stretching tight against a yellow button-down shirt and a brown sports coat.

Navarro laughed, then ran his hand through his thinning hair. "Actually, I've been going for the Friar Tuck look."

Donnally tapped his thumb against his chest. "And I take it I'm supposed to be Robin Hood?"

"I'm not sure you'd look all that good in tights."

Donnally smiled. "You're not likely to find out."

They fell silent as they surveyed the street and the sidewalks, now overpopulated with mothers pushing strollers, wandering coffee drinkers in North Face parkas, couture-clad children of privilege, and red bandana-necked golden retrievers with their earnest noses sniffing the air.

"Sometimes this feels more like Aspen than a big-city neighborhood," Donnally said.

Navarro waved his hands toward the surrounding hills. "Or an enormous set constructed to shoot Eddie Bauer commercials."

Donnally watched two women walk by, holding hands. "You think these folks realize how lucky they are?"

Navarro stared ahead at the women for a moment, then said, "I suspect they mostly just feel deserving."

Donnally nodded toward a bearded man wearing three layers of coats and carrying a cloth sleeping bag. He was walking toward the bakery, eyes fixed on the sidewalk in front of him.

"Until somebody like Charles Brown shows up," Donnally said.

Navarro held up a decades-old mugshot, then glanced back and forth between it and the man. "Maybe those folks are right who say that the mentally ill don't age like the rest of us."

"I'll cross the street and come up from behind," Donnally said, opening the passenger door.

"You sure you don't want me to call some uniforms?"

"I'm sure." Donnally climbed out. "I don't want to spook him and I don't want anybody reading him his rights until I have a chance to talk to him."

Navarro leaned over and looked up at Donnally. "I don't know, man. It's sort of a gray area."

"Not the way we're doing it."

By the time Donnally had made the circuit down the block and across the street, Rover was sitting with his back against the low, black-tile façade of the bakery.

Rover paid no attention as Donnally walked up since his jeans and windbreaker made him unremarkable among the men standing around chatting and drinking their coffee with copies of the *New York Times* or the *Wall Street Journal* tucked under their arms.

Donnally pretended to read the take-out menu taped inside the bakery window until Navarro positioned himself near the news racks on the opposite side to block Rover's escape. He then lowered himself to one knee and bent down close to Rover. The aromas of blueberry muffins and cinnamon rolls swirling around them couldn't mask the stench enveloping Rover's body.

"Are you Charles Brown?" Donnally asked, adopting a sympathetic expression.

Rover looked up and licked his sugar-caked lips. He held a half-eaten donut in his left hand, with crumbs sticking to his spongy beard.

"Rover?" Donnally asked.

Rover squinted at Donnally and then nodded.

"I'd like to talk to you about Anna Keenan."

Rover's head jerked side to side. "My cathe is clothed." The lisp that changed "case" to "cathe" and "closed" to "clothed" sounded authentic. "They clothed it. I wath in jail thirty-theven yearths."

"Who told you they closed the case?" Donnally asked.

"My lawyer. My lawyer told me that."

"You mean the public defender?"

"Yeah, my public defender came and told me."

Donnally sat down next to him. "Since the case is closed, maybe you can tell me what happened."

Rover threw down the donut, then wrapped his arms around his knees. Donnally could see mangled knuckles and scarred skin, and recent lacerations and scabs. Rover's head twitched side to side, eyes darting. His breathing became heavy, verging on hyperventilating.

"Take it easy," Donnally said, touching Rover's left arm. "Nobody's trying to hurt you."

"They told me I killed her." Rover lowered his head and rocked back and forth. "They told me I killed her." He looked at Donnally. "Do you know if I killed her?"

Donnally nodded. "That's what they say."

"They said I strangled her. And that I was crazy." Rover lowered his head again. "I didn't understand what was going on. They put me in Atascadero. I began to remember . . ."

"Remember what?"

Donnally caught sight of a stroller slowing to a stop on the sidewalk next to them. He looked up at a thin, young mother smiling at Rover and him, as if he were a city mental health worker checking on a client. She reached out with a dollar and let it fall into Rover's lap. Donnally gave her an acknowledging nod, then she moved on.

Donnally turned back to Rover. "Remember what?"

"Looking down at Anna in her bed. Reaching at her."

"And then?"

Rover didn't answer. His head was still lowered.

"Did Anna like you?"

Rover looked up, grinning. "Anna liked me. She wanted me to touch her."

"Touch her how?"

Rover's grin turned sly, mischievous, embarrassed. "You know."

"Did you touch her?"

"Yes." Rover frowned. "But she got angry."

"Then what happened?"

Donnally watched Rover's body tense, his eyes hardening.

"Why are you asking me this? My cathe is clothed." Rover's voice rose. "I did thirty-theven years. My cathe is clothed."

Rover pushed himself to his feet, then spun and smashed his fist into the bakery window. Donnally grabbed Rover's collar and yanked him backward as the glass shattered and ragged fragments fell and exploded on the sidewalk. Donnally lost his balance and the two of them crashed down onto the concrete. Rover thrashed, throwing elbows at Donnally's side and face and kicking at his legs. Donnally slid his right arm under Rover's neck and locked his hand behind his head. He then felt the thud of Navarro diving in, rocking their bodies. Navarro yanked Rover's left arm behind his back, snapped on a handcuff, then pushed himself up and kneeled on Rover's shoulder. Rover's body stiffened with pain and his legs stopped kicking. Donnally rotated Rover's right arm down and back and Navarro snapped on the second handcuff.

When Donnally rolled off, he found himself nose-to-rubber wheel of the same stroller. He looked up at the women, now glaring down as if Rover was somehow a victim and as if she'd been betrayed by a pretender to goodness. Donnally reached over and picked up her dollar from the sidewalk and held it out toward her. She stared at it for a few seconds, then turned away and used the stroller as a battering ram to break through the gathering crowd.

Donnally looked over at Navarro as they stood up. "Apparently one woman's murderer is another woman's mascot."

Navarro grabbed Rover by his left upper arm, Donnally took his right, and they hauled him to his feet.

Donnally rubbed his left elbow as they drove away from the North County Jail in Oakland where they had dropped off Rover.

Navarro glanced over. "Seems like your old bones can't take this anymore. You ought to get yourself some better padding like me."

Donnally smiled. "When you dove in, I thought you were going to croquet both him and me into the street."

Navarro's face flushed. "I wasn't exactly diving."

"You tripped? So it was really my padding that protected you?"

"I guess you could say that."

Donnally reached for his cell phone and called Katrisha. Her voice mail picked up. He left a message about Brown's arrest and assured her that he wouldn't let the DA know that she'd helped out.

They then rode in silence until Navarro had merged into freeway traffic heading toward the Bay Bridge.

"Man," Navarro said, "that guy sure didn't want to go to jail."

"Maybe he realized that once we got him locked up, he'd never get out again."

"You think he's sane enough to go to trial?"

Donnally had thought through that question during the time he'd spent searching for Rover.

"I think there are three issues," Donnally said. "Does he remember what happened? I think he does. Does he know he'll go to trial for murder? That's why he fought us so hard. Can he help his attorney formulate a defense? Probably. He's even got his defense ready: She got angry and they had a fight."

"Except he'll only be putting on a defense if the court finds him competent." Navarro looked over at Donnally. "What do you think the shrinks are going to say?"

Donnally had also thought that one through.

"That depends on who's paying them."

CHAPTER 13

The assistant public defender reached down and rested her hand on Charles Brown's shoulder at the defense table in the arraignment department of the Superior Court in Oakland. It was as if to say to the judge about Brown, *Poor, tormented man*.

The pretense reminded Donnally why so many court proceedings had repelled him as a cop. They too often devolved into theater in which every person and every thing—every fact and everything done and suffered—was reduced to an image to be manipulated.

And he suspected Brown's competency hearing two decades earlier had begun the same way: with a wordless attempt by his attorney to cast him in the role of the victim.

What the public defender said aloud was "I'd like the defendant sent under Penal Code 1368 to determine whether he's competent to stand trial."

Judge Julia Nanston looked down toward Chief Assistant District Attorney Thomas Blaine.

"Do the People have any objection?"

Her raised left eyebrow told everyone in the courtroom the People had better not.

"No, Your Honor," Blaine said. "We've already

discussed the selection of psychiatrists with the defense."

"So the People are contesting the issue?"

Blaine glanced back at Donnally sitting in the front row of the gallery, then back at the judge.

"You bet the People are."

Despite his annoyance, Donnally let his eyes go dead as the judge looked down at him. Like the public defender's gesture, Blaine's had been a performance: a pretend solidarity that falsely included Donnally in a process over which he had no control.

The courtroom door opened, followed by a rush of footsteps. Donnally turned to see a pack of reporters hurry to take seats in the second row. A longtime *San Francisco Chronicle* crime reporter recognized Donnally, then pointed at his open notebook.

Donnally shook his head, then shrugged and mouthed the words, *I'm just a spectator*, then rose and walked out.

His cell phone rang as he was driving back across the Bay Bridge to Janie's.

"How did the fucking press find out about this so soon?" Blaine said, his voice rising.

Donnally pictured the flush-faced prosecutor stomping around his office.

"It wasn't me," Donnally said. "What's the storyline?"

"What do you think it is? How the fucking DA's office fucked up and let a fucking maniac get away with a fucking murder for over twenty fucking years."

Donnally heard the beep of an incoming call. "Hold on." He connected the call. "Harlan Donnally."

"It's me." It was his waitress at the café. "I got a couple of calls from the press. Apparently you're the hero."

"What did they want?"

"A picture of your handsome face and to find out how you got involved in this."

"What did you tell them?"

"What could I tell them? I don't have a clue."

Donnally imagined camera crews camping out in front of Mauricio's junkyard and ex-prosecutors and marginal defense lawyers standing by in a cable news studio, all made giddy by a truth-is-stranger-than-fiction elixir of murder, attempted rape, a maniac on the loose, incest, and patricide.

"Tell them I was doing research for a book and happened to run across the case."

"Really? What's it about?"

"I don't know yet."

She laughed. "I get it."

"Try to sound sincere."

Donnally reconnected to Blaine. "You seem a little deficient in the adjective department today."

"Asshole."

"And the noun department."

Donnally heard Blaine drop into his chair.

"You know what else is going on?" Blaine said.

"All I know is what you're telling me."

"The Crime Victims for Justice group held a press conference on the courthouse steps. They want the state attorney general to take over the prosecution, claiming that we're incompetent. And get this. The Albert Hale Foundation jumped in."

"The what?"

"Albert Hale Foundation. Some kind of do-gooder organization put together by some rich guy who's never been robbed."

"What's their angle?"

"That Brown has been abused by the courts and failed by the mental health system."

Donnally's anger shifted from Brown to his equally misguided defenders. "Sounds like they've forgotten who the victim is."

"Hey, man, this is California."

CHAPTER 14

Brown was already seated at the defense table, handcuffed to his chair, when Donnally and Blaine had walked into the courtroom. He was bracketed by two attorneys that neither of them recognized.

One bailiff sat five feet behind Brown and another next to the low swinging doors leading to the gallery.

"People versus Charles Brown."

Donnally sat down behind the barrier as Blaine walked up to the prosecution table and faced Judge Julia Nanston.

"Thomas Blaine for the People."

The thickset woman sitting next to Brown rose to her feet.

"Margaret Perkins substituting in for the public defender."

Blaine glanced at Perkins, then said to Judge Nanston. "Your Honor—"

Judge Nanston raised her palm toward Blaine, then glared down at the new attorney.

"Ms. Perkins, two weeks ago I gave the public defender a date certain. And that date is today. The people of this state have waited over twenty years for a resolution in this case." Nanston removed her half-height reading glasses, then pointed a thin finger at Perkins. "If this is some kind of stunt to get a continuance . . ."

Perkins smoothed the front of her gray suit. She looked to Donnally like an army captain adjusting her dress uniform.

"No, Your Honor. We're ready to proceed."

"And your colleague, for the record?"

"Doris Tevenian of my firm, Schubert, Smith, and Barton."

Blaine's head swung toward Tevenian, then toward Donnally, his eyes asking, *Who's paying for this?* Then he mouthed the question, *Albert Hale?*

Donnally knew SSB's reputation as one of the most expensive firms in the nation. Because of their ages, Donnally guessed that Perkins and Tevenian were partners, which meant that between them and their two assistants, the case was costing more than two thousand dollars an hour.

"Just to make sure we understand each other," Judge Nanston said. "I hope you don't think you're making a special appearance to give yourself some time to see whether you want to take the case. You're in for the duration." Nanston nodded twice, expecting Perkins to nod along. She did. "Even if that means a forest of motions and a three-month trial."

Tevenian rose. "Yes, Your Honor."

Judge Nanston looked at Blaine. "Any objection?"

"No, Your Honor, but the People want some assurance that the defendant consents to the substitution. There are appeal issues to be considered."

The judge looked down at Brown. "Mr. Brown,

would you like Ms. Perkins and Ms. Tevenian to represent you?"

"I don't want no public defender. I want a real lawyer."

Judge Nanston smiled, then looked at Blaine. "May I take that as a yes?"

"What the hell is SSB doing in this case?" Blaine asked Donnally as they walked down the ninth floor hallway toward his office.

"Does it make a difference?"

"No. But I'll tell you something that will." Blaine stopped and turned toward Donnally. "The jailhouse informant that we were going to use in Brown's original trial died of a heroin overdose ten years ago. He was the only one who heard Brown confess."

"Did he testify in any pretrial hearings?"

"Nope. So we've got no testimony that would be admissible now."

They walked a few more steps, then Donnally realized that Blaine's complaint was a setup.

Donnally stopped. "What are you saying?"

"Maybe we should . . ." Blaine let his voice trail off.

Donnally's fists clenched. "Let him be found incompetent again?"

"But we'll keep an eye on him."

"Like you did for the last two decades?"

"At least we're sure to keep him locked up for another ten years—"

"And then he falls through the cracks again and walks out the door?"

Blaine folded his arms across his chest. "The risk of going to trial is that he walks out sooner, either on a not guilty by reason of insanity or on a lesser offense."

"You mean a manslaughter?"

"Exactly. Say Brown gets up there and says it wasn't premeditated. It was just an accident or heat of passion or some kind of sex play that went bad. Nobody remembers what a gem Anna Keenan was. Most jurors will think she was just a Berkeley weirdo and will be prepared to believe anything."

Donnally pointed a finger at Blaine's chest. "It's your job to make sure they don't."

"Not mine alone, pal. If you want to bury Brown, then you'll have to be my first witness at the competency hearing."

"And testify to what? I'm not a shrink."

"You'll testify that even with you catching him by surprise, he was able to articulate that he'd been accused of murder and that he was thinking clearly and quickly enough to come up with a fake manslaughter defense that would cut his jail time in half."

Blaine spread his arms to encompass the courthouse.

"That alone makes him more competent than ninety percent of the crooks that come through here."

Blaine chuckled, but Donnally didn't laugh with him.

"Most of them don't figure out how they're going to fight their cases until halfway through trial."

CHAPTER 15

Donnally watched Thomas Blaine jump to his feet and shoot his hand out toward Margaret Perkins.

"That's not the issue, Your Honor. The question isn't whether the defendant is mentally ill or even developmentally disabled. It's whether he's competent to stand trial. Now. Right now. Not twenty years ago."

Judge Julia Nanston glared down at the prosecutor.

"For the third time I'm telling you. No . . . speaking . . . objections. The only words I want to hear out of you are 'objection' and 'relevance.' If the basis of your objection isn't obvious, I'll ask for an explanation."

Nanston made a note on the yellow legal pad before her. The flourish of her pen stroke gave Donnally an edgy feeling, as though she viewed the evidentiary battle as just a game and she was keeping score.

The judge looked back at Blaine and said, "Please don't try to tell the court something it already knows. Denied."

Blaine sat down and glanced at Donnally sitting

behind him, who acknowledged the prosecutor's frustration with a shrug.

The judge then focused on Perkins.

"Please bear in mind, Ms. Perkins, that I'm allowing you to present background information as context, not to make a current argument."

Perkins leaned down toward her cocounsel, Doris Tevenian, who handed her a handwritten note. She read it, then looked up at Dr. William Sherwyn sitting in the witness box.

"Again, Doctor, what was your impression of Mr. Brown's demeanor when you interviewed him just after his original arrest?"

"As I recall, the first time I saw him was in the locked ward of the county hospital."

Donnally's peripheral vision caught the motion of Brown curling forward as though resisting a painful memory. Tevenian squeezed his shoulder, trying to calm him, but Brown pulled away and yelled, "Not true. Not true."

Judge Nanston slammed her gavel, then pointed at Tevenian.

"Counsel, control your client."

Sherwyn held up his twenty-year-old report toward the reporters in the gallery and the news cameras in the jury box as if to say, *The records don't lie*, then continued.

"Mr. Brown bore all of the signs of bipolar disorder, what we referred to back then as manic-depression. Racing thoughts. Irritability. Grandiose ideation. Agitation. Delusions."

Blaine rose.

"Your Honor, is he describing all the symptoms

of bipolar disorder or just the ones the defendant displayed?"

Nanston glared at Blaine.

The prosecutor's hands clenched. He looked to Donnally like a little boy who'd suffered a reprimand from his mother. But his voice stayed even:

"I'll withdraw that. Objection. Nonresponsive."

"Objection sustained." Nanston looked at Dr. Sherwyn. "Please let's limit yourself to the precise symptoms Mr. Brown displayed when you evaluated him."

Sherwyn nodded, then said, "He was in a manic state that we would now call bipolar type one." He scrunched up his nose and smirked at the prosecutor. "All of the above, combined with psychotic episodes."

Perkins scanned her legal pad, then flipped back a few pages.

"Pardon me, Doctor, I should have asked this earlier. How did it happen that you were chosen to evaluate the defendant?"

"In addition to my private practice, I had a contract with the county to perform these evaluations. A second psychiatrist would be brought in if my conclusions were contested by one side or the other."

"Good afternoon, Dr. Sherwyn."

Blaine stood at the podium, his cross examination laid out in front of him.

The swagger in Blaine's steps from the counsel table had told Donnally that the prosecutor believed he could win his competency argument through Sherwyn's testimony alone.

And Donnally hoped so. He didn't want to be forced to explain under oath how he'd gotten onto Brown's trail and feared that Mauricio's original sin might taint the jury's view of Anna.

"As I recall," Blaine said, "the majority of your practice in those years was the treatment of sexually abused children. Is that correct?"

Sherwyn smiled at Blaine. "It was the basis of your objection to my qualifications during Mr. Brown's first competency hearing."

"Objection," Perkins said. "Irrelevant."

Judge Nanston cast a disapproving look at Blaine.

"You already lost that battle, Counselor." Nanston pointed at his list of questions. "Maybe you should move on."

Blaine shrugged and made a checkmark on his pad.

"Dr. Sherwyn, did you medicate the defendant at any time during the period he was undergoing evaluation?"

Donnally caught the motion of Brown's head nodding in quick, precise motions.

"You mean did I attempt to restore him to competency?"

"Dr. Sherwyn," Judge Nanston cut in. "It works better if the attorney asks the questions."

Sherwyn reddened. To Donnally, he looked like a scuffling football player a referee had caught throwing the second punch.

"Yes," Sherwyn said, "I medicated him."

"And what was that medication?"

"Medications, plural. Lithium and an anticonvulsant to address its side effects."

"And did these have the result of restoring him to competence?"

"As you well know, his attorney obtained an order preventing his further involuntary medication."

Blaine glanced at Donnally, then at Perkins, and finally back at Sherwyn.

"Doesn't that suggest that the defense wanted to ensure that Mr. Brown would remain incompetent so he'd never have to face trial for the murder of Anna Keenan?"

"Objection!"

CHAPTER 16

"I'm reminding you again, Ms. Perkins, please stop trying to bootstrap his mental history into an argument for his current competency."

Studying Perkins from where he sat behind Blaine, Donnally realized that she'd been quicker than the judge and she already had. But he wasn't sure why.

"I gave you a great deal of latitude in examining Dr. Sherwyn," Nanston continued, "but they're separate issues."

Perkins glanced down at Charles Brown sitting next to her at the counsel table, then back up at Nanston.

"The problem we're facing is that my client has refused to cooperate with the psychiatrist we hired to evaluate him. We're in a Catch-22. She can't even determine whether his refusal to speak to her is an indication of his incompetence."

Judge Nanston paused for a moment, then said, "If the only evidence you have is historical, then you may need to forgo this competency hearing altogether, proceed to trial, and put on an insanity defense."

Blaine reached his hand behind his back and

flashed Donnally a thumbs-up. It seemed to Donnally that it was too soon to celebrate. Perkins hadn't made partner at SSB by failing to get what she wanted.

Perkins shook her head. "That's impossible at this point."

"Why?"

"There's no way to recreate the defendant's mental state leading up to the time of the homicide. Very few of his psych records prior to that date still exist."

Nanston leaned forward. "Excuse me, Counsel?"

"The county hospital records have long been purged and just a few moldy fragments remain of the file that traveled with him from Atascadero to the various developmental centers. The only complete report that exists is Dr. Sherwyn's and it contains almost no history."

Nanston looked toward the prosecutor, brows furrowed, eyes accusing.

"Did you know about this, Mr. Blaine?"

Blaine rose.

"We informed the defense as soon as we discovered the records were missing." He looked at the defense table, then smiled. "At this point I believe that the most complete record of the defendant's mental history is contained in the public defender's file Ms. Perkins received when she entered the case."

Perkins glared at Blaine, then held up a few handwritten pages and almost unreadable fragments from the Elsa's Home for Men file Donnally had passed on to Blaine.

"This is all we have, Counselor."

Nanston's voice turned harsh. "Ms. Perkins, please direct your comments to the court."

Perkins looked up at the bench.

"I'm sorry, Your Honor. But I resent the district attorney's implication that this burden falls to the defense. After all, it was his office that didn't bother to preserve these records."

"Your Honor," Blaine said, "I hardly—"

Nanston held up her palm. "Just a moment, Mr. Blaine."

The judge turned her gaze toward her law clerk sitting in the jury box taking notes. He didn't look up, unaware that all eyes in the courtroom bored down on him.

"Let's take a ten-minute recess."

Nanston rose and walked down the two steps from the bench and into her chambers, followed by her staff.

Blaine stepped toward the low barrier behind which Donnally stood.

"What's she doing?" Donnally asked.

"I don't know, but I sure hate it when judges get ideas on their own. They just screw things up and make unnecessary work for both sides."

They looked over at Perkins to gauge whether she'd divined what the judge was thinking. She rolled her eyes and walked over.

"What wheel is the judge trying to reinvent this time?" Perkins asked.

"I haven't the slightest idea," Blaine said, then looked back and forth between Perkins and Donnally. "You two know each other?"

"No," Donnally said, reaching out his hand. It annoyed him that she seemed so likable.

Perkins gave it a firm shake, then asked, "What brought you into this?"

Donnally shrugged and flipped the question back. "I was wondering the same thing about you."

"I'm surprised to be here." Perkins smiled. "The Albert Hale Foundation's choice in causes is sometimes rather bizarre."

Donnally smiled back. "I take it you got your fee up front?"

"We gave them a discount rate. Half price. A case this big fulfills most of the firm's pro bono obligations for the year." She glanced over at her two legal assistants sitting at the defense table. "And it gives the kids some experience."

"I don't understand why Albert Hale picked Brown," Donnally said. "I did some research. On crime issues, the foundation is usually on the other side."

"I think you may be looking at this backwards. It may not be about Brown being some kind of victim, but"—Perkins glanced at Blaine—"more about embarrassing the prosecution. The theme that runs through most of their causes is government incompetence and weakness."

Blaine smirked. "So they try to prove their point by helping a murderer go free? Hale must be nuts."

"I know it's crazy," Perkins said. "We tried to explain it to him—"

"To Hale personally?" Blaine asked.

Perkins shook her head. "I'm not sure anyone

has actually seen Hale in years. He put millions of dollars into the foundation, then disappeared from public view."

"But you think he remains the invisible hand?"

Perkins nodded. "The president of the foundation says Hale is on a mission he's not sure even Hale comprehends." She looked at Donnally. "Did you see that environmentalist on television the other day, the idiot who said he'd give his life to save a damn tree frog?" She didn't wait for an answer. "That's Hale, except his tree frog today is a lunatic."

Donnally rotated his thumb toward Brown sitting hunched over and rocking back and forth at the defense table.

"You sure you want to refer to your client as a lunatic?"

Perkins smiled again. "As often as I can." She winked. "Maybe I'll even convince myself."

The bailiff's "All rise" stifled the courtroom conversations.

Donnally returned to his seat while Blaine and Perkins walked back to the counsel tables.

Judge Nanston was on the bench when Donnally looked up.

Nanston's gaze shifted back and forth between Perkins and Blaine, then she took off her reading glasses.

"Ms. Perkins, would you outline for me the materials the prosecutor has given to you in discovery?"

Perkins squinted up at Nanston. "I'm not sure why you want—"

"You don't have to be sure why I want to know."

Perkins turned to her cocounsel, Doris Tevenian,

who searched through a banker's box, then handed her a list. Perkins showed it to Blaine, then read off the items.

"We have the original crime scene reports, witness statements, and forensic analyses. A two-page psych report from Dr. Sherwyn when the defendant was taken for the evaluation on the day of his arrest. We have the reports of the psychiatrists from his first competency hearing—"

"Do those address his mental history?" Nanston asked.

"Only tangentially, Your Honor."

"Have you contacted the doctors to determine whether they retained the defendant's records?"

Perkins looked at Blaine.

"Both are deceased and their files have been destroyed," Blaine said.

"Anything else, Ms. Perkins?"

Perkins leaned down close to Tevenian and whispered a few words. Tevenian pointed toward the bench. Perkins glanced at Blaine, then straightened up.

"May we approach, Your Honor?"

"Maybe we better do this in chambers."

CHAPTER 17 ═══════════════

"What do you mean the public defender lost the rest of their file?" Nanston's voice rose in anger. "I worked in that office for fourteen years. I know exactly what their procedures are. Files don't get lost."

Blaine had asked Donnally to come along and no one had objected. He leaned against the wall by the door, understanding that he had no more status in the meeting than the coatrack in the corner.

Perkins shrugged. "That's what they're telling me."

Nanston searched the county directory on her computer, then reached for the telephone.

Five minutes later the chief public defender, Izel McAdam, stood before her, alternating between fidgeting with the pendant hanging from a chain around her neck and brushing away strands of gray hair from in front of her eyes.

Behind her lurked the chief assistant, bearing what Donnally had come to recognize during his years in the criminal justice system as the cowering countenance of a bureaucrat who'd been promoted far beyond his competence.

The judge looked at the two, her lips thin, her

expression communicating bewilderment at how an office in which she'd worked for over a decade and had come to love had fallen into the hands of buffoons.

"Your Honor," McAdam said, "our office handles sixty thousand cases a year. More than a million since Mr. Brown was arrested. One case among all of those—"

"This isn't a lottery, Izel. This is a homicide."

McAdam reddened. "But—"

Nanston held up her finger, then looked at Blaine.

"Our file is intact," Blaine said. "And we've turned over everything except our work product."

Blaine then glanced over at Donnally as if for confirmation, but he didn't react. He had no way of knowing what Blaine had handed over to the defense. He only knew what he had given Blaine.

"I'll need your assurance that you aren't using an overly broad definition of what that is," Nanston said.

"The only thing we didn't turn over is some legal research and my own handwritten notes."

"What about psych records you collected?"

"The burden wasn't on us. It was on the public defender, so we didn't subpoena any. If the defendant had been found competent to stand trial and had put on an insanity defense then, of course, we would've gathered a war chest of them."

Nanston looked at McAdam. "When was the last time you're certain the file was in your possession?"

McAdam glanced at her chief assistant. It seemed to Donnally as though she was trying to slough off the responsibility onto someone who didn't seem capable of even serving as a fall guy.

When he didn't respond to the judge's question, McAdam said, "About fifteen years ago. That's when the defendant was transferred into the civil system and we withdrew from the case."

Nanston turned to Blaine. "When was the last time the developmental center submitted a report regarding Mr. Brown's progress toward the restoration of his competency?"

"I haven't looked at the court file," Blaine said, "but the last report our office received was twelve years ago."

Nanston glanced back and forth between Blaine and McAdam, her eyebrows furrowed.

"You mean no one in your office or in the public defender's office has paid any attention at all to this case in over a decade?"

Blaine and McAdam answered with silence.

Nanston leaned back in her oversized leather chair and gazed out of her window toward the glass and concrete County Administration Building across the street.

After a long moment, she pointed at her law clerk.

"Get me *Louis Craft v. Superior Court of Orange County* and *People v. Simpson*. It's a Fourth Appellate District case from the 1970s."

She then pushed herself to her feet.

"Let's go back."

Donnally followed Blaine into the courtroom. The DA was shaking his head and biting his lower lip as he walked Donnally to his seat, then faced him across the low barrier.

"We're in big trouble," Blaine said in a tense whisper.

"How do you figure?"

The bailiff again. "The court will come to order."

Blaine turned around and took two steps, stopping behind his chair, his shoulders slumping, his head lowered as if facing his executioner.

Nanston scanned the reporters in the gallery and the news video cameras in the jury box as if to say, *You folks will want to get this down.* Her eyes then bored down on Blaine.

"As the loss of evidence over the years may have impaired the ability of the defendant to put on a defense, the court is willing to entertain a defense motion to dismiss *People v. Brown* on speedy trial grounds."

Donnally felt his body rock backward.

Blaine raised his hands in front of his chest as if to block a blow.

"Just a second, Your Honor—"

Donnally leaned forward, trying to hear the rest of the prosecutor's complaint, but he couldn't make it out over the gasps and confused chatter among reporters, each asking the other if the judge had said what they thought she had.

Nanston struck her gavel once and the room fell silent.

"This is not the time, Mr. Blaine." She looked back and forth between him and Perkins. "And this isn't brain surgery. I want all the briefing done in a week. Work out the schedule between you. Court is adjourned."

CHAPTER 18

Blaine threw his file down on his desk and kicked his trash can across the room, smashing it into a bookcase. It bounced, then rolled in a semicircle on the linoleum floor.

"I knew it the second she asked for *Craft* and *Simpson*. That bitch. She's never stopped being a public defender."

Donnally cast Blaine a sour look.

"Skip the performance," Donnally said. "It was your job to get this guy to trial and now you're dead in the water."

Blaine spun toward Donnally, his finger jabbing.

"You—"

Donnally raised his palm.

"Now you're going to blame me?"

"I don't know why you opened up this can of worms in the first place."

"That's not the point. The question is what you're going to do about it."

Blaine dropped into his chair, thought for a moment, and then said, "Since it looks like Nanston has already made her decision, I'll try to smoke her out and make a record for the appeal."

He glanced out of the window, then looked back at Donnally with a half smile.

"Wait a second . . . wait a second. Maybe we can block the speedy trial hearing altogether. Maybe we can argue that no decision can be made on anything in the case until he agrees to talk to the shrink and is found competent. That way Nanston can't dismiss the case and he stays in custody."

Donnally locked his hands on his hips.

"Let me get this straight," Donnally said. "You're going to trade places with the defense? You arguing he's not competent and them arguing he is?"

Blaine's smile turned into a grin. "Exactly. You saw how Brown has been acting in court. If his own lawyer calls him a lunatic, I sure as hell can."

"Who are you trying to kid, me or yourself?"

The prosecutor's grin faded. "Apparently not you."

Blaine tapped his pen against the edge of his desk. His eyes blurred, then he started to nod.

Donnally sensed the prosecutor's mind gaining traction on the slope of his impromptu strategy.

Blaine's head snapped up and he aimed a forefinger at Donnally's chest.

"You're still going to be my first witness," Blaine said. "But this time to show that he's crazy. You're gonna testify about Brown's delusion that he was in the nut ward for *thirty-theven yearths.*" Blaine laughed as he imitated Brown's lisp.

Donnally glared down at the prosecutor. "Not . . . a . . . chance."

Donnally walked down the courthouse steps and turned toward the eight-story county parking garage a half block away. It loomed over the surrounding buildings like a nuclear cooling tower. He stopped at the corner crosswalk.

I did my part, Donnally said to himself as he stared at the red "Wait" sign. *Maybe I delivered a different message to a different recipient, but it got delivered.*

Moments later, Donnally found himself crossing the intersection, away from his car and toward the lake. He felt suffocated by the rumbling of traffic that reverberated off the government offices behind him and the faces of the apartment buildings along the encircling boulevard.

Donnally traversed the grass between the sidewalk and shoreline trail, sickened by the trash littering the bank: the squashed malt liquor cans and scattered pork rinds, the yellow-brown butt ends of joints, the Taco Bell wrappers.

He stopped along the shore and watched the foamy water lap up against the moss-covered rocks. He took in a breath infused with the decay bubbling to the oily surface.

The air was thick with an odor of rot and deceit that seemed to seep through his clothes and into his skin.

He exhaled.

It was time to head home.

I'm done playing postman.

CHAPTER 19

"Hey, Harlan, you in there?"

Donnally's body jerked forward, as if the voice had jabbed him in the back of the neck. The sound broke his mind free from the accounting scrawl lying before him on top of Mauricio's desk.

In the previous two hours he had discovered that the little guy had done well by living cheap. He had about thirty thousand dollars in cash in the bank and at least ten times that amount in equity in his property.

The question that had been troubling Donnally as he stared at the figures was what to do with the money now that Anna wasn't alive to collect it.

He looked over and saw Will with his hands cupped around his eyes and pressed against the dirty office window, his cook's apron splattered with beaten eggs and pancake batter.

"Harlan?"

"Yeah, what do you need?"

Donnally walked over and worked the bottom of the weathered double-hung window back and forth until he could raise it a few inches.

"Nothing," Will said, tilting his narrow head to speak through the gap. "Deputy Sheriff Asshole came by the café a few minutes ago. Said he had to speak with you, personal. I told him I didn't know where you was, and I didn't, till now."

"He say why?"

"Nope."

"You ask?"

All the skin not concealed by Will's black eyebrows and the wide soul patch springing from beneath his lower lip flushed red.

"I didn't think to do it until he drove away."

"That's okay. Thanks for the heads-up."

Donnally glanced over at the few cars left in the café's gravel parking lot. Two had snowboards clamped onto rooftop racks.

"How many came in for breakfast?"

"I think forty. I wish it had been thirty-nine. Deputy Asshole was saying that if his father was still sheriff there'd already have been some kinda investigation of Mauricio to find out what he was hiding. Asshole kept calling him Pancho just like his father used to. Can't we just ban him from the café?"

"You mean put up a sign? No brains. No sense. No service."

Will laughed. "But you'd have to add, This Means You, Deputy Pipkins, otherwise he wouldn't be able to figure out that it was aimed at him."

Donnally stood by the window after Will returned to the café. He wondered whether Wade Pipkins Jr. was just doing what his father would've done, but for which he no longer had the authority beyond what he commanded as the patriarch of his Sunday dinner table.

Whatever the answer, Donnally knew he had to destroy what remained of Mauricio's real identity.

Three hours later, Mauricio's fireplace had consumed all the documentary remnants of his hidden life, and five hours after that, not one of Mauricio's fingerprints remained on a countertop, refrigerator, doorknob, bed table, or dresser. Even his truck interior, which had never seen a dust rag or vacuum cleaner, had been wiped clean and now bore a coating of Armor All.

If latents still existed from the forty-five-year-old murder, now they'd never be matched to Mauricio.

Deputy Pipkins appeared again at the café during the dinner rush.

"I need to talk to you, Harlan," Pipkins said, standing in the kitchen doorway, blocking the waitress's path.

"Coming through," she said, jabbing him with her elbow and squeezing by with a tub of dirty dishes.

Donnally glanced over from where he was grilling a steak.

"We're kind of busy around here."

Pipkins straightened his five-foot-nine body that matched his father's pound for pound, mustache for mustache, pudgy jowl for pudgy jowl, and said, "That's not my problem."

Donnally pressed down on the beef with a fork. The meat's slight resistance told him it was medium rare and ready to come off the fire. He slid it from the pan to a plate, then passed it down the stainless steel counter to Will, who was waiting with a ladle of mashed potatoes.

Only then did Donnally turn to face the deputy.

"If you're going to use one of your father's lines, you better learn to use it at the right time." Donnally gestured toward the chaos of the dinner rush. "Otherwise you're just going to keep sounding stupid."

"Fuck you, Harlan, one way or another we'll be having a little talk about your pal Mauricio."

Donnally lowered the fork.

"You find out who stole Pete Johnson's mare?"

The deputy shook his head.

"What about the backhoe from Tractor City?"

Another shake.

"The graffiti at the elementary school?"

Clenched teeth.

"Unless you've got a victim claiming that Mauricio did them wrong, you better get back to doing your job."

Donnally turned again toward the stove.

"And I'll get back to doing mine."

CHAPTER 20

Moments after Donnally passed him on the forest road, Deputy Pipkins flicked on his overheads and siren, and then spun a U-turn that took him off the blacktop and into the gravel. Even in the twilight, Donnally could see in his rearview mirror a cascade of rock and dirt enveloping Pipkins's cruiser. The stunt reminded him of Will's golden retriever who once knocked itself dizzy running into a tree stump while chasing a cat.

Looking over at Mauricio's mutt, Ruby, sitting in the passenger seat, Donnally saw an expression as close to a smile as he'd ever seen on a dog and wondered whether Ruby had made the same connection.

Donnally had already parked his truck in a turnout and was leaning against it by the time Pipkins pulled up. Frozen air sliding up the canyon from the Trinity River where Donnally had spent the day fishing bit at his face and hands, but he wasn't about to give Pipkins the satisfaction of watching him reach for the jacket behind the bench seat.

"You should've just called and asked me to stop by if you wanted to talk about something," Donnally said as Pipkins approached, bundled in a department-issued green parka and wearing a cowboy hat.

Pipkins reddened. "How come you're always telling me what to say and when to say it? You're not my—"

"Father?"

"Fuck you."

Pipkins rested his right hand on the butt of his gun and his left hand on his baton.

"I'm sick of you screwing with me, Harlan. You may've been a big-city detective once, but you're just a short-order cook now."

Donnally glanced back and forth between the two weapons, their outlines framed by Pipkins's headlights. He then noticed that the silence of the forest hadn't yet been broken by voices over the deputy's radio, not even background static.

Pipkins had gone ten-seven. Out of service.

"You follow me across two counties to tell me that?" Donnally asked.

"Nope." Pipkins smirked as he reached into the inside breast pocket of his parka. "To give you this." He unfolded a subpoena and handed it over. "A DA down in Alameda County wanted this served ASAP."

Donnally didn't look at it. He just reached into his truck window and said, "Ruby, how about do me a favor and ruminate on this."

Pipkins laughed like someone had just played into his hand at poker.

"He said you'd do something like that and that he'd be just as happy to have you testify in handcuffs."

"And I guess you've already assigned yourself the task of hooking me up and hauling me down there."

"I'll be waiting for my phone to ring on Tuesday morning with the DA's call. You're either going to be on the stand at 10 A.M. in Oakland or in the back of my patrol car at 10:05."

Donnally grinned. "Don't let the anticipation keep you awake the night before."

"It won't, but something else will." Pipkins leaned back against Donnally's truck and crossed his arms over his chest. "I hear you're good with numbers, Harlan. How about helping me with a little addition?"

The self-satisfied expression on Pipkins's face told Donnally that they'd finally arrived at the real reason Pipkins was putting a dismal end to his good day on the river.

"I get this subpoena," Pipkins continued, "then I call a guy I know in the Sheriff's Department down there and he fills me in about the Charles Brown case. So I backtrack a little bit and find out that you headed on down there right after Mauricio kicked off. It gets me to wondering if there's a connection."

"Apples and oranges," Donnally said. "That's all."

"I don't think so. When the DA called to see if the subpoena arrived, I asked him about how you got into the case. He said you didn't tell him and he doesn't know. That alone tells me you got something to hide. And combine that with the name on the headstone . . ." Pipkins arched his eyebrows. "It kinda gets me thinking that there's a lot more to that little wetback than I thought."

"Which means what?"

"That maybe we should have the city attorney—"

"You mean, your uncle Bud—"

"The city attorney . . . tie up Mauricio's assets until we figure out if it's all legit."

With that comment, Donnally grasped the Pipkins family's preoccupation with Mauricio. They wanted his land. For twenty-five years Pipkins Sr. had used rigged auctions, usually of property seized from pot growers, to build a real estate empire. Everybody in town knew it, but nobody wanted to risk a marijuana plant showing up on their property followed by a zero-tolerance seizure. Now Pipkins Jr. was playing a variation on his father's theme, maybe trying to prove to his father that he'd someday be ready to sit at the head of the family table.

And what more satisfying way of doing it than by robbing a dead Mexican of his land and his legacy.

Pipkins grinned, then reached down and turned on the radio holstered on his belt. He then spoke into the mike attached to his shoulder strap.

"This is Pipkins. I'm ten-eight again."

CHAPTER 21

"There's no way you're going to put me on the stand," Donnally told Blaine over the phone the following morning. He was sitting at his desk in the café office. "You're just covering your ass."

Donnally had it figured out even before he'd driven a mile from where Deputy Pipkins had pulled him over to serve him with the subpoena. As soon as the judge dismissed the case, Blaine would call a press conference and praise Donnally as the one who exposed it, then hint that it was Donnally's fault for losing it because he'd refused to testify in support of the DA's motion to have Brown declared incompetent to stand trial.

Blaine laughed. "Fun, isn't it? It must remind you of what you left behind when you got out of police work. This is like one of those noir movies from the forties, hard to tell who the good guys are."

"Maybe I should go all the way and sign on as a defense witness. I'm sure Margaret Perkins would be glad to have me on her team."

"You missed your chance, pal. We cut a deal late last night."

Donnally's body stiffened and he caught his breath.

"You what?"

"Brown pleads guilty to voluntary manslaughter and gets credit for the time he served in the loony bin."

Donnally's hand clenched the telephone receiver. "And that means he gets out . . ."

"The end of next month."

Donnally pushed himself to his feet, as if the force of his body in motion would deflect the course of the case.

"Is that what a life is worth down there?"

"It's the best we could do," Blaine said. "The judge didn't want to take the political heat for dismissing a murder on speedy trial grounds. The defense gets to wash its hands of the case. And I get a conviction. It works for everybody."

"It sure as hell doesn't work for Anna Keenan."

Blaine snorted. "Well, she's never gonna find out, is she?"

CHAPTER 22 ═══════════

For the first time in his life, Harlan Donnally felt like he'd become a hick. Sitting on a leather couch in the lobby of Schubert, Smith, and Barton, looking out at the San Francisco financial district, wearing jeans and a Levi's jacket, with his gray Stetson lying on the coffee table.

He could've worn a suit. He had one left over from his detective days that still fit.

But when he was getting dressed to drive down from Mount Shasta, he felt like he needed to let Margaret Perkins know that there remained a real flesh-and-blood working world where people still cared about the truth and tried to do the right thing.

But now he wasn't so sure.

After all, what was the real difference between the Blaines and the Nanstons, and the Pipkinses and the Mauricios?

Sitting there, watching the starched shirts and silk ties and eight-hundred-dollar shoes walk from the elevators into the glass-walled conference room bordering the lobby, he concluded that the only difference was the area code.

Donnally rose when Perkins came out from the hallway to the left of the receptionist. He was surprised not just by her genuine smile, but by her pink tennis shoes.

Perkins stuck out her hand as she approached and said, "Maybe we should get out of here and take a walk. There's never been a conversation inside here like the one I think we're about to have."

Donnally nodded, then picked up his hat.

"Do I think he did it?" Perkins said as they walked up Stockton Street toward Chinatown. "I assume so, but I'm too scared of him to give you a rational answer." She reached over and took Donnally's hand for support as the hill steepened, then pointed at her hip. "Brand-new. I'm still getting used to it."

Donnally wondered if she'd done some research on him, learned about him being retired out on disability after the ambush, and was trying to position herself on common ground.

"Then why plead him out?" Donnally asked. His voice was more accusatory than he wanted it to be. "If you believe he's incompetent—"

"No, we *argued* that he was incompetent—"

"Then how can it be ethical to go through with it?"

"Because it's the best disposition for him and I'm obligated to do what's in the interest of my client. And it's not like a felony conviction will change his life. I don't see him applying for a job requiring a top-secret clearance."

Donnally wasn't sure what he'd had in mind as he'd driven down through the Central Valley toward San Francisco, but he'd expected that it would look a lot more like an argument than the conversation it was turning into. He'd even fantasized that Perkins would come into the reception area gloating like all the rest of the imbeciles in the defense bar who celebrated every murderer going free and couldn't grasp that it was a tragedy, not a victory, when the criminal justice system failed.

In thinking back to the smile with which she greeted him, it now seemed like the kind that fellow sufferers offer each other in doctors' offices.

He now wondered whether she'd been swept along by events just as he had been.

"The Albert Hale Foundation mustn't be too thrilled with their poster boy pleading guilty," Donnally said. "Makes Brown look a whole lot less of a victim. In fact, it shows he worked the system better than the folks who run it."

Perkins stopped to take a breath next to one of two potted orange trees bracketing the entrance to a Chinese restaurant.

"The word from on high is that Hale is fine with it," Perkins said. "And his underlings are finally acknowledging what we told them at the start. It was a mistake to jump into the case without looking into it a little deeper. Charles Brown was the wrong guy to build a cause around."

Donnally looked at his watch. It was almost 12:45.

"You hungry?" he asked.

Perkins nodded.

He pointed at the framed menu hanging on the green stucco wall next to the front door.

"How adventurous are you?"

Perkins grinned. "I think we're about to find out."

"What do you call this, again?" Perkins pointed at her almost finished bowl of hand-rolled wheat noodles, beef, pork, scallops, shrimp, mussels, and onions in a spicy red sauce. Her face was pink and sweating.

Donnally smiled at her.

"In Chinese it's called *ma mien*. Horse noodles. The Koreans call it *jambong*. The name of this restaurant is Yantai. It's a city in China right across the Yellow Sea from Seoul."

"And you know that because . . ."

"I had a fascination with maps as a kid."

She set down her chopsticks and spoon and wiped her lips with her napkin.

"Why was that?"

Donnally felt himself stiffen. He hadn't come down to San Francisco to talk about himself, but to find a way to torpedo Brown's deal.

Perkins must have seen something in his eyes. "Come on," she said, "spill it."

He pushed his bowl forward, then folded his arms on the edge of the table. While some of his childhood memories came back to him like half-remembered episodes from the storybooks his mother had read to him, this wasn't one of them. This was real and he knew it was the incident that started his downhill slide from the innocence of childhood.

"I was in the third grade," Donnally finally said. "It was after my brother was killed in Vietnam. I went outside into our backyard, up in the Hollywood Hills—"

Perkins stopped him with furrowed brows.

"My father is in the entertainment business."

Donnally pushed on before she could begin the line of who-what-where questions everyone asked.

"Up there, above the city lights, before I could identify constellations, it just looked like a chaos of stars. And that night they all seemed to be moving together, like you could actually see the universe expanding. Looking back, I suspect that it was a thin layer of clouds passing by that made the stars look like they were moving the opposite way." He paused for a moment, then shook the image from his mind. "In any case, it was unnerving. Ever since that moment I've needed to know where I stand."

"So you're always triangulating your position."

"I guess you could say that."

"And now Charles Brown has been sprung free from the place he was supposed to hold."

"And where he was supposed to spend the rest of his life." Donnally paused as a wave of sadness passed through him, followed by anguish and then anger. "Brown tried to rape Anna Keenan and she resisted. That's not manslaughter. It's capital murder."

Perkins closed her eyes and took a breath.

"What am I supposed to do?" she said, looking at him again. "I also have a place in the world where I fit in. And it comes with obligations not of my own choosing."

Donnally sat in silence for a moment, letting the hollowness of Perkins's final sentence linger, then said:

"At your age and at mine, with money in the bank and a place to live, everything is of our own choosing."

CHAPTER 23 ═══════════

"I understand we have a disposition in this matter," Judge Nanston said, after sitting down behind the bench in the crowded courtroom.

Donnally sensed relief in her voice, and he knew why. Brown's guilty plea had excused her from the obligation of acting on her legal conclusion that the case had to be dismissed on speedy trial grounds. By accepting the deal, she'd escaped a week of infamy on conservative talk radio, maybe even a recall election.

Charles Brown, no longer chained and hand-cuffed to the chair next to Margaret Perkins, stared up at Judge Nanston. His hair had been cut and his beard had been shaved, and he looked ten pounds heavier. Donnally guessed it was from lithium or another manic-depressive drug he'd been given in custody. The innocent expression and gray suit Brown wore gave him the appearance of a minis-ter who was stunned and bewildered by his drunk-driving arrest. Only Brown's eyes betrayed the racing thoughts within.

Perkins rose. "I'm sorry, Your Honor, but I don't believe we have a disposition."

Donnally felt his body tense with expectation. Maybe Perkins had found an escape from what seemed like an ethical straitjacket. Maybe justice would be done after all.

Perkins continued, "The defendant's position is that he's not guilty of the offense."

Blaine's head jerked toward Perkins, his face flushing with fury and betrayal.

Judge Nanston slumped back in her chair.

"Does this mean you want to renew your incompetence motion?" Nanston asked.

"No, Your Honor. We'd like the court to set a trial date."

Donnally spotted Blaine's left hand hanging by his side, rubbing his fingers against each other like he was trying to wipe off pine sap. Donnally didn't expect Blaine to look back. He had avoided Donnally from the moment he'd entered the courtroom ten minutes earlier.

"May we approach, Your Honor?" Blaine asked, his voice taut, suppressing the anger raging within.

Judge Nanston nodded. She rolled her chair to the edge of the platform on which the bench stood, and then leaned over into the huddle of Blaine, Perkins, and the court reporter. Every few seconds, one of them would glance over at Brown, who sat staring down at the defense table.

Donnally glanced up at the courtroom clock, at the silent second hand lurching along against the background of the unintelligible whispers at the front of the courtroom. He scanned the faces of the reporters sitting in the gallery behind him, each one's head angled toward the bench, as though their ears were parabolic microphones.

The group dispersed.

All eyes followed Perkins as she returned to the defense table and sat down. She and Brown leaned in toward each other. He stared at Perkins as she spoke. Finally he swallowed hard and nodded.

Perkins stood and looked up at Judge Nanston.

"We have reached a disposition, Your Honor. Mr. Brown will plead no contest to the count of manslaughter."

Donnally pushed himself to his feet. Everyone in the courtroom turned toward him, except Blaine.

"No contest?" Donnally said, eyes fixed on Blaine's back. "No contest? Like it was a crime that nobody committed?"

Both bailiffs rose, hands on their guns.

Donnally saw the clerk reach under her desk, finger poised to press the alarm that would flood the courtroom with sheriff's deputies.

Perkins faced toward him, her hands extended as though pleading for forgiveness for an act her duty required.

Judge Nanston glared at Blaine like a neighbor demanding that he control his off-leash dog.

Blaine turned and took the few steps toward the low barrier behind which Donnally stood.

"Take it easy, man," Blaine said, reaching for Donnally's shoulder. "This isn't the time—"

Donnally pushed away his hand.

"I know this isn't *the* time, it's the *last* time anybody will have a chance to stop this. What the hell do you think you're doing?"

"The best that I can, under the circumstances."

"Then change the circumstances. Nothing says you have to take this deal. Make him go to trial."

"For what? Given a choice between letting him walk on reasonable doubt and a first-degree murder conviction, the jury would've compromised on manslaughter anyway."

"I'll tell you for what," Donnally said, jabbing a forefinger against Blaine's chest, ignoring the approaching bailiffs. "So Anna Keenan, wherever she is, can hear the word 'guilty.'"

CHAPTER 24

Donnally thought he'd probably looked like a lunatic as he pushed past the television cameras and reporters outside the courthouse on his way to the parking garage.

Watching the eleven o'clock news in Janie's living room confirmed it, for him and for her.

But at least Blaine hadn't blamed him for the outcome of the case during the press conference afterward.

Donnally leaned back on the couch and closed his eyes as he listened to Blaine uttering hateful platitudes about justice and closure, spoken with prosecutorial authority, calculated to make the obscene disposition palatable to the public.

For a moment, the target of Donnally's fury oscillated between Blaine and his audience, both now willing to put someone else's past behind them.

Then another wave of embarrassment.

Donnally cringed as he thought back on his final words to Blaine. He didn't believe in an afterlife, and he sure didn't believe that dead souls wandered among the living, waiting for human justice to release them from the mundane world of their battered flesh.

He knew that it wasn't Anna who needed to hear Brown say the word "guilty."

It wasn't even Mauricio who needed to hear it.

It was himself: a short-order cook in a two-bit town dwarfed into insignificance by its namesake lump of dirt and rock towering above it.

Janie reached over and touched his arm as a reporter quoted Donnally's final words in court.

He looked again at the screen. The woman stood with the lake behind her, face framed by auburn hair, the microphone held high. She said again, now whispering, "So Anna Keenan, wherever she is, can hear the word 'guilty.'" She lowered the mike as her eyes welled up and the camera panned past her toward the shimmering water.

Donnally then knew why he chose those words. He was yelling fire in a complacent world's theater, only to have it transformed into melodrama for the eleven o'clock news.

He also knew that his father would be so very, very proud.

Donnally rose from the couch and walked upstairs to the bedroom. He closed his eyes after he lay down, wondering if that melodrama had been his plan all along, wondering if he'd once again let himself be seduced by his father's magic in turning life into fiction.

He thought back to his father entering his ICU room at SF Medical where he lay after he had been shot. Even in the gray haze of morphine, he'd seen his father hesitate in the doorway as though framing the scene, choosing the camera angle, the point of view, the distance.

In that moment, Donnally had felt himself break in two, as though his mind had risen above his body, suspended like a lens, watching, recording, as if what happened to him had actually happened to someone else, to a character in a movie.

OPENING SCENE: Squad Room. Undercover operation run-through. Homicide Detective Harlan Donnally will park his car next to Morelia Taqueria and walk past the Norteño bodyguards and into the restaurant. He'll slide into a bench seat across from Alberto Villarreal and make the trade: a get-out-of-jail-free card for a name.

CUT TO: Shootout. Donnally firing at Norteño Gangster Number One and Sureño Gangster Number Three, both too preoccupied with shooting at each other to notice the detective with the double-handed grip leaning over the hood of his car.

JUMP CUT/HIGH ANGLE: A top-down view of Donnally sprawled on the Mission Street sidewalk next to the wheel well of his bullet-ridden undercover Chevy. Unmoving legs. Back riveted to the pavement. His Levi's and leather jacket soaking up splotches of Coke and salsa.

TRAVELING SHOT: The whoop-whoop of patrol cars bursting through the South of Market intersections from the police station a half mile away.

PAN SHOT: Following behind the siren blasts reverberating against the storefronts lining the street: Carniceria Michoacan, Tortilleria Juarez, Tacos Guadalajara.

FREEZE FRAME AND CLOSE-UP: A bra and panty-clad manikin in a store window. A bullet hole in her throat.

POV: Donnally's vertigo as the paramedic flops him away from the curb and toward the shattered plate-glass shop windows. Then a view past the black boots of the EMT squatting near his head and toward the Starbucks fifteen yards away.

"Cut!" his father yells.

Donnally watches director Donald Harlan point his finger at the couple slumped over the wrought-iron table in front of the coffee shop, their fake blood dripping through the latticed top onto the sidewalk.

"Don't just slump," his father says, throwing up his arms. "Audiences don't want slumping. They want wrenching, spasmodic writhing. And knock over the goddamn coffee cups. Nobody's going to believe you've been killed unless you knock over the goddamn coffee cups."

VOICE-OVER:

NEWSCASTER

Officer caught in a crossfire.

CRANE SHOT: Dead Mexican gangsters lying in the street, all but their snakeskin boots covered by the medical examiner's plastic sheets.

JUMP CUT: The shooting review board.

VOICE-OVER:

SFPD CAPTAIN

Let's hear your version, Detective. Tell us what led up to the ambush.

"Ambush," Donnally mumbled.

"What?" Janie leaned up on an elbow. It was still dark out. "What did you say?"

Donnally rubbed his eyes. "Nothing."

"It sounded like you said 'ambush.'"

"I must've been dreaming."

"About the shooting?"

"No, not now. It was last night as I was falling asleep."

Janie reached over and ran her hands through his hair. "Are you fighting a battle in there, or planning one?"

Donnally stared up at the invisible ceiling.

"I don't know what I was doing."

"I can't let this go until I hear him say it," Donnally said to Janie, as they walked along the fog-curtained Ocean Beach after breakfast. Far ahead of them in the semidarkness stood a shivering crowd drawn to the shoreline by a rough tide's exposure of the wreckage of the *King Phillip*, a clipper ship that went aground in the nineteenth century.

"Because of how you think you looked on television?"

"No," Donnally said. "This isn't about me."

They stopped and watched the fog reach inland, over the surf and sand, insulating them, isolating them, the gulls wheeling away, their calls and shrieks fading like distant echoes.

Donnally took in a long breath and exhaled, then looked over at Janie.

"Tell me," Donnally said. "Which is worse? Them failing to get Brown convicted over all those years or letting him plead no contest and drift away like he did nothing at all?"

Janie didn't answer right away, her eyes moving, seeming to search the gray around them for something solid to attach her thoughts to.

Finally she said, "I'm not sure there is a worse." She looked up at him. "Or even that they're all that different. It seems to me they did the same thing twice."

Donnally nodded. "And I'm not going to let it end this way."

CHAPTER 25

The burglar wasn't after money.

Donnally recognized that the moment he stepped into Mauricio's office. The petty cash tin lay open with the same fifty dollars inside that had been there since Mauricio checked himself into the hospital. Someone was either looking for something more valuable or trying to send a message, or both.

The voice on the blinking answering machine gave Donnally the answer.

"Interesting thing, Harlan," Deputy Pipkins said on the recording. "I checked DMV and birth records and the only Mauricio Aguilera born in California on January 14, 1956, died on January 15, 1956. What do you make of that, Detective?" Pipkins chuckled. "Oh, yeah, there's one other thing. Strictly speaking, can you call them wetbacks if they snuck in across the desert?"

The next voice he heard was Will's, but coming from within his own head:

Deputy Asshole.

Donnally extracted the tape and slipped it into his shirt pocket. He didn't put in a new one. Mauricio was done receiving messages.

While he straightened the papers on the desk,

Donnally wondered what difference it made whether Pipkins found out the truth about Mauricio. Maybe he'd been resisting not because the truth would hurt anybody, but simply because Pipkins was Pipkins, or maybe because Pipkins was his father's son.

By the time he'd stepped back and uprighted a chair, he realized that it made a difference for the same reason that promises made to the dying did.

And it sure as hell wasn't because the dead cared afterward.

It was because the living had to live with themselves.

Donnally checked the rear door and each of the rooms until he found where Deputy Pipkins had broken in. Scuff marks showed that he had climbed through a bedroom window that was concealed from the café parking lot by an overgrown pyracantha.

After retrieving a flashlight from the kitchen, Donnally leaned over the sill and shined the beam toward the ground and among the intertwined and leaf-cluttered branches.

A glint of silver flashed back.

He swept the beam past the same spot a second time.

Another flash.

He locked on it and squinted until he could make out the outline of a basket-woven rectangular square of leather with a chrome clasp: Deputy Asshole's ticket book.

A metallic pop and a "Jesus fucking Christ!" startled Donnally awake as he lay in Mauricio's bed at 2 A.M.

Branches thrashed against the glass and the wood siding as Pipkins flailed, each yank on the badger trap onto which Donnally had tied the ticket book driving the jaws deeper into the deputy's wrist.

Donnally grabbed his shotgun and racked it.

He heard an "Oh shit," then the crunching of Pipkins fighting his way toward the ground, deeper among the thorns and out of the line of fire.

"Don't shoot, you son of a bitch," Pipkins yelled.

"Give me a good reason."

Pipkins didn't have an answer that wouldn't embarrass him in front of his department or make him appear even more pitiful than he already was, and they both knew it.

Donnally reached for his cell phone, located a number, and pressed "send."

"This is Donnally. I'm at Mauricio's. Come get your idiot kid."

CHAPTER 26 ═══════════

Rain thudded against his truck's windshield and hammered the pavement as Donnally sat in the parking lot of the Santa Rita jail, spread out in a central Alameda County valley.

He looked at his watch. It was nearly 3 P.M., kick-out time for Charles Brown and the rest of the prisoners who had completed their sentences.

Donnally wondered how much the place had changed since the few trips he'd made out to the campuslike facility more than a decade earlier. The long, wide hallways and the bare interview rooms, with their unscuffed paint and inmate-waxed linoleum, were then as sterile as hospital floors and lacked the grime of despair and hopelessness that sometimes made the guilty want to purge themselves. As he watched the entrance at the end of the rising, grass-bordered walkway, Donnally wondered whether the place had now deteriorated enough to make detective work possible.

The slow clunk-swish of his wipers provided more rhythm than clarity as he waited for Brown to emerge. A couple of defense attorneys ran from their cars toward the entrance, attaché cases gripped with one hand, legal newspapers held above their heads for shelter with the other.

He recognized one of them: Mark Hamlin, Sonny Goldstine's lawyer, and wondered whether Sonny had finally been arrested for the gun he wasn't supposed to own, and whether Hamlin had come to represent him, or maybe just to shut him up in order to protect others connected to the Tsukamata murder all those years earlier.

In any case, Sonny would surely have to wonder where Hamlin's loyalties lay: with him or with former clients among the remnants of the sixties and seventies radicals whose secrets Sonny might want to trade to buy his way out of a third-strike life sentence.

For a moment, Donnally enjoyed thinking through the trajectories and anticipating the collisions, for time and distance and weariness had broken the gravitational pull of caring about Sonny's future.

But then he remembered the dollar that tied him and Sonny together and that was still in the pocket of his Levi's jacket. It made him feel queasy, doubting whether he should've accepted the money. Not only had he gotten nothing for it, but it felt like a leash around his throat.

A few minutes later, inmates began filing out through the front door and into the rain. They looked to Donnally like refugees who were still dressed in the clothes they were wearing when the bombs fell or the earthquake struck and destroyed their homes. He turned his wipers on high and peered out through the windshield, inspecting the men first for race, then size, then features.

The men streamed out one-by-one, then collected at the bus stop at the foot of the walkway. The weak stood in the rain and the strong under the surrounding trees.

But no Charles Brown.

Maybe he'd been moved to the county hospital psych ward, Donnally wondered.

Maybe he got released earlier.

Maybe—

The door opened again. It was Hamlin. Walking backward. His arms spread wide like he was trying to herd an escaped goat back into a pen.

Then Brown walked out, shaking his head and holding his hands out in front of him as though he was blocking an assault.

It wasn't Sonny after all who had brought Hamlin to Santa Rita.

Hamlin backed down the walkway another twenty feet, moving side to side as Brown tried to slip around him with his eyes lowered and his body hunched. Hamlin reached into his shirt pocket and pulled out a business card. Brown pushed it aside, then cut across the grass, angling west away from the bus stop and toward the two-lane road leading to the freeway.

Hamlin watched him go, then stared at the receding figure like a salesman whose deal of a lifetime had been rejected by a customer.

In that gesture, Donnally saw Hamlin's plan expose itself like a pervert opening his raincoat. Hamlin had intended to sign up Brown as a client, then call a press conference and display the hangdog lunatic as a victim of judicial abuse. He'd claim

that the harmless, innocent man-child had pleaded
no contest solely to end a miscarriage of justice,
and then he would leverage that claim into a lawsuit against everyone who'd laid a hand on Brown,
maybe even Donnally himself.

But Brown had walked away from it.

Why? Donnally asked himself. Too crazy to
grasp his own self-interest? Rushing to reclaim his
square of sidewalk in Noe Valley? Hurrying to get
a blow job from a homeless crack addict behind a
bush in Golden Gate Park?

Donnally watched the rain soak into Hamlin's
three-piece suit, then smiled to himself as the lawyer's hair flattened to his head like seaweed on an
exposed rock. Hamlin took a last look at his forty
percent fee slipping away and then ran inside out of
the rain.

CHAPTER 27

Brown, head down, seemed to Donnally not to be following a chosen route, but merely his feet, as he walked the maze of streets, lanes, courts, drives, and parkways that composed the Dublin Commons housing development.

Donnally tracked him from a distance, the space between them stretching and contracting like an accordion, Donnally pulling to the curb while Brown made progress, then catching up to close the gap.

Brown finally made it out of the neighborhood and under the freeway and into an office park. Another campus, but this one for software developers, temp agencies, and Internet startups.

The rain let up, but a cold breeze from the Pacific catapulting the hills bore down, causing Brown to shiver as he stood across the parking lot from the Sweet & Savory Café at the edge of a five-acre business complex.

Brown finally walked toward the entrance, but instead of going in, he sat down next to its double glass doors and wrapped his arms around his bent legs and rested his head on his knees.

A creature of habit, Donnally thought. A mascot again.

After Donnally pulled to the curb, he noticed that the restaurant served only breakfast and lunch. If Brown had reverted back to Rover the Mascot, he'd picked a bad place to start. Lunch was long over and breakfast wouldn't be served until tomorrow morning.

Donnally glanced at this watch. In ninety minutes the sun would fall behind the hills and the valley temperature would begin sinking toward the forecasted twenty degrees. At some point in the descent, Donnally figured, Brown would be ready to accept the truck as the closest, warmest, safest escape from an alien, frozen suburb whose only refuges for the transient bore the names of Hilton, Hyatt, and Radisson, not Rescue Mission or Salvation Army.

When Donnally looked up again, a security guard was rolling up in a golf cart. The cart rocked and its miniature American flag whipped as a blockish man with a bovine face twisted into a scowl climbed out and approached Brown.

Donnally recognized the swagger. It was of a failed cop-wannabe whose life had already peaked, either when he'd made a game-saving tackle during his junior year in high school or when he got laid for the first time later that night.

The guard stopped a foot away from Brown. He scanned the parking lot, then kicked Brown in the ribs with the reinforced toe of his black work boots. Brown grunted, flopped to his side, and then shielded his head with his hands.

The restaurant door swung open and a woman in a baker's apron pushed her way between the two and then slapped the guard's face with a wet dish towel, all the while screaming words that were unintelligible to Donnally from where he sat inside his truck.

The guard raised his hands in self-defense, but didn't grab for the cloth or strike back.

She screamed at him again, then turned toward Brown, now looking up from the wet concrete, cowering and bewildered.

Donnally decided that he couldn't take the chance of Brown either being rescued by the woman or escaping into the complex beyond, so he jumped down from the truck.

Brown alerted to Donnally crossing the parking lot toward him. His eyes went wide, then he scooted backward, trying to rise and run away at the same time.

The woman and the guard turned toward Donnally and, like domestic combatants interrupted by the police, joined each other against him. As the woman pushed the security guard into Donnally's path, the hulk transformed himself from a misbehaving puppy into her Doberman.

Donnally flashed his retirement badge as he ran by them, the sight of the gold shield first freezing the pair in place, then uniting him and the guard in common cause against Brown. Donnally grabbed the back of Brown's jacket, swung him down to the concrete, and kneeled on his back. The guard held his feet while Donnally snapped handcuffs on his wrists.

"What did he do?" the woman asked as Donnally rose to his feet.

"He murdered somebody."

She gasped and covered her mouth with the towel. "I'm sorry. I had no idea."

Donnally glanced at Brown lying mute on the wet walkway, then looked back at her.

"You've got nothing to be sorry about."

He turned toward the security guard.

"I appreciate your help, but don't go kicking people. Nobody appointed you judge and jury."

A flash of lighting and a crack of thunder gave Donnally an excuse to haul Brown away before the two had a chance to ask enough questions to figure out that he'd already appointed himself.

CHAPTER 28

"It's called kidnapping," Janie said, standing at the foot of the stairs in the basement, her eyes locked on Brown. He sat handcuffed and chained to a metal workbench that was anchored to the concrete floor. She'd just returned home from a late group counseling session in the psych ward at Fort Miley VA hospital a few blocks away.

"He said he came here voluntarily," Donnally answered, pointing at the tape recorder lying on the chair next to where he sat.

Janie glared at Donnally.

"Voluntarily? Like the way a cornered criminal surrenders voluntarily?"

"You could say that."

"You've gone overboard on this." She glanced back and forth between him and Brown. "I'm not sure which of you is more crazy."

"I'm not crathy," Brown said, rotating his head toward her. "It wath a lie. I've never been crathy."

Donnally grinned at Janie. "I'm not sure you're supposed to use the word 'crazy.'"

"It's not a diagnosis. It's what we call otherwise sane people who go out of their minds just long enough to destroy their lives." Her face flushed and she jabbed her fingers against her chest. "And take other people down with them."

Donnally flicked on the tape recorder and held it out toward Brown. "You don't blame Janie for anything that's happened today, do you, Charles?"

Brown stared at her for a moment, then at Donnally, and shook his head.

"The tape recorder can't see you. You've got to say it aloud."

"No, I don't blame Janie."

Donnally switched it off.

"See?" Donnally said. "If he's competent enough to enter a plea in the case, then he's competent enough to let you off the hook."

"What about the handcuffs?" Janie asked.

Donnally looked down at the tape recorder. "I don't see any handcuffs."

Janie was sitting at the kitchen table when Donnally returned from serving Brown his dinner. She had a half-finished glass of wine in her hand and an unopened box of Chinese takeout in front of her.

Donnally had the feeling he was about to lose his appetite, too. He set Brown's plate in the sink, then sat down across from her.

"I shouldn't have brought him here," Donnally said. "I'm sorry. This is your house."

"Until now, I liked having it as our house, whatever 'our' means."

"Look, I'll testify that you had nothing to do with it."

"You won't have to. It's not like he's going to run

to the police, and even if he did, nobody would pay attention."

They sat in silence for a moment, then she took a sip of wine and said, "I think it's time for me to move out and move on. I've just been in orbit. Circling the same spot in the universe and not really bumping into anything."

Donnally felt gravity give way. "But we're—"

"What? We're what? People who occupy the same space every few months, or like now when you happened by on a mission that you don't even understand."

"I understand it perfectly. The truth has got to come out."

"If you're worried about the truth, you should've started a little closer to home, like with your father. It's the blood on his hands, not on Charles Brown's, that drives you." She smirked as if she didn't care whether their relationship ended that second. "Or is that just a little too much truth for you?"

"He's got nothing to do with this."

"He's got everything do to with it. Every murderer you ever hunted down was a surrogate for your father."

Donnally leaned back in his chair and folded his arms across his chest. "I didn't realize that you've been psychoanalyzing me."

"I should've started a helluva lot sooner. I'm not sure why I gave you a pass all these years."

"Maybe because then you'd have to figure out what, exactly, you've been up to. After all, it's the Vietnamese that he always portrays as either monsters or cannon fodder, or as prostitutes."

It was like every other argument they'd ever had, Donnally thought as he kicked at the Ocean Beach sand. Start someplace real, spin onto a tangent, re-create the past for whatever was the current need, and then he or she would say something meant to hurt worse than heartache. Somehow the real point, the real source of the pain, would get lost.

Donnally stopped a few feet from where the high tide died. It was only then, within the sound of the breaking waves and against the cold wind off the water, that he grasped why Brown's no-contest plea had torn into him. It was as if no one had snuck into Anna Keenan's bedroom, no one had climbed on top of her, no one had put his hands around her throat, no one had restrained her desperate thrashing, no one had muffled her screams, no one had felt her body go limp, no one had climbed out of her window—

Donnally felt his line of thought get hijacked and yanked off course.

Climbed out of her window?

He closed his eyes and locked his hands on top of his head.

Why would Brown climb out of her window?

Was it panic?

Was it guilt?

Did people like Charles Brown even feel guilt?

Donnally tried to visualize the police diagram he'd copied from the court file.

Why didn't Brown just walk to the kitchen and out of the back door, or even out of the front door, like nothing happened?

But neighbors said they'd spotted Brown climbing the back fence and running away.

Donnally lowered his hands and opened his eyes.

Maybe it really was just a manslaughter. A premeditating murderer would've concealed both his approach and his escape in the normalcy of everyday life, not drawn attention to the crime or to himself by climbing over fences and running through yards.

Even so, Donnally swore as he turned back toward the city. *I want to hear him say it. No contest isn't good enough.*

CHAPTER 29 ═══════════

Donnally slipped through the kitchen door into the house. He wanted to force the words out of Brown, then drive him to Golden Gate Park and point him toward the bushes.

And he didn't want to risk another argument with Janie.

The house was quiet, not even the sound of Janie's bedroom television.

The basement stairs creaked as Donnally walked down. He wished he'd fixed them last year when she'd complained. The sound foreclosed the surprise he wanted. Without it, Brown would tense. Lock himself up. Bury his face in his hands and pretend the world away.

Donnally imagined Brown looking over at the stairs, watching his feet come into view where the overhead fluorescent fixture cast light on the steps, then his legs, and his torso and the semiautomatic holstered on his belt. Fear building in Brown's mind. Maybe he'd even panic at the delusion that Donnally was coming down to kill him, cut up his body with the power saw on the shelf, and bury the pieces in the backyard.

Why not march down the stairs, Donnally asked himself, *pound his heels into the wood, match crazy with crazy?*

But he didn't want Brown just to say the words, he wanted Brown to mean them.

He slowed his pace and lightened his steps. Just a friend coming to visit.

Donnally took the final turn.

Brown's chair was empty.

The chains that had held him lay snaked on the floor.

Donnally grabbed a two-by-four, cocked it like a baseball bat, and ducked toward the space under the stairs.

Empty.

He tossed down the board and ran back up the steps.

Brown wasn't hiding in the downstairs bathroom or in Janie's office.

Janie.

Donnally ran up the next flight. Her bedroom door was open and her bed was in disarray. The bathroom light was on. He pulled his gun, imagining Brown standing over her bloody body lying in the tub.

Four steps later, he faced an empty bathroom.

He heard a muffled sound from down the hallway, then spun back toward the door and ran to the next bedroom. The door was closed.

He heard a voice from within. Janie's. "No."

At least she was still alive.

An image of Brown strangling Anna flashed

through Donnally's mind. He was sure Brown was kneeling over Janie. If he shot at Brown and missed, he'd hit her. He slipped the gun back into his holster, wishing he'd brought the board from the basement and imagining the thunk of wood against the back of Brown's skull.

Donnally eased his hand around the doorknob and turned it. He heard a soft click of the bolt sliding past the strike plate. He pushed the door inward an inch, then allowed the knob to turn back. He lodged his forearm against the door and set himself to spring across the ten feet between it and the bed, grab Brown by his shoulders, and throw him to the floor.

He flung the door open, took a step, then froze.

Brown was curled into a fetal position at the head of the bed. Janie was sitting at the foot, dressed in her robe. They both flinched and looked up at Donnally, Brown in terror, Janie in anger.

"What are you doing?" she asked, raising her hands in complaint.

"I should be asking you that."

"You said it's my house. And in my house I can do what I want."

Donnally extended his palm toward her. "Don't put him in the middle of us." He stepped forward. "Let me do what I brought him here to do."

She rose and blocked his path. "No."

"No what?"

"I've decided to make him my patient."

"And have him do to you what he did to Anna when she took him in?"

"How do you know he did anything to her?"

Donnally glanced at the ceiling and rolled his eyes. "You're as nuts as he is."

Janie reached toward the dresser and picked up a plastic pill bottle. She tossed it to Donnally. He looked at the label. Lithium prescribed at the Santa Rita jail.

"He's been on that since he first appeared in court. His attorney insisted on it. Perkins wanted him to be competent to stand trial. She wanted to know the truth, too."

"The truth? You think he was ever going to tell the truth to her? Or you?"

"In time."

Donnally locked his hands on his waist and glared past her at Brown. "The time is now." Then back at her. "Ask him why his fingerprints were on the windowsill?"

"I already know."

"How could you know? You haven't seen the ID tech's report."

"Which way were the fingerprints facing?" Janie asked.

"The way they'd be if someone let themselves down."

"Or pulled himself up to look in?"

Donnally drew back, feeling himself wrenched around by the change in perspective.

"What?"

"He says he pulled himself up to look inside."

"More likely he climbed inside to attack her after she locked him out."

Janie pointed down toward the dining room. "Get the report."

Donnally walked downstairs. His legs were weak. The fixed point toward which he had been marching had tumbled away.

He gave his head a shake. *Not yet.* Brown had years to figure out a story that matched the evidence. Surely he had moments of clarity long enough to accomplish that.

The reports lay in an accordion file on the table. Donnally slipped off the rubber band and flipped through them until he found the crime scene diagram and photographs.

He dropped into a chair and inspected a photograph of the outside of the house below the window. Scuff marks. Wide at the top. Thin at the bottom. Someone trying to push himself up. His shoes slipping. But none higher than two feet off the ground.

He then rose and walked to the double-hung window behind him. He imagined himself climbing in. His hands first gripping the sill, then twisting as he pulled himself over and in.

He turned around and looked down at the photograph. No twist. Just the fingers and palm of each hand facing inward, a little smudge forward and a little smudge back.

Donnally closed his eyes.

What had Brown said in front of the Noe Valley Bakery?

"They told me I killed her. Do you know if I killed her?"

Then what did he say? Something about Atascadero.

"They put me in Atascadero. I started to remember."

Remember what?

Donnally felt gravity sucking him down as he forced himself to climb back upstairs, struggling under the weight of his misplaced certainty. He paused on the landing, recalling Saam Ji telling him in the park that Brown gave him the willies because of the way he looked at women.

"Rover's really gonna hurt somebody someday," Saam Ji had said.

But Brown hadn't. He'd mostly only hurt himself, punching walls and trees and news racks. Even the injury to Katrisha had been the result of a similar kind of blind lashing out.

Maybe Brown did have delusions about women, about Anna, maybe even now about Janie. Maybe he truly did believe that Anna wanted him to touch her, and it was the delusion alone, and not the evidence, that had made him seem guilty, even to his own lawyers, over all these years.

CHAPTER 30

Donnally, Janie, and Brown sat the kitchen table, their breakfast plates before them.

"Did you want to take lithium after you were arrested?" Janie asked Brown.

"They said it would help, but it didn't. It made me sick. They tied me to the bed, but it gave me diarrhea and they wouldn't let me go to the toilet. And I kept throwing up, laying on my back. I was choking. I begged them to stop."

Janie looked over at Donnally. "They gave him too much at the beginning. In those days, dosing amounts were still a mystery."

"And you told your attorney?" Donnally asked him.

"The judge made them stop." Brown stared down at his half-eaten scrambled eggs. "Anna told me Dr. Sherwyn was bad, but I thought he wanted to help me."

Donnally glanced at Janie, his expression telling her that Brown was delusional, unable to recall the sequence of events that led him to meet Sherwyn only after Anna was dead.

"Are you sure it was Anna?" Janie asked.

Brown's head jerked up and down with such force that his body shook.

"That was after they argued about *Star Wars*."

Donnally slumped in his chair and exhaled.

"R2D2. They argued about R2D2 and RT. She said to Dr. Sherwyn, 'I know who you are. A rabbit.' She said he was a rabbit. And he called her Alice in Wonderland."

Donnally looked into Brown's eyes, now darting. Obviously hallucinating.

"Where were they talking?" Janie asked.

"In Anna's living room."

"Where were you?"

Brown looked around. "Here."

"What do you mean, here?" Donnally asked.

"The kitchen. I mean her kitchen. I peeked around the door. He looked like a rabbit."

Donnally smiled to himself. Despite his delusions, Brown had gotten that right. Even in his mid-sixties and probably thirty pounds heavier than back then, Dr. Sherwyn still had a pointy face and disproportionate ears.

Brown scrunched up his nose, exposing his upper teeth. "He did that when he was thinking."

That was a tic that Donnally had noticed during Sherwyn's testimony, but he thought it was just a defensive grimace prompted by Blaine's attacks.

"Did anyone else hear the conversation?" Donnally asked, hoping that something in Brown's story had a bit of truth, some kind of starting point from which his stream of consciousness flowed and toward which Donnally could work back.

"Anna's mother, Trudy. Trudy was there." Brown grinned. "She knows R2D2. She told me so."

CHAPTER 31 ══════════════════

Katrisha Brown's flight from Seattle to San Francisco arrived an hour late. The fog layer eclipsing the airport had kept incoming planes grounded all over the country under the theory that if there was no place to land, there was no reason to take off.

She handed her black duffel bag to Donnally, who was waiting by the TSA security checkpoint, then looked past him toward the terminal's automatic exit doors.

"I need a cigarette," she said, "and to have my head examined."

Donnally smiled at her. "You'll be going to the right place."

Katrisha had told Donnally over the telephone that she'd never divorced Charles Brown. She'd filed in San Francisco, but her process server couldn't find him. Then, after Brown was arrested for the murder of Anna Keenan, there was no way she would chance letting him know where she was living, much less appear in court to face him, until Donnally called her.

The consequence was that since she was a navy veteran and Brown was still her spouse, he was eligible for psych treatment at Fort Miley.

Janie was waiting just inside the monolithic Mayan Deco entrance to the hospital lobby. Donnally introduced Katrisha, and then Janie guided them toward a waiting room crowded with hobbled veterans and their families. Katrisha paused at the threshold and scanned the faces until she spotted Brown sitting by himself in a corner, head down, face shaven, hands in his lap.

Katrisha jutted her chin toward him. "You clean him up for the occasion?"

Donnally glanced over at Janie and smiled. "It was a joint effort. You want to talk to him?"

"Let's just get the paperwork over with." Katrisha jerked her thumb over her shoulder. "There's a bar stool a couple of blocks down with my name on it."

Brown rose and walked toward them.

"Shit. If that asshole touches me," Katrisha said, "I'll break his neck."

Donnally intercepted Brown a few steps away, then put his arm around his shoulders and whispered, "Just do what we agreed, nothing more. Okay?"

Brown nodded, but Donnally could see in his eyes that his mind was racing, on the edge of a manic episode.

Janie walked over and took hold of Brown's hand, now trembling like he had Parkinson's, a side effect of the new drugs she'd put him on. Finding medications he could live with had been one of the things Janie hoped to accomplish once he was admitted.

They approached Katrisha. Brown pulled his

arm free of Donnally. Katrisha half turned and raised her palms in defense, but Brown simply extended his hand and looked at her, his face wide and innocent with an expression of hesitant expectation.

Katrisha accepted his hand.

Brown looked at Donnally, then back at her and said, "Thank you, Katrisha. I'll try my best."

Her eyes welled up as if she had just glimpsed the twenty-year-old she'd married concealed inside the wreck he'd since become. She let go of his hand and wiped away her tears with the cuff of her jacket.

"I know you will, Charles."

An hour later, Katrisha was perched next to Donnally on the bar stool she had coveted. She took a sip of her beer, then flipped the bird at the "No Smoking" sign hanging by the tavern door.

"You know how many times I've heard him say he'd try?" Katrisha said, spinning her cigarette pack on the bar in front of her. "Dozens. You know how many psych wards I went trekking to, getting him committed? How many court appearances I made begging them to keep him locked up?"

Donnally nodded. "I know it was a struggle."

She looked over at Donnally.

"It's not going to work," Katrisha said. "He'll be off his meds and back on the street in no time. That's just the way he is."

CHAPTER 32

Sonny Goldstine grinned when he saw Donnally walking toward where he sat on his porch in West Berkeley. The yard was as overgrown as when Donnally last saw it.

"I saw you on television a while back," Sonny said. "Man you looked pissed."

"I still am."

"I figured. I went the no-contest route myself a couple of times. Practically made me feel innocent. Kind of like a purification ceremony." Sonny looked up at the noon sun, then rose to his feet. "You want a beer?"

Donnally nodded as he climbed the three steps. Sonny pointed at a second rocking chair, then walked inside the house. He returned a few minutes later with two cans of Coors and handed one to Donnally.

Donnally held his up and inspected it. "I didn't think you sixties types drank Coors. Something about their right wing politics. Heritage Foundation and all that anti-farmworker stuff."

"I draw the political line at beer." Sonny took a long drink, smacked his lips, and said, "I got . . . to have . . . my beer." He dropped into the chair next to

Donnally. "What brings you back to Shady Acres?"

"I need to talk to Trudy."

Sonny smirked. "You and everybody else. It ain't gonna happen."

"Yes it is."

"How do you figure?"

"You're going to take me."

"Not a chance."

"Either that or I'll start tearing things up."

"The cops have tried that already."

"I can do things they can't."

"What? Kidnap me and make me take you to her?"

Donnally looked over. "It'll be my second one this week."

Sonny's head snapped toward Donnally, who shrugged, as if to say, *Don't ask. I'm not telling.*

Sonny gazed toward the street for a few moments, then took a sip of his beer.

"I'm too old to hide out," Sonny said. "I'll call somebody who'll call somebody who'll call somebody. I'll let Trudy be the one who decides whether or not she wants to talk to you."

Two days later, Donnally sat in the passenger seat of Sonny's 1955 Willys Wagon. The springs in the seats creaked as Sonny backed into the street, and the gears ground as he shifted into first and headed toward the freeway.

"You sure this thing is going to make it?" Donnally asked.

Sonny grinned as if to say that he knew Donnally didn't have a clue where Trudy was living.

"Just how far do you think it has to go?" Sonny asked.

"Nineteen seventy-five."

Sonny skirted north around San Francisco Bay, dropped off the freeway at San Rafael, headed though the rolling hills of Marin County, then along the coast. The gusting ocean wind buffeting off the rattling Willys made it sound like an airplane taking off.

They pulled into a parking lot in Fort Bragg just after sunset and entered the Dead End Café. Sonny pointed at a table along the window facing the commercial fishing harbor, then walked through the swinging double doors into the kitchen.

Donnally wondered whether Trudy Keenan would follow Sonny back out.

He got his answer two minutes later.

Sonny returned alone.

"What was that about?" Donnally asked, after Sonny sat down across from him.

"Just checking to make sure nobody followed us up here."

"How would they know?"

Sonny tilted his head toward the freeway they'd traveled. "The hills have eyes."

"And what did they see?"

"Two guys in a Ford Expedition were on our tail as far as San Rafael, but they got trapped in city traffic."

"Trapped?"

"Let just say that somebody who used to live with us at New Sky still hasn't learned to parallel park."

A waitress in a tie-dyed shift walked up and took their orders. She was old enough to have been at the commune in the seventies, but Donnally couldn't detect any sign that she was Sonny's contact at the café.

Sonny grinned at Donnally as she walked away. "Nice try, pal, but it's not her. She's a divorcee from Boston just arrived to pursue the new age dream."

"I thought metaphysics was all in your head and you could do it anyplace, even while serving clam chowder at Fenway Park."

"Some people need the scenery."

"Is that why Trudy is up here?"

"No. She's so trapped inside herself. It doesn't make any difference where she is."

"Then why Mendocino County?"

Sonny glanced toward the waitress, who was handing the order form to the cook.

"She blends in."

After dinner, Sonny led Donnally across the dark parking lot to the back of the Willys and lowered the rear gate.

"Let me see your cell phone," Sonny said. "I need to make sure your GPS isn't activated."

Donnally removed it from his jeans pocket, punched his way through three levels of the menu, then showed the screen to Sonny.

Sonny nodded, then pointed back and forth between Donnally and the interior and said, "You'll be riding back here." He glanced around to see if anyone was watching them, and then reached inside and withdrew a ski mask with the eyeholes sewn closed.

"If you trust me to get you to Trudy," Sonny said. "I'll trust you to keep your head down and this covering it."

Donnally lay down on the sleeping bag–covered bed and slipped on the mask. Moments after Sonny closed him in, he pulled out his gun and checked the safety. He was able to keep track of Sonny's first few turns, then he was lost. He could tell the kind of roads they were on by the vibrations and the jolting, but not the direction or the distance.

Gravel ticking up from below and rattling against the undercarriage an hour later told Donnally that Sonny had turned off the pavement. The wagon bucked, bumped him into the air, and then slammed him down.

"Sorry, man," Sonny said. "I didn't see that one coming."

A half hour of bouncing and jostling later, Sonny stopped. The abrupt end to the chaos of squeaking springs and shuddering metal made the silence seem hollow.

"You can take off the mask," Sonny said, opening his door.

Donnally lowered the tailgate and climbed out into the night, grateful to be breathing mountain air instead of the Willys's exhaust. He flinched at the light emerging from the first floor of the two-story log cabin, then heard footsteps behind him. He turned toward the soft crunch of boots on pine needles. The bearded man ignored Donnally and walked up to Sonny.

"You search him?" the man asked.

"Yeah, Bear. Before we left."

Bear turned toward Donnally. "Raise your arms."

The man patted down Donnally's chest, sides, and the inside and outside of his legs, then nodded.

"He's clean," Bear said.

Sonny looked over at Donnally, eyebrows narrowed. Donnally hooked his thumbs over his belt buckle and patted the top of his zipper as if to say that amateurs are too squeamish to squeeze another guy's crotch.

"See. I told you," Sonny said.

Bear shrugged and pointed at the cabin door, then turned and walked off into the darkness.

"Bear?" Donnally said to Sonny. "These folks couldn't come up with a nickname more original than Bear?"

Sonny grinned. "They're strong believers in recycling."

Donnally followed Sonny inside. A sixty-five-year-old woman sitting wrapped in an afghan next to the stone fireplace looked over and directed a weak smile at Sonny. She then gazed up at Donnally. Her face was as emaciated as Mauricio's on the day he died. Pale, thin, and drawn. Eyes sunken. Gray-blond hair hanging long and frizzy. Bony fingers interlaced on her lap.

Donnally hesitated to approach her for fear she would disintegrate like a ghost in daylight.

Trudy gestured toward the rough-hewn pine couch to her right, facing the fire.

Donnally sat down while Sonny stoked the embers, and then picked up some chunks of oak and walked to the kitchen behind them. Donnally recognized the creak of the opening and closing doors of a wood-burning stove and the clang and scrape of a teapot on the cast-iron surface.

"I didn't come here to ask you about Tsukamata," Donnally told her. "I'm not trying to figure out why the cop was killed or who did it. I only want to know about Anna."

Trudy gazed at Donnally. It struck him that there was a hardness and calculation behind her gaze that her appearance otherwise belied.

She had fugitive's eyes.

"Sonny said that you found Rover and made the court convict him," Trudy said.

Donnally shrugged. "Sort of."

"Why?"

"Why what?"

"Why did you go looking for him in the first place?"

"I didn't start out trying to find him, but Anna. Her brother asked me to."

Trudy's eyes widened as if it hadn't crossed her mind since the day Anna was dropped off at New Sky that she had a birth family.

Donnally nodded. "Her brother."

"Where is he?"

"Dead." He anticipated her next question. "And her parents were already dead when he dropped her off at New Sky."

"Why, after all these years . . ." Her voice trailed off into a sigh.

"He wanted to leave her something," Donnally said, knowing that the implication was different than the fact. Mauricio intended to leave her not just money, but a lifetime of confusion.

"He didn't know she'd been murdered?"

"Not a clue."

Trudy stared at the fire. It crackled against the rumbling of Sonny's water, near boiling in the kitchen.

"Why didn't he look for her sooner?"

"There'd be too much to explain and he was on the run."

"What did he do?"

Donnally shrugged. "That's not important. He figured there were good people at New Sky who'd take care of her and not call the police."

The teapot whistled, then fell silent when Sonny slid it to a cool part of the stove.

"It's sad that he never knew what a wonderful person Anna grew up to be," Trudy said.

"He saw her once outside of Berkeley High School. I think he knew you did a good job raising her."

Trudy inspected Donnally's face. He felt she was setting him up to confirm what she was about to say.

"I guess it's finally over," she said. "Now with Rover convicted."

Donnally cringed. She sounded like a delusional relative of a murder victim, the sort who give press conferences talking about the closure they'd get if the killer was executed, as if the memories would die just because a murderer's breath ceased.

But he didn't say what he was thinking. He hadn't come up there to attack Trudy's self-deceptions.

"That's what I wanted to talk to you about." Donnally let the thought linger for a moment, then said, "I'm not sure Brown did it."

Trudy's body pulled back. Her hand flew to her open mouth, but her eyes remained dull and fixed and emotionless. Donnally thought she looked like a second-rate actress playing herself in a third-rate production of her life. He didn't want her to see his disgust, so he looked away. He felt like walking into the kitchen and shaking Sonny, make him wake up to the fraud she was and stop putting himself at risk protecting her.

She found her voice. "The police said—"

"They were wrong."

Donnally pushed himself to his feet and stepped to the fireplace. He wasn't sure what to say next. He was relying on a delusional man to guide him to the truth, and he didn't yet know what she was hiding.

"Then who did it?" she asked.

He turned back toward her.

"Who is R2D2?"

Metal crashed against metal in the kitchen as Sonny slammed the teapot down on the stove.

"You son of a bitch," Sonny yelled as he charged into the living room. "I didn't bring you up here to talk about Tsukamata."

Sonny stopped next to Trudy's chair and jabbed a finger down at her. "Don't answer him."

Trudy looked up at Sonny. "The police already know who they are. What difference does it make if he does?"

"They?" Donnally said.

"It's not R2D2," Trudy said, "but R2T2. Two brothers who lived at New Sky in 1975. Artie and Robert Trueblood."

"They're who the police think killed Tsuka-mata?" Donnally asked.

They both nodded.

"And the police want to get to them through you?"

"That's what they've been trying to do since 1975," Trudy said, then closed her eyes. Her shoulders slumped as if the effort of disclosing the pivotal truth in her life had depleted her.

Sonny stepped forward like a referee and held out his arms as if separating them.

"That's enough," Sonny said. "We're getting into accessory-to-murder territory."

Sonny looked back and forth between them until Donnally shrugged his consent.

"This has all been too much of a burden on her," Sonny said to Donnally as he reached out and rested his hand on her shoulder. "She's been sick for decades." He glanced toward the doorway. "Bear and the others look after her."

Donnally sat back down on the couch.

"Sometimes my muscles and bones ache so much I can't move. If I do housework, even for an hour, it takes a week in bed before I can do anything else."

Trudy reached up and laid her hand on top of Sonny's.

"It's like I have arthritis all over my body and I can't move without excruciating pain."

"Maybe we should finish talking in the morning," Sonny said, looking first at Trudy, then at Donnally. "About everything but R2T2. They're off-limits."

Sonny escorted Trudy down the hallway to her

bedroom and returned with some blankets for Donnally.

"There's one thing you need to understand about Trudy," Sonny told him. "She carries the weight of the world on her shoulders, that's what makes her sick. It's like she has the consciences of ten people. It paralyzes her."

Donnally accepted the blankets from Sonny's hands, then said, "I think it's just the opposite. It frees her to do and believe pretty much anything she finds convenient."

"How do you figure?"

"One person's conscience prevents him from lying, stealing, or torturing, another's insists that he do them all, as long as he can justify the goal."

Sonny stared at Donnally for a moment, then said, "Jeez. That's kind of a mind spinner. I never looked at it that way before."

CHAPTER 33

In the dawn light, Donnally surveyed the living room from where he lay on the couch.

Crocheted pillows lay on all the chairs. Embroidered cloth on the tables. Quilts with American Indian motifs hung on the walls along with paintings in a dozen styles. One of them was of the New Sky Commune. Carvings of bears, wolves, and salmon stood on shelves and in bookcases.

Donnally slipped outside. The forest was silent except for the croaking of two ravens on the peak of the A-frame roof. The second floor windows were shuttered. He realized that he'd heard no sounds emanating from upstairs since he arrived: no footsteps, no voices, no flushing toilet. Holding his breath, he listened for road traffic or jet noise or even the buzz of high-voltage wires. Nothing.

He looked up at the blue sky, and then at an outbuilding to the northwest and at a barn to the north, imagining how the house and the two structures would look from a low-flying plane. The three buildings formed a triangle, twenty yards across the clearing from point to point. He surveyed the rest of the property. A long dirt driveway entered from the west and dead-ended at the house. A ten-year-old Ford pickup was parked next to the front steps. He memorized the license plate.

Trudy wasn't as far off the grid as Donnally had first imagined, for an electric power line emerged from the forest and connected to the southeast corner of the house, just below a satellite dish.

Donnally looked around for Bear, then walked past Sonny's Willys to the barn. A heavy lock barred the door, but through the slats he could make out the contours of a thirty-year-old water truck with a twelve-foot-long tank and a gasoline-powered generator.

By the time Trudy and Sonny emerged from the hallway next to the kitchen, Donnally had the table set and pancakes cooked.

"Smells wonderful," Trudy said, as she sat down. She was dressed in Levi's and an oversized Pendleton wool shirt, not looking as pale as the night before.

"Secret ingredient," Donnally answered.

"Can't be secret." She smiled. "I know everything that's in the kitchen."

Sonny sniffed the air. "Nutmeg. Got to be."

Donnally shifted the pancakes onto plates and carried them to a dining table that separated the kitchen from the living room. He watched them spread homemade blackberry jam and begin eating. Both were nodding within seconds.

"You've got lots of beautiful things here," Donnally said, glancing around the living room, then sitting down.

Trudy smiled with pride. "I made most of them myself. I sell them at the flea market in Fort Bragg."

"Not herself," Sonny said. "Bear and some of the others run the booth."

The comment returned them to the previous night's conversation. Trudy's smile faded.

Donnally wanted to ease back to where he'd left off, but recognized that anywhere he began might provoke another one of Sonny's outbursts. He stirred sugar into his coffee before he said, "Did Anna know a psychiatrist named William Sherwyn?"

Trudy set down her fork. "Why do you ask that?"

"Something Rover told me."

"What did he say?"

"That Anna called Sherwyn a rabbit."

"Not a rabbit," Sonny said. "Just Rabbit. That was his nickname at New Sky."

Donnally felt a jolt. "Sherwyn was at New Sky?"

"Only for a few months in the late seventies," Sonny said. "The son of a bitch." He looked over at Trudy. "You want to tell him or should I?"

She lowered her eyes.

"The problem with being outside the system," Sonny said, "is that as a matter of principle you can't use it even when you really need to."

"Which means?"

"We caught him molesting one of the kids. But instead of hauling him down to the police station, we kicked him out."

Donnally dropped his hands to the table with a thunk.

"You did what?"

"Don't give me grief, Donnally. The principle

that allowed us to help Anna's brother by taking her in is the same one that kept us from going to the police."

"Letting a child molester walk away was a matter of principle?"

Sonny smirked. "Don't say it like that. You're the guy who took a dollar to create attorney-client privilege. Is that principle any different? Even if I told you I murdered somebody, you couldn't turn me in."

Donnally now had another reason to wish he hadn't taken the money, but he wasn't going to argue about consistency. The answers he wanted from Trudy weren't philosophical.

"If Anna said to Sherwyn, 'I know who you are,'" Donnally asked Trudy, "is that what she meant?"

"Did Rover tell you that?"

"He said you heard her say it, too."

In her hesitation and her twitching eyelids, Donnally got his answer. She was there, in the house with Anna and Sherwyn and Brown. He pushed on before she could lie.

"I'm thinking that Anna wanted to expose Sherwyn, but he threatened that if she did, he'd snitch you off about R2T2 and Tsukamata."

Trudy bit her lower lip, then nodded.

"It was a stalemate," Donnally continued. "Neither of them could do anything."

Sonny cut in. "And Anna wasn't about to embarrass the ex–New Sky people. A lot of them had moved away and gone straight. College professors, lawyers, shop owners. They all had a secret that made them feel dirty and would've made them look dirtier."

"Which? About the molestation or the murder?"

Donnally couldn't suppress the sarcasm in his voice.

"The molestation. The murder had nothing to do with New Sky. R2T2 were just hiding out there. They were Black Guerilla Family members on the run from an armored car robbery in New Jersey."

"We had no idea who they were at the beginning," Trudy said. "We took them in like we took everybody else in. No questions asked."

"Was Anna the child Sherwyn molested?"

"No. It was a boy."

Donnally closed his eyes, trying to imagine Anna and Sherwyn arguing in the living room, and Rover and Trudy listening in the kitchen. The image led him to a question: What brought Sherwyn to the house in the first place? He directed it at Trudy.

"Did she tell you why Sherwyn had showed up after all those years?"

Trudy shrugged. "Anna said she wanted to look into some things first, but promised to tell me about it. She used the phrase, 'do some research.'"

"She was murdered a week later, before she had a chance," Sonny said, reaching over and taking Trudy's hand.

"Did you find anything about Sherwyn in the house afterwards?" Donnally asked.

Sonny shook his head. "We looked through all of her papers, her diary, everything. Nothing with his name on it."

Donnally looked at Trudy. "You still have all that stuff?"

Trudy looked at Sonny, then back at Donnally. The same hesitation. Then the same twitch.

"No."

CHAPTER 34

"Trudy fell in love with Artie and bought the guns they used to kill Tsukamata," Sonny said, as he drove them from the property that night.

"Why'd they kill him?"

"He suspected that Artie and Robert weren't who they claimed to be and they were afraid he'd eventually figure it out. Artie got Tsukamata to pull him over for speeding and Robert was already set up on a rooftop with a rifle. The police came knocking on Trudy's door a week after the murder. They just couldn't prove she knew what the guns were for when she bought them, otherwise they would've charged her as an accessory."

Donnally was lying in the back of the wagon, his head once again covered with the ski mask. But this time, instead of holding his gun, he held his cell phone, pressing "send" to call his home number, then disconnecting after his voice mail picked up in order to create a cell site trail back to the area of Trudy's house.

"So she fled up here so she couldn't be used as a witness against them?" Donnally asked.

"That's what she thinks. But it's no more real than her symptoms."

"You mean they're all psychosomatic?"

"Of course. You saw all the craft stuff she's made. She's like everybody else in the world. People do what they want to do. While most people rationalize when they don't want to face something, Trudy paralyzes herself physically."

"Why don't you all confront her instead of coddling her?"

"It's not my problem, it's Bear's. But he ain't gonna do it either. She pretends he's suffering from post-traumatic stress from the Vietnam War and he pretends she really is sick. It's a perfect marriage of neuroses."

"Where was he last night?"

"On guard duty."

"Against who?"

"Everybody." Sonny chuckled. "Real and imaginary."

They rode in silence for a few minutes, then Donnally asked, "What's upstairs?"

"Which upstairs? Anna's?"

Donnally laughed. "You know I'm not asking about Anna's."

"Let's just call it their workshop."

Donnally rolled from his side to his back on the hard wagon bed and waited for Sonny to explain what he meant.

"You want to drag this out or just tell me?" Donnally finally said.

"You'll never find the place again, so why not? They make most of their money sorting and cleaning marijuana for the growers up here."

"I figured it was something like that, but I assumed they were the growers. I saw the tanker and generator."

"Not for twenty years or so. Now they rent the equipment out to others. I think they're nuts to keep doing what they're doing. A lot of people would kill to find out where this place is so they could bust in when they're sorting and steal the crop. It would be the quickest hundred grand anybody ever made."

"Would kill or did kill?"

"You're quick," Sonny said. "That was one of the theories in the days after Anna was murdered. Some people thought that R2T2 did it. Trudy had made a run up to supervise a harvest. People were thinking that R2T2 were trying to get Anna to give up where the grow was so they could rip it off. Life on the run costs a lot of money, and it wasn't like they could hold day jobs. But Rover getting busted put that theory to rest."

"Did Anna even know what was going on up here?"

"Sure. She didn't like her mother doing it, but couldn't stop her. Anna grasped what Trudy had refused to. Peace and love were dead and marijuana had become a business no different than heroin and speed. By the early 1980s even the Hare Krishnas were into the drug trade and had left a trail of bodies from Twin Peaks in San Francisco to the New York harbor."

"Somehow I don't see Trudy being capable of marijuana growing. It's tough work. Hiking the hills, planting and harvesting."

"She wasn't always that way."

"You mean she didn't have these symptoms when Anna was growing up?"

"They kicked in later."

"When?"

Sonny laughed and accelerated down the dirt road. "I'll let you answer that one yourself."

It wasn't until Donnally once again heard the popping gravel that he got it: Trudy hadn't gone into hiding after the police knocked on her door to question her about Tsukamata, but only after her daughter's murder in 1986. And her guilt revealed itself, to everyone but herself, in the form of her psychosomatic symptoms.

"You mean it really was R2T2 who killed Anna, trying to find out where the marijuana operation was?" Donnally asked. "And Trudy had once protected the guys who later came back and killed her daughter?"

The question died in the rumbling of tires and grinding of gears, and Sonny answered with his silence.

Donnally was glad that Mauricio's cowardice had kept him from looking for Anna himself. It had saved him from the truth, and from the tragedy that he'd delivered his sister up to an equally cowardly woman that Anna had sacrificed her life to protect.

He remembered a line spoken by a janitor, leaning on his broom in an army hospital hallway during one of his father's movies: A hypochondriac is just a sociopath without courage.

That was Trudy Keenan.

And in that moment, Donnally felt sadder for Anna than at any time since he first read her name in Mauricio's letter.

CHAPTER 35

"Where is she, Sonny boy?"

A grim voice shook Donnally awake. He looked out from the bed of the Willys and recognized the side of the apartment building bordering Sonny's driveway. He propped himself on an elbow and looked over the driver's seat toward the front of the wagon. Two men, one black, one white, both in their mid-fifties, stood facing Sonny, who was leaning back against the hood.

"We're tired of screwing around, asshole. You've been fucking with us for over thirty years. It stops tonight. Where's Trudy?"

Sonny held his hands out and looked at the black one.

"Come on, Jenkins, I don't know where she is."

Donnally glanced toward the street to see if there was backup. A vacant Ford Expedition blocked the driveway, probably the one that got cut off in San Rafael. He heard a thud and a grunt, then looked back to see Sonny doubled over.

Jenkins pointed a leather-gloved finger at Sonny's head. His other hand was still formed into a fist.

"I'll tell you all I know man," Sonny said. "Just go through my lawyer."

Jenkins punched down toward Sonny's face. His head rocked to the left.

"Fuck your lawyer."

Donnally eased toward the rear door.

The white one stepped between his partner and Sonny.

"Take it easy. He won't be able to talk through a broken jaw." He then set his hand on Sonny's shoulder. "You better come up with something, Sonny. I'm not sure how long I can control him."

"Give me the address," Jenkins said.

Donnally turned the handle to flip up the top half of the gate and gripped the lower latch. He yanked it hard and in one motion kicked the bottom gate and slid out. By the time he'd pulled his gun and crouched down at the back of the truck, there were two Glocks pointed at him.

"I'm a cop," Donnally called out. "Back off."

"You used to be a cop, asshole," Jenkins yelled back. "Why don't you go back up to Mount Shasta and flip your flapjacks?"

"Not a chance."

A light came on in a second-story apartment window. Donnally glanced up as the curtain was pulled aside.

The window slid open and a female voice called out, "Everything okay?"

Donnally lowered his gun and slipped it into his back pocket. Jenkins and his partner holstered theirs.

"Yeah, fine," Donnally said to her, "Sonny just got drunk and passed out. We'll take care of him."

"Why don't you just cut a deal and get this over with?" Donnally asked.

Sonny pressed the ice pack against the side of his head as they sat at the kitchen table, then quoted back Donnally's earlier line about Mauricio: "There'd be too much to explain." He took in a long breath, then exhaled. "Look, man. Anna was everybody's baby, not just Trudy's. She was a little goddess that appeared out of nothingness. Everybody showed up at the house after she was murdered. I mean everybody. Crooked and straight. People who were still in the movement and some who'd long left it behind. Even that asshole Sherwyn showed up, but we chased him away.

"We were going to handle it ourselves. It was insane, man, a crazy fantasy. People who'd never touched a gun were buying them on the street, ready to posse up like it was some Western movie."

Sonny paused, his eyes went vacant for a moment, then he continued.

"Some already had them. The guys that had gone into the drug trade. They're the ones who figured out that Artie was in Berkeley the day Anna was killed, that he needed money and was trying to find Trudy. He was broke and homeless. Everybody knew it."

"And he figured Trudy was making a lot of money from marijuana?"

"That wasn't it. They'd loaned Trudy most of the cash from the armored car robbery to buy her house. If they hadn't done something like that, it would've rotted where it was buried. Artie came back to collect what she owed him, and he was desperate, desperate enough to show his face in Berkeley."

"What happened?"

"You can guess."

"Tell me."

"What's the point?"

"You want the dollar back and I'll go find out myself?"

Sonny smiled, then winced and touched his busted lip.

"All I can say is that some people . . . some people . . . tracked Artie down. He blamed Robert and led the folks to where he was hiding. Things went sideways and it got kind of bloody."

"Does Trudy know what happened to Artie and Robert?"

"Nope."

"Why not?"

"She can't keep her mouth shut. She admitted buying the guns they had used to kill Tsukamata the first time the cops leaned on her. The last thing anybody wants is for the police to start testing DNA from every unsolved double murder in those years to see if it matches any ex-members of New Sky."

"So all this time she's been hiding from dead people and she doesn't know it?"

Sonny shrugged. "I guess you can say that."

Donnally walked over to the kitchen counter and refilled their coffee cups. He turned back toward Sonny.

"And for over thirty years you've been fending off the cops for her?"

"It wasn't just for her." Sonny touched his swollen eyes. "I had no choice." He tried to smile. "But like the paranoid, at least I was never lonely."

Donnally returned to the table and set down the cups. He remained standing, arms folded over his chest.

"And that means that you folks were willing to let Charles Brown take the fall for a murder he didn't do?"

"We knew that wasn't going to happen."

"You knew that because . . ." The last piece fell into place in Donnally's mind before Sonny could answer. "Because of Sherwyn. It was Sherwyn's job to make sure Rover never went to trial."

Sonny nodded. "He was the only one in a position to do it and we had leverage to make sure he did. And things went along fine for decades. Until you showed up. Trudy collapsed into a pile of symptoms because she was terrified, afraid that Rover, as nuts as he is, would go to prison for the rest of his life for a murder that R2T2 did. Everybody knows what happens to mentally ill people in the joint. But then he pled no contest and she thought it was finally over."

"Then why'd she see me? And why was she so sick-looking if she really believed it was over with? I would've thought she'd be dancing among the pine trees."

"I guess she needed to feel like the book is finally closed on the past."

"But it isn't."

Sonny shook his head. "No matter how hard she tries to slam it shut."

CHAPTER 36

"**Y**ou mean it was true?" Janie said, as she moved a stack of books from a shelf to a box in her bedroom.

It was 8 A.M., an hour after Donnally had left Sonny's house.

"Don't change the subject," Donnally said, standing in the doorway. "I'm sorry about what I said. You don't need to move out."

"You don't have to be sorry. You did me a favor by knocking me out of orbit. It's not as bad as I thought it would be."

Donnally shrugged. "Have it your way."

"You may want to try it, too."

"So this is for my benefit?"

She stared at him for a moment. "Your orbit was never around me."

But it was once.

He knew it and she knew it, from the moment he'd entered her office, sent by SFPD under the assumption that he needed to get his head straight after being shot and killing the two gangsters. He had taken a look at her, underwent what felt like the Big Bang, then asked, "Can a patient date his shrink?" She smiled and told him no. He then turned around and walked back out the door. Thirty seconds later, her phone rang, she said yes to a new question, and he hadn't asked another woman out since.

Standing there looking at her now, he realized the problem was not that there wasn't an orbit, but that there was.

For too many years, they had been like bodies in motion, pulled together by attraction and pulled apart by inertia, and it was momentary acceleration in one direction or another that had replaced the exhilaration that had swept them along for the first few years. In the end, there hadn't even been enough passion to carry them through with their plan for her to join him in Mount Shasta and work in the nearby VA clinic.

Donnally walked out of her room, already imagining the house empty. Then he noticed a worn spot on the hallway carpet and scuff marks on the wall and a chip out of the paint on the corner near the top of the stairs.

All of that had been invisible just two minutes earlier.

He couldn't decide whether he was already starting to think like a landlord or it was just guilt about how he had let the house deteriorate.

By the time he arrived at the bottom of the stairs he'd almost worked himself around to the sort of place he always did: It didn't make any difference which it was or how he felt about it.

Things just are the way they are.

He'd fix the place up, rent it out, and head back up to Mount Shasta.

Except there was a new void in his life. An emptiness. And not just because Janie was leaving, but because the trail from Mauricio's deathbed to Anna's killers had ended almost a generation earlier, in a history he wasn't part of and that didn't feel real to him.

Donnally walked into Janie's office and used her computer to run a news archive search for articles about Artie and Robert Trueblood, but he couldn't find any murder victims with those names. He discovered that the true names of the suspects in the New Jersey armored car case were Willie Carley and Julius Moran, but those didn't show up in local homicide reports either. Finally he searched for double murders during the weeks after Anna was killed, and there it was.

BODIES FOUND IN HUNTERS POINT
Thomas Peele
Chronicle Staff Writer

Two unidentified men were found bludgeoned to death in an abandoned Hunters Point warehouse on Sunday night. The bodies were discovered by a homeless man looking for a place to sleep. Police reported that it appears the men were beaten to death after being tortured, and they suspect the homicides were the result of a drug deal gone bad.

Sergeant Pete Peterson said the hands of both men had been cut off, most likely in an attempt to prevent their identification by fingerprints.

"What's this?" Janie said, her soft footsteps coming to a stop on the carpet behind him.

"I'm just tying up some loose ends that Sonny left me with. It doesn't all seem quite real yet."

"That's the problem with history."

"The tragedy is real," Donnally said, staring at the monitor, "it's just not anchored to anything." He thought for a moment. "If Mauricio was still alive, it would be different."

"I know," she said, squeezing his shoulder, "and he would've been proud of her. Charles told me that Anna helped out lots of people. Food, medicine, advice. Some would come right to her door once a week, like clockwork. She'd give them boxed lunches or, for the ones she trusted, money to buy things for themselves."

He looked up at her. "Like clockwork?"

Janie nodded. "My phrase, but his idea."

"Did he say who?"

She shook her head, then sat down next to the desk.

"He told me she even borrowed money to pay for all the charity." She smiled. "He said she took out a 'mortuary.' It took most of the session to figure out why he picked that word. It turned out that the bank she went to was next to a funeral home and what she got was a mortgage."

Donnally raised his eyebrows as he looked over at Janie. It sounded less like charity and more like guilt.

"It seemed a little excessive to me, too," Janie said.

"When are you seeing him again?"

She glanced at her watch. "Ten o'clock."

By noon Donnally was sitting before a different monitor, this one at the Alameda County Recorder's Office, and paging through scans of Anna Keenan's loan records. He became more and more puzzled as he looked through the documents. Between the day her mother signed the house over to her in 1980 and when she was murdered, she'd refinanced three times.

He wondered whether she'd discovered the violent origin of the money that went into buying the house and had decided to turn evil to good by giving it away.

Then why not just sell the house and give the money back to the armored car company?

The answer again arrived in Sonny's words. "There'd be too much to explain."

And with her remaining in the house, Artie and Robert would believe their money was still invested there.

Is that why they killed her? Because they found out she'd given their money away? And because they wanted to get past her to Trudy so she could make good their loss?

Donnally leaned back in his chair and stared up at the tiled ceiling.

But then strangling her? Kneeling over her on her bed and strangling her?

It didn't make sense. Not with his years investigating homicides. A knife at her throat, yes. A gun at her temple, yes. But strangling? Not very likely. And by hand? Even less likely. Strangling hands were a weapon of passion, not calculation.

Donnally found that his eyes had lost focus. He blinked, then logged off the computer.

It just didn't make sense.

Donnally's cell phone rang as he drove across the Bay Bridge. It was Janie.

"Charles said that one of the two regulars she gave money to was named Art or Artie. Does that name mean anything to you?"

CHAPTER 37

Donnally flashed his badge for just the second time in his ten years of retirement. He couldn't tell whether he felt like a priest of lapsed faith giving Communion or an actor playing a part that just happened to reveal his true self.

The cellular company's security chief in San Francisco bought Donnally's lie that he was investigating the theft of his cell phone. His raised eyebrow and slanted grin revealed his conclusion-by-fantasy that the thief was a woman who'd run out on Donnally.

The chief handed him off to a clerk who walked him to a windowless office and printed out a list of the cell sites that had picked up Donnally's calls as Sonny drove him from Trudy's cabin back to Berkeley. Donnally got the clerk talking about everything but the report he was printing out so he wouldn't notice that all the calls from the cell phone were to the same landline and only a second in length, and wouldn't then ask whose number it was.

The electronic trail dissolved into the coastal range northeast of Fort Bragg. The clerk displayed a topographical map on the screen that showed a road heading north from the highway, and pointed out that for the first half hour, the signal had alternated back and forth on the border between two cell sites. The sites covered a little more than five square miles. Donnally was grateful that Trudy had chosen a hideaway in the hill country. Unlike the flatlands where cell sites can be twenty miles apart, antennas in the mountains are stationed close together so reception isn't lost in the canyons.

Two hours of inspecting satellite maps on Janie's computer narrowed his search down to three probable locations, each composed of a cabin and two outbuildings laid out in the form of a triangle within a clearing. He plotted a course from one to the other, starting at Fort Bragg along the coast and ending at the east end of the highway bisecting Mendocino County.

Each route would take him far to the north of his targets, then down fire roads to within hiking distance, and each would require camping overnight in the forest.

None of the routes was one he would've taken during pot-growing season, when the hills were patrolled by armed guards, patches were booby-trapped, and the earth was damp enough for the anonymous burial of an intruder.

The first two days were a washout.

Even as he hiked up toward the ridge-top trail above the dormant marijuana fields, he suspected that he was a victim of wishful thinking that made him choose the easiest first.

And a moment after setting up his spotting scope on the outside walkway of an abandoned fire lookout, he discovered he was right: The outbuilding was too large, the barn was too small, and the cabin was just one story.

Only with that failure did he feel the aches in his muscles and hip, and the bruises on his legs and arms inflicted by shrubs and tree branches as he had bushwhacked the deer trails.

The search for the second site took him down a forest service road into a canyon about four miles north of the highway and deep into marijuana country.

He climbed out of his truck and inspected the dirt to make sure there were no fresh footprints or tire tracks, then hoisted on his pack and began a cross-country trek that would begin with a hike up eleven hundred feet in two miles, then almost down to sea level two thousand feet below over the next eight miles, and back up again.

A handheld GPS kept him on track as he hiked the growers' trails through the pines and oaks. He stepped over rows of macheted trunks of harvested plants and over hundreds of sections of black plastic piping, the drip systems veining the hillsides, waiting to be fed in the spring and summer by water trucks like Trudy's.

At 9 A.M. on the second day he crested the final ridge and looked for a place to spot on the property. He found a rock outcropping shaded by a mature oak and set up his scope. He held his breath as he turned the focus ring, then a moment of relief: Bear's red truck emerged against the brown and green background of the clearing.

Donnally set up camp on the level ground under

the tree and moved the scope to a flatter section of rock fifteen feet higher. He then laid out a bird-watching guide next to it in case he needed to explain his presence to hikers or growers happening by.

A chilly ocean breeze stung his face and eyes as he lay prone, watching for movement. He didn't want to break into an occupied house, but didn't know whether Trudy ever left. He realized that he should've asked about her medical treatment, how often she went to visit doctors or herbalists or acupuncturists or Indian shamans, or whoever it was who was prepared to treat her psychosomatic illnesses as real. He figured Bear would be the one who ran their errands, but didn't know whether she ever went with him.

Nothing stirred all day in the clearing below, not even Bear emerging from the shadowed forest making his rounds.

Mist filled the valleys below him in the late afternoon, blocking his view of the cabin. He used the time to cook spaghetti on a one-burner kerosene stove and was back at his scope when the dropping temperature condensed the moisture and turned it to drizzle.

By then it was dark, and the cabin lights, now filtered by the swirling silvery droplets, burnished the clearing with what seemed to Donnally, watching through the lens of Trudy's delusions, like nothing more than the plastic innocence of a department store nativity scene.

CHAPTER 38

The fog to which Donnally awoke the following morning encased the ridge like the slumber he'd left behind in the night. The world around him, along with the images that had populated his dreams, was lost in gray.

Water dripping from the oak leaves overhead tapped the plastic tarp protecting him and ran off the edge and down the hillside in rivulets. He reached for his cell phone and searched the Internet for a local weather report.

The coastal range wouldn't see the sun all day.

Donnally decided that what was concealment for the cabin and Bear was also cover for him, and that it didn't make sense to lose another day waiting for the weather to clear. He ate breakfast, then packed up his gear and hid it thirty yards farther up the hill under a brush-concealed rock overhang.

The trail near the ridge where he began his descent soon merged with crisscrossing paths cut by growers through the pines, firs, and manzanita. The ten-foot visibility meant that he had to watch his GPS as much as his feet as he worked his way down the gullies and crossed small streams.

Halfway down the mountain, he tripped over a

drip line and tumbled forward, rolling and bouncing down through ferns and deer brush. The impact of his shoulder glancing off a tree trunk ejected the GPS from his hand. From his back at the edge of a plot of harvested marijuana stalks, he watched it make a cartoonlike pause in the air, then drop into the mud next to him with a comical smack.

But the Mexican pointing the shotgun at Donnally's head wasn't laughing.

Donnally looked past the single barrel at the impassive eyes of the rain-slickered man and then spread his hands in the air.

"*Usted habla inglés?*" Donnally asked.

The man shook his head.

Donnally sat up and glanced around as he wiped his hands on his pants. Bags of fertilizer, jugs of pesticides, and coils of black pipe were stacked under a lean-to fifteen yards to his left. Next to it was a shack constructed of branches and covered by a camouflaged tarp. The grow seemed to possess the sophistication of a cartel operation, and the man's knockoff jeans and new rain jacket suggested that he had been smuggled in from Mexico not more than a few days earlier.

Donnally cupped his hands and held them in front of his eyes like binoculars and pretended to scan the trees surrounding the field.

"*Pájaros.*" Birds.

The Mexican smirked and gestured toward the fog with a dismissive wave of his arm.

Donnally held up one hand, eased it into his jacket pocket, then pulled out his bird-watching book and held it up.

Another smirk and a shake of his head.

"*Policía*," the man said, racking the shotgun.

"*No. No policía.*"

The Mexican waved the barrel in a small circle, indicating that Donnally should roll over.

He complied.

Seconds later, Donnally felt his gun jerked out of its holster and his wallet pulled from his back pocket.

Donnally guessed the moment when the Mexican would flip open the wallet and spot his retirement badge, then kicked the man's kneecap. The leg buckled and the shotgun discharged as he fell backward, sending buckshot skyward. The Mexican grunted when his back hit the ground. Donnally pawed through the mud and yanked the shotgun from his hand and aimed it at his grimacing face.

Bracketing the grower on either side were the angled, four-inch stumps of last year's harvested pot plants.

Donnally winced when he realized that the Mexican was impaled on the one between them.

After searching him for other weapons, Donnally raised him up and rolled him onto his side. The man gritted his teeth but didn't scream. A bloody stump matched the hole in his back, just below his ribs on his left side. Donnally knew from observing dozens of autopsies that the wound wouldn't be fatal if he could get it treated soon enough.

"*Su nombre?*" Donnally asked. Your name?

The man didn't answer, his expression saying that giving up his name would be the first step in giving up his bosses, and that he was ready to be buried in a nameless grave in an alien land rather than do it.

Donnally remembered a noun from his high school Spanish, but had to struggle to recall the verb tense he needed to assure the man that he meant him no harm.

"*Le llamaré Afortunado,*" Donnally finally said. I'll call you Lucky.

The Mexican tried to smile, but it ended again as a grimace.

Donnally worked Lucky's rain slicker down his arms and spread it out under him. He then unbuttoned the man's wool shirt and slid it off his shoulders to expose the wound.

The only clean piece of fabric Donnally could find was a towel hanging from a clothesline next to the shack. He used it to cover the wound, then cut a piece of rope from a roll and bound it around Lucky's torso to hold the bandage in place.

But it wasn't the external bleeding that worried him, it was the internal.

He checked his cell phone. No service this far down in the canyon. He retrieved the GPS. Muddy, but unbroken. It told him that it was another five hundred feet down the hillside and a quarter of a mile to Trudy's.

Donnally untied the tarp from the shack, ripped out a couple of supporting posts, and made an Indian-style stretcher. He knew it would be a rough ride, but there wasn't an alternative.

The stretcher bounced behind Donnally like a buckboard on a rutted road as he dragged it down the deer and grower's trails, with Lucky grunting and groaning at each bump.

After a fifteen-minute descent, Donnally set down the stretcher among the pine and scrub oak a hundred feet from the edge of Trudy's clearing, then snuck through the trees until he could see the property.

The truck was missing. The inside cabin lights appeared to be off, and no smoke wisped up from the chimney.

The fact that Lucky was still conscious told Donnally that he probably wasn't bleeding out internally. At the same time, he hated the idea of rolling the dice with someone else's life—

But he needed Anna's papers. Even if the Mexican refused to describe him to Trudy and Bear, they'd know that someone had been in the nearby hills, and increase their vigilance.

There'd be no second chance.

After peeking through the windows and satisfying himself that the cabin was empty, Donnally kicked in the back door. A quick search of the two bedrooms, the upstairs marijuana sorting room, and Trudy's craft workshop turned up no paperwork other than recent sales records. He took thirty dollars that was lying on the dresser, a bottle of Oxycontin tablets, and a baggie of marijuana, hoping that Trudy and Bear would assume that these items alone were the target of the burglary.

Donnally returned to the Mexican, gave him one of the painkillers, and dragged him to the front steps. He then walked to the outbuilding and broke a back window with a piece of firewood and climbed in. Sheets of dust jumped off the workbench and the stacks of boxes when his feet hit the plank floor, and then plumed into clouds as he scanned the room.

The first boxes he opened contained an archive of Berkeley in the sixties, seventies, and eighties: copies of the *Berkeley Barb* newspaper, antiwar handouts, Black Panther manifestos, books on colonialism and imperialism: evidence of Trudy's past, stored away and sealed against time.

In a box on top of the third stack he found Anna's decades-old lesson plans printed on the Berkeley Unified School District letterhead. He pulled it down and searched through the next and the next, setting aside everything handwritten or typed that didn't seem related to her teaching. He extracted spiral notebooks, date diaries, and financial records, pausing every few minutes to listen for the sound of Bear's truck. He piled everything into a suitcase, and when that was full, began a second.

A downshifting transmission broke the silence, then the vehicle accelerated. Donnally figured that the driver must have spotted Lucky.

It skidded to a stop. Two doors opened.

"What the fuck?" It was Bear's voice.

Donnally peeked between the blinds. Trudy and Bear were standing over the Mexican.

"What's wrong with him?" Trudy asked.

"Who cares?" Bear scanned the property. "What I want to know is how he got here?" He glared at the Mexican. "English?" He kicked one of the branches that formed the stretcher. The Mexican winced. "You speak English?"

The Mexican shook his head.

Trudy kneeled down and felt around and under the man's back.

"I think he's been shot," she said. "We need to get him to the hospital."

"You get him to the hospital. I'm gonna find where he came from."

Bear climbed into the truck, made a three-point turn, and backed toward the stretcher. He propped the head end on the lowered rear gate, then pushed it in the rest of the way.

"Maybe you should come, too," Trudy said.

Bear didn't respond, just handed her the keys. He scanned the clearing until he spotted the scrape marks left by the stretcher when Donnally had dragged the Mexican from the forest, then pointed toward the hill.

"I'm gonna check the house, and then get a gun and head up there."

The ninety-minute hike that Donnally had taken down from his campsite turned into a four-hour struggle back up through heavy brush and rocky canyons, scraping his face and wrenching his hip along the way.

It wasn't just the two forty-pound suitcases. It was finding a route that wouldn't lead him back through the Mexican's plantation, where he was sure Bear would be waiting.

Bear had impressed Donnally as a paranoid but patient man, and he knew that patient men, like deer hunters in tree stands, wait for targets to come to them.

Donnally wasn't going to chance walking into Bear's sights, no matter what the cost to his body.

CHAPTER 39

When Donnally drove into Mount Shasta, he found it quiet in the comfortable way that mountain towns get around midnight, especially when the ground is wet and the air heavy. He rolled down his window. The only sounds were the occasional shush of tires on pavement and the whoosh of pneumatic truck brakes, the surface water somehow canceling the low rumble of the gasoline and diesel engines.

The fog that had followed Donnally in from the coast haloed the streetlights and neon signs, rendering them three-dimensional. And his Lone Mountain Café seemed to him more lone than mountain, standing in the middle of its empty parking lot, locked up for the night, next to Mauricio's junkyard, locked up forever.

After stopping at a pay phone to make an anonymous call to the Mendocino Coast Hospital to confirm that Lucky had survived, Donnally drove back across the freeway and north into the foothills to his house.

If a woman had been living there, the neighbors would've described it as cozy.

Without one, it was just small.

Detached garage. One story. Square. Shingled. With a hipped roof and dormers that brought winter sunshine into his attic office.

Donnally hauled the suitcases upstairs, then took a shower and made himself a sandwich. He stood in the kitchen as he ate, wondering how he'd strayed so far from fulfilling what had seemed a simple request: find Anna, show her the letter, and give her the money Mauricio had left. Instead he had committed one felony after another. Even the injury to Lucky happened because he was on his way to commit a burglary.

As a yawn came over him, he wondered who he was becoming.

And then the answer arrived: a vigilante.

He yawned again and stretched his arms high over his head, and then smiled. Until that moment, he'd always thought vigilante justice was a bad thing.

But as he undressed for bed, Donnally felt less like a vigilante than a viewer of one of his father's early films, made after he had returned from Vietnam and had abandoned advertising to pursue his dream of becoming a new Truffaut or Godard or Chabrol or Rohmer. He had situated them in wartime France and Indochina and made the protagonists enemy collaborators and gangsters: antiheroes. Each film was riddled with irrelevant shots of manikins or garbage cans that were supposed to impart a mysterious meaning accessible only to the initiated, of which Donnally discovered he wasn't one. It seemed to him, even then, that the stories were not reflective of great truths, or even a search for them, but of a psychotic break.

Now lying in bed, staring up at the ceiling, it struck Donnally that while his father's fragmented films had been shot in the present tense, he himself had been wandering in a very imperfect past, one captured in a series of jump cuts by a handheld camera that never stopped moving, one that jerked him around in time and space like energy and matter in a physicist's thought experiment.

Everyone he'd been thinking about seemed to be living parallel lives in two separate places, at two separate times—Mauricio, Charles, Anna, Trudy, Sherwyn—and he wondered whether he'd be any more successful in comprehending the universe in which they existed than his father had been.

But he knew he could do no worse.

Donnally remembered at age fifteen sitting in the Grauman's Chinese Theatre in Hollywood during the premiere of his father's first mainstream Vietnam War movie.

And his own bewilderment.

It was a coming-of-age film in which maturity meant insanity, and the single soldier who survived the battle had gone on a berserk rampage, had been awarded a Silver Star, and then had returned home unable to remember what he had been fighting for.

Donnally now saw himself, felt himself, walking out of the theater, confused and distraught, wondering who the film was really about, for the only soldier he'd known during the war had been his brother, who hadn't been insane, who hadn't gone berserk, and who hadn't won any medals while he was alive. Eventually, of course, like the character in the movie, he did come home, but in a body bag.

As Donnally relived his brother's funeral, a side view of Janie's face popped onto his mind's screen. And with it a memory of one of their conversations prompted by a call from his father.

"Haven't you ever wondered why your father always chooses a fool to speak the most significant lines in his movies, and always has him staring right at the camera?"

She'd been propped up in bed, sipping from a cup of tea.

"That's just his form of ridicule," Donnally had answered. "A way of painting a bull's-eye on a piñata and hanging it in the middle of screen."

"Not the doofus in Shooting the Dawn who says, 'Wouldn't it be weird if the best and the brightest confessed after we lost the war in Vietnam that they knew all along we couldn't win it?'"

"I don't remember that line."

Looking over at him she'd said, "I'm starting to wonder whether you've ever watched one of his films, or paid attention when you did."

"I stopped a very long time ago."

"I think it's time you started again."

"I've seen the trailers on television. Nothing has changed. He's still making self-indulgent movies about how Americans feel about war, not what war is really about and who it is we're fighting and why they're fighting us. His message that life is hell and only the insane survive doesn't explain why my brother died. My father's fool never seems to get around to answering those questions."

Then his own voice speaking inside his head. *Who's the fool this time, Donnally? And what's he saying?*

And it was morning.

CHAPTER 40 ════════════

After two hours and two pots of coffee, Donnally had separated Anna Keenan's records into four stacks on his desk: school, personal, financial, and other.

"Other" was the tallest.

Donnally realized that his arms would've hurt a whole lot less if he'd had time to sort through Anna's papers at Trudy's, instead of having to carry the two suitcases up and down the hills.

Most of it looked useless.

Surveying the damp, musty heaps, Donnally remembered why he'd disliked paper cases like insurance scams, check frauds, and auto repair shop swindles when he was a cop. That was one of the reasons he'd passed on a couple of promotions and waited for a spot in homicide to open up. What had happened in a violent crime scene would be visible and measurable and reconstructable from the blood, from the angles of attack and defense, and from the markers of identity sloughed off by the killer. Everything would be right there in front of him, with the hypotheticals constrained by the evidence.

But paper was just words upon words, with their

meaning sometimes only evident in the eye of the reader.

He decided to start with the least malleable: the numbers.

A file labeled "Appraisals" told him that Anna had gotten the house reappraised every March, just before the spring home-buying season, frenzied during those years by first-time buyers hoping to get into the market and rushing to catch the appreciation wave as it built among the tight inventory. If Charles was right about how she spent her money, the increase in home value of five or ten thousand dollars a year was enough to feed a lot of hungry people.

The original purchase agreement between Trudy and the seller called for seller-financing and a balloon payment in five years. But the handwritten ledger showed it was paid off in three years, four thousand dollars a month, in cash, and all long before Trudy moved north and went into hiding.

He couldn't determine from the paper alone whether the source of the money for the down payment was marijuana profits or the stash from Artie and Robert's armored car robbery. He imagined Trudy pulling up a floorboard or digging in the backyard, withdrawing stacks of money from her private bank, and slipping it to a seller happy to receive cash he wouldn't have to report to the IRS.

Donnally laid out the purchase agreement, the payment records, and the refinancing papers side by side. The numbers were equal. Money in, money out.

A ledger of expenditures was in a folder of its

own. Food, clothing, medicine, cash. Organized by dates, separated into years, with initials alone to identify the recipients. He matched them to Anna's tax returns. She had taken just the standard deduction. None for mortgage interest or property taxes or charity, even though she had receipts from homeless shelters and the Salvation Army. Donnally guessed that she had forgone the deductions because they would've been a way of getting back the dirty money that she'd been trying to give away.

As he reached for the next stack, Donnally alerted to a break in the pattern of cars passing on the street. He then noticed a low rumble of an idling motor. He peeked between the curtains and spotted Deputy Pipkins parked in front of the house, blocking the driveway, the driver's window open, his bandaged wrist exposed and looking like the result of a failed suicide.

Pipkins's face wasn't visible, but Donnally imagined him scanning the windows, either checking to see whether Donnally was inside or maybe hoping for eye contact in order to make a point Donnally couldn't yet fathom.

Donnally heard his phone ring downstairs. He suspected it was Pipkins checking whether he was home. He let it go, then called the café on his cell and told Will that if Pipkins called asking for him to say that he was busy taking an order from a customer.

A minute after the ringing stopped, Pipkins climbed out of his patrol car and walked down the driveway carrying a KFC take-out bag.

Donnally smiled to himself. Whatever Pipkins was up to, he'd decided to do it in daylight. No way would he chance reaching into another spring-loaded trap.

Donnally's cell phone vibrated after he'd walked to the rear dormer and was looking down into his backyard. It was Will reporting that a man sounding like Pipkins had called asking for him.

Ten seconds later, Pipkins came into view from the side of the house. Donnally raised his cell phone and videotaped the deputy as he walked toward the five-hundred-gallon propane tank that supplied fuel for heating and cooking. Pipkins pulled a crescent wrench out of his bag and kneeled down next to the copper fittings at the front.

Donnally raced down the stairs, arriving at the kitchen window in time to video Pipkins backing away down the driveway and snapping off the cover of a road flare. He struck it against the igniter button and then disappeared from view. Moments later, the burning flare came flying from along the side of the house and rolled to a stop five feet from the tank. Donnally stepped onto the back porch, ready to run over and grab the flare before it ignited the gas. He looked up at the pines bordering the yard. They were motionless in the calm air. He found himself rolling the dice again, this time with his own life, as he waited for Pipkins to drive off.

The rising whine of Pipkins's engine sent Donnally running toward the flare. He dived and rolled, then drove the lit end into the dirt and covered it with his body. He felt the last of the smoldering chemicals eat through his shirt and singe his skin, but the smell of propane now surrounding him made him keep his body tight to the ground.

A few minutes later a gust cleared the gas for a moment and Donnally ran to the garage, retrieved a wrench, and retightened the fitting.

Despite the pain, Donnally felt a kind of relief standing in front of his bedroom mirror five minutes later, inspecting the craterlike wound on his stomach. Not just because his house hadn't blown up, not just because he had evidence that would end Pipkins's grab at Mauricio's land, but because unlike the delusions of Charles Brown and Trudy and Sonny, unlike what awaited him in the attic, unlike the reconstructed life of Anna Keenan that seemed more fiction than fact, the burn was real and would remain real as a scar, as a piece of reality, that tied the crimes of a generation to this single day in his life.

As Donnally finished cleaning and taping the wound, he heard a car slow in front of his house, and then accelerate away.

He didn't need to look out of the window to know that it had been Pipkins and what he had seen: the flare hanging by a fishing line from the porch roof and rocking in the wind.

CHAPTER 41

Donnally returned to examining Anna's records, now trying to follow the trail of cash payments, looking first for a code sheet to match the initials of the recipients shown on her ledger and then for an explanation for why she chose to give money to those she did.

He pulled out her calendars and organized them by year, latest to earliest, then opened to March 1986, the month of her death, thinking that if there were any leads to be found, they'd show up near the end. He had expected to find shopping lists, birthdays, scheduled meetings, and plans for spring vacation. There were none. It was a diary, not of her life or of her introspections, but of the lives that impinged on hers.

The last entry was on the day of her death.

> Father Phil claims that the problem has been resolved. He's been reassigned to Holy Names in San Francisco. I told him that it wasn't over and he was deluding himself.

Donnally wondered what sort of problem brings a priest to a teacher's doorstep. Had she become

Catholic and gotten involved in church politics? Had he been her confidant? Or she, his?

The day before her death:

A came by. He's ready to go back to New Jersey and turn himself in, even if R doesn't. I gave him the name of Mark Hamlin.

Donnally sat back and folded his arms across his chest. If A was Artie Trueblood and R was Robert Trueblood, then Mark Hamlin probably had known their true identities for decades.

Did Hamlin try to arrange Artie's surrender? Did he try to convince Robert to go along? And who paid Hamlin's fee? Anna? Trudy? Sonny?

Did Hamlin also know they were dead?

Two days before:

Melvin came by crying. Confused. Heard that Father Phil has been assigned to Holy Names in San Francisco. Will go see him.

Who is Melvin? Another crazy homeless guy like Charles Brown? Did he want money to go see his priest? Or maybe it was Anna who was going to visit Father Phil.

Three days before:

R came by looking for A. Said A had given him last week's money like we agreed. I told him that he couldn't keep living like he was. He was going to kill himself.

Suicide? Was Robert planning to kill himself? Then what was the point of killing Anna? If he was dead, she couldn't have hurt him anymore. And if she was giving him money, there was no reason for him to rob her.

Four days before:

A heard his mother died. Afraid to go to her funeral.

A killer who's a mama's boy? Nothing unusual in that, Donnally thought. Death row was lined with them.

A week before:

Sherwyn showed up. Unannounced. Said I should stop interfering. I was damaging to his progress.

Whose progress? Sherwyn's? In doing what? Two weeks before:

Dr. Sherwyn got my message. Came by. Acknowledged he was called Rabbit. Said he got caught in the middle of an internal conflict at New Sky and that everyone knows it. Asked him about the theory behind his treatment methods. RT. Referred me to a textbook. Said he had a contract with the church.

The notes mirrored what Brown and Trudy said they'd overheard, except the letters R2T2 were missing.

Donnally wondered whether what was said about R2T2 wasn't important enough, or maybe too dangerous, to write down. Maybe that was why she wrote only the letters RT.

He reread the notes. Treatment methods? Treatment of whom? Melvin? Father Phil? Someone else? Sixteen days before:

A came by, gave him some more money. Looks bad. He will pass on R's share. Thinking about surrendering.

A guy thinking about turning himself in isn't going to commit a murder. Suicide, maybe. Murder, no—unless something changed in the weeks leading up to it.

Donnally read back through the notes. Artie had later decided to turn himself in, Anna had hooked him up with Hamlin, and Robert had gotten his money. No motives there.

Eighteen days before:

Melvin asked to talk to me after class. St. Mark's. Father Phil. Twice. Sent for counseling. Called the church. Father Phil not available. Message left.

Melvin must have been a student, and whatever his problem was, he first got counseling with Father Phil. Maybe that's why Anna wanted to talk to the priest, to check on Melvin's progress.

Donnally then searched further back through the calendar looking for entries relating to Melvin,

Sherwyn, and Father Phil. He found none. The few references to A and R seemed to relate only to handouts of money.

Leaning back and rubbing his eyes, Donnally realized that he'd been talking to himself for the last two hours in the voices of people he'd never met, except Sherwyn's. He took in a long breath, then read through the entries he'd highlighted, but this time in chronological order.

A was dead and R was dead.

What about Melvin?

And Father Phil?

Sherwyn was alive. But if Sonny was telling the truth about the doctor's role in covering up the murders, Sherwyn wouldn't be talking, at least to Donnally.

CHAPTER 42 ═══════════

Donnally hadn't worn a suit since his grand-
mother's funeral nine years earlier. He felt
like a clown at a wake as he sat in the Holy Names
Church library after services among the screaming
Hispanic kids who'd been herded inside by their
Sunday school teacher.

But it was worth the awkwardness.

The 1986 church directory he located on a shelf
with others had a color photograph of Father Phil
and a last name: McGrath. There wasn't a picture
of him in the directory for the year before or the
year after.

Father Phil looked to Donnally more like a man
who'd spent most of his fifty-five years sitting on a
barstool drinking neat bourbons, rather than in a
confessional, with his cheeks becoming more ruddy
and his eyeglasses becoming less fashionable in the
eternal semidarkness of a neighborhood bar.

Donnally wasn't sure how he'd pry Melvin's last
name out of the priest when he tracked him down,
but he hoped that with the passage of time, the de-
mands of confidentiality would give way to an old
man's nostalgia.

The church secretary's eyes turned to glass when

Donnally spoke the father's name. The beatific afterglow of the morning service that had greeted him when he walked through her office door vanished just as fast. It was replaced by a waxen face and a defensive stare.

"He's no longer here," she said, looking up at Donnally, her voice even. "He left many years ago."

She didn't use his name. Just "he," spoken as if she'd used the word "it."

"Do you know where he might be now?" Donnally asked, guessing that the answer would be some form of a snide *for me to know and you to find out*.

The secretary's voice was not at all singsongy when she answered; it was shaky, as if she'd already used up her allotment of self-control.

"I . . . I don't know where he is."

"Don't you have some sort of directory of priests?" he asked. "Or somebody I can call?"

She reached for a message pad and wrote out a telephone number.

"You can call the diocese. Maybe they'll help you."

Donnally accepted the slip of paper, then thanked her and turned away. It wasn't lost on him that she'd said "maybe" rather than "can." Even before he reached the threshold, he grasped that the answer from the diocese would be "won't."

Moments after the door closed behind him, he heard the secretary's muffled voice.

"I'm sorry to bother you on Sunday, Mr. Pagaroli, but a man was just here asking about Father Phil . . . I didn't give him your name or the name of your law firm . . . I'll let the monsignor know . . . sure . . . I'll do that."

Donnally smiled like a former altar boy at two elderly women walking past him and down the hallway, their short, plump bodies shrouded in black. But he wasn't smiling inside as he drove away, for he now understood that whatever Father Phil McGrath had done twenty years earlier lived on in the present like a cancer in remission.

A half hour after leaving the church, Donnally walked into Fort Miley and asked the receptionist to page Charles Brown. A few minutes later, Brown walked unescorted into the lobby. He was still clean shaven, his hair was trimmed, and he was wearing a brown sweater and black pants. His face aimed at an earnest expression, but his eyes betrayed him. Donnally followed Brown's leer toward a young woman sitting alone along a wall, then he stepped in front of her, so she wouldn't be forced to see herself in Brown's predatory reflection.

Brown finally looked up and greeted Donnally, then led him to the visiting room, where they sat facing each other across a metal table.

It seemed to Donnally that the medications Janie had put Brown on were now working, or at least he was at a lucid mid-point between the extremes.

Donnally opened the church directory and pointed at the photo of Father Phil. Brown squinted at it, then nodded.

"He came to see Anna." Brown grinned. "He was drunk and Anna made him go away. But he came back, even more drunk. He said that Anna was going to ruin him."

"Why would Anna want to ruin him?"

"Because of Melvin. He was Anna's student. Melvin was unhappy with that man." He pointed at the photograph. "That's why Dr. Sherwyn came, because of him."

"Was the father a patient of Dr. Sherwyn?"

"I thought so, but Anna didn't say. She didn't talk to me much."

"When was the last time the father visited Anna?"

Brown shrugged. "I don't remember. I get confused."

Donnally heard the click of high heels pass behind him, then watched Brown's eyes track the woman, left to right, below waist level, as if he could see her crotch through her skirt. Donnally now suspected that this was the real reason Brown played the role of Rover the Mascot. He could sit on the sidewalk and look up between the legs of women walking by. He wondered whether Anna's endurance of this creature was a form of penitence, or maybe repentance in the old, biblical sense of returning to sorrow, returning to her own sexual abuse by her father.

"What about Artie and Robert?" Donnally asked.

"I don't know," Brown said, forcing himself to look back at Donnally. "Anna liked Artie, but didn't trust Robert. I heard her tell Trudy that Artie felt guilty all the time and Robert used drugs. I didn't understand what she meant. I thought it would be the other way around." His eyebrows furrowed. "Maybe Janie can explain it to me."

"Do you know Melvin's last name?"

Brown shook his head. "He was just Melvin."

As Donnally walked through Janie's living room toward her office to run Internet searches on Mc-Grath and Pagaroli, it struck him that she hadn't made much progress in packing. The bookshelves were still half full and her photographs remained propped at their oblique angles, half looking at one another, half looking out into the room. The resignation to which he'd become accustomed lifted for a moment, then he realized that her preemptive boxing of books was more symbolic than pragmatic, since it would take her a month or two to find another house to rent.

Maybe that was the problem all along, he said to himself as he sat down at her desk. *Somehow we started communicating only through symbolism.*

He paused and looked around at the walls and windows and doors, and it struck him that the house, which could've been a home in some people's lives, had devolved into just a way station in which both of them had gotten stranded.

CHAPTER 43

"I didn't expect ever to see you again," Margaret Perkins said to Donnally as she walked into the Schubert, Smith, and Barton conference room. Her pressed slacks and steaming Starbucks cup gave her a fresh Monday morning look. She held up the records release signed by Charles Brown that Donnally had faxed over the night before. "And I sure as hell wasn't expecting this."

Donnally smiled and extended his hand. She slipped by it and gave him a hug.

"And I wasn't expecting that," he said.

Donnally turned and pointed at the Golden Gate Bridge framed by the floor-to-ceiling window.

"Nice view."

Perkins shrugged. "Just one of life's illusions. Most of the world is composed of trampled dirt. Not so pretty."

She then pointed at a chair and they sat down next to each other at the table.

"I somehow thought we were on the same side from the beginning," she said. "I wanted to know the truth, too. The problem is that court is rarely a place to discover it."

Donnally smiled. "Maybe something should be done about that."

"It won't happen in our lifetimes."

Perkins looked toward the glass wall separating the conference room from the reception area where two suited men waited, hands gripping briefcases as if afraid they'd spring open and confess to some uncharged crime.

"We spend most of our time around here trying to keep the facts and the truth from getting into court."

"I guess that's because your clients are usually the ones with something to hide."

Perkins nodded. "You got that right. Charles Brown may turn out to be our single exception this year." She smiled. "Of course, we didn't think so at the time."

She took a sip of coffee and then set down her cup.

"I ruined a paralegal's Sunday evening and had him do some research on Lou Pagaroli and his firm, starting with what you discovered on the Internet. The child molesting case you found wasn't the only one he's done. The church has become his cash cow over the last ten years."

Donnally raised his eyebrows. He had also researched Schubert, Smith and Barton's clients. SSB represented the Vatican in litigation in U.S. courts.

"Different church," she said. "The work we do for the Vatican is entirely separate. Both from a financial and a legal perspective. You can't get there from here. Trust me. Lots of plaintiff's lawyers have tried. There simply is no Vatican-controlled entity in the United States."

"What about the pope's dominion over his flock?"

"That's hearts and minds, not corporate structure." She grinned. "That you'll find in the Cayman Islands."

"Which means?"

The playfulness disappeared from her face.

"I'll do everything I can to help you nail that child-molesting priest."

"Just because Pagaroli is involved—"

"Yes, it does. It means exactly that. You know that old hymn, 'His eye is on the sparrow?' Well, Pagaroli is the shotgun the church uses to blast it out of the sky. All Pagaroli has done for the last decade is represent California dioceses in their worst sexual abuse cases."

"But I didn't find any cases where Philip McGrath was named as a defendant."

"That just means that no victims have come forward."

"Why not? There's a lot of money in it."

"Most are too ashamed," Perkins said. "Would you want to get up on the stand and get cross-examined about some priest sticking his—"

"Other people do it."

"And it truly, truly amazes me."

Perkins reached for the banker's box containing Brown's file and pulled it closer. "I'm not sure the police were even aware that Father Phil had ever been at Anna's house. His name doesn't come up at all."

"What about guys named Artie and Robert?"

Perkins cast Donnally a puzzled look. "Who are they?"

Donnally shrugged. "It's not important."

"Important enough for you to mention."

The question was hard to answer without raising other ones, so he asked, "You ever been to a crime scene?"

"Only the occasional corporate headquarters," She smiled. "But I'm sure that's not the kind you have in mind."

"The idea is to search through and collect or record everything that might be relevant."

"And Artie and Robert are in the 'might be' category."

Donnally nodded.

"And should have been noted at the time if the detectives were doing their jobs properly?"

"Along with Father Phil and Sherwyn."

Perkins's eyes widened. "Sherwyn?"

"Sherwyn. Now that I know how Pagaroli fits in, my guess is that Father Phil molested Melvin, and the church sent Father Phil to Sherwyn for treatment instead of turning him in to the police. Sherwyn testified in Brown's hearing that most of his practice was in the area of sexual abuse."

"Sherwyn never disclosed that he—"

"And the police were tunnel-visioned in their focus on Brown."

"But how could that happen?" Perkins said, voice rising. "What are the chances that Sherwyn would be picked to do the competency evaluation?"

"Easy. There were only a handful of shrinks in

the whole Bay Area who did them. It was a little cottage industry. Still is. For the defense one week, for the prosecution the next, whoever called first. Maybe Sherwyn saw Brown in the legal pipeline and elbowed someone else aside."

Perkins's eyes moved like searchlights shining on an internal battlefield, trying to pick out the enemy from among the shadows.

She finally looked at Donnally and asked, "You think Father Phil murdered Anna to keep her from going to the police?"

"He was the one facing living in prison as a child molester," Donnally said. "And he was the last one we know for certain who was at Anna's house, and her diary says that she warned him that he was deluding himself if he thought her investigation of him was over. He left, then probably snuck back in and killed her. And Sherwyn put himself in a position to keep the case from ever going to trial."

Donnally didn't say it, but finished the thought in his mind: That meant that Artie and Robert had been murdered in revenge for a crime they hadn't committed and that Sherwyn had been protecting himself, not the former New Sky members who'd beaten them to death.

Perkins glanced at the banker's box. "But I thought Sherwyn put Brown on lithium so he'd become competent. That's what his lawyer sued to stop."

"It was just the opposite. Sherwyn overdosed Brown on lithium. It made him physically sick and even more crazy."

She exhaled, almost a whistle. "Why would he take a risk like that?"

"Maybe money. Who knows how many priests he was treating. A hundred and fifty dollars an hour, eight hours a day. Over a quarter of a million dollars a year. Maybe because Sherwyn's first attempt at treating Father Phil had been a failure, and Melvin was the father's second victim."

"And if Brown went to trial, the defense might have figured out that the real killer was Father Phil—"

"And complete the circle back to Sherwyn. He'd be seen by the public as a failure and the church wouldn't—couldn't—hire him anymore."

Donnally watched Perkins shake her head, as if clearing her lawyer's mind.

"But all this assumes that Melvin, whoever he is, really was a victim of molestation," she said. "And you've got no proof of that. It's what we call in the netherworld of law a lack of foundation."

"Maybe I should drop by Sherwyn's office and ask him."

"He'd just make that little rabbit face he does, then slam the door. You'd probably have better luck with Father Phil."

Donnally's cell phone rang as he was driving past the gold-domed San Francisco City Hall on his way back toward Janie's.

"Got some bad news for you," Perkins said. "Father Phil is permanently exercising his right to remain silent."

"You mean—"

"Dead as a church doornail."

"How'd you find out?"

"I went to law school with one of the plaintiff's lawyers in the lawsuits against the San Francisco Diocese."

"You mean they had a case against him?"

"Never got that far. They couldn't turn up a victim."

"Back up. You've got me confused." Donnally pulled into a yellow zone in front of a bank. "Try it again."

"My friend told me that a parishioner at St. Mark's in Berkeley had some suspicions about Father Phil. Her name was Theresa Randon. She warned the monsignor, who sent Father Phil packing. She later became a member of Holy Names in San Francisco and was shocked to find him there. She complained a second time and was told that they'd discovered no evidence that he'd molested anyone."

"But the church sent him for therapy with Sherwyn," Donnally said, "so they must've had some proof."

"The plaintiffs' lawyers didn't know about that until I told them just now."

"They would've found that out from church records. The plaintiffs must have subpoenaed—"

Perkins cut him off with a bitter laugh.

"I guess you've forgotten what shredders are for. And no one owns more of them than the church and its lawyers."

CHAPTER 44 ═══════════════

Finding Theresa Randon wasn't as easy as Donnally had hoped. Ninety-year-olds typically don't have driver's licenses. They don't apply for credit. They stop doing any of those things that get their names into databases. She had almost disappeared into the vast emptiness of anonymity that Donnally himself sometimes craved.

Almost.

Donnally had learned from his grandmother that elderly church ladies tend to keep track of one another. They visit old folks' homes. They keep lists of people to pray for when they're ill. They bring meals to the homebound.

And they tend to be well organized.

The eighty-year-old woman looked up at Donnally with a grin when he stopped her on the sidewalk at the bottom of Holy Names' front steps. He had timed his visit for just before the start of a meeting of church volunteers. He described himself as a former Sunday school student of Theresa's.

She withdrew a photocopy of a two-page spreadsheet from her purse, titled "Holy Names Visiting Schedule."

"I don't know how we used to keep track of all this without computers," she said.

Donnally could see that about a dozen names, addresses, and telephone numbers were highlighted. He guessed that they were the woman's own assignments.

She scanned the list, then pulled out her cell phone, punched in a number, and repeated Donnally's story to the person at the other end of the call.

"Is Theresa back from the hospital?" she asked.

A frown came to her face, which soon transformed into a smile.

"Just a false alarm. That's wonderful. Thanks, dear."

She disconnected and turned the sheet toward Donnally and let him write down the address.

"I hope you won't be disappointed, Mr. Donnally." The frown returned. "Theresa is no longer Catholic." She brightened. "But we still consider her one of the girls."

"It's not nice to lie to old people," Theresa Randon said to Donnally an hour later. She was still dressed in the pastel green sweat suit she'd worn to her Stretch and Tone class at the San Francisco Woods Retirement Center.

"I never taught Sunday school," she said. "I was banned like a modern Socrates. They were afraid I'd corrupt the youth."

"I didn't think the lady would help me if I told her the truth."

Theresa smiled. "You got that right, buster."

Donnally looked around the atrium from where

they sat at a small marble table next to the fountain. The running water muted the classical music filling the room.

"Nice place," Donnally said.

"I bought Microsoft at five dollars a share." She held up two fingers, close together. "Bill Gates and I are like this."

"Not like you and Father Phil were."

Theresa's cheeks wobbled and her silver hair shook as her body shuddered. "Creepy. He was damn creepy."

"But you never found any proof?"

"His being booted out of St. Mark's in Berkeley and later from Holy Names over here was proof enough for me. He molested boys in every parish they tried to hide him in. What we never got was justice."

"And that's why you left the church?"

"I didn't leave the church, it left me."

She folded her arms on the table and inspected Donnally's face.

"You haven't exactly told me what you're up to. How do I know you're not part of a secret Vatican plot?" She glanced around and hunched her shoulders. "They have agents everywhere, you know."

Donnally felt himself stiffen. *Not another Berkeley lunatic like Trudy.*

She straightened up and laughed. "Gotcha."

Donnally smiled. "Yes, you did."

"Spill it."

He nodded, then lied to another old person.

"I'm trying to help a lawyer prove that the diocese knew about the molestations by Father Phil and others, but I've dead-ended. The last lead I have is the first name of a kid that he may have molested. Melvin."

"Melvin." Theresa squinted up toward the chandeliers, then looked back at Donnally. "Did he have a nickname?"

"Not that I know of. Just Melvin."

Theresa went back to her upward squint. "Melvin. Melvin. Melvin." She slapped the tabletop, then fixed her eyes on Donnally. "I know who that is. Little Mel Watson. During high school he worked at The Sweet Tooth. Pale-faced, earnest little runt, but man did he know how to pile chocolate ice cream on a cone."

She paused and her brows furrowed.

"You're not going to believe it, but he became a goddamn priest."

As he walked to his car, Donnally repeated in his mind the thought that Theresa had left unspoken: Molested children sometimes become molesters themselves. And what better place for someone like Melvin Watson to disappear than back into the scene of an unprosecuted crime.

CHAPTER 45

Brother Melvin rested his forearms on his thighs and stared down at his thin hands. He and Donnally were sitting on a concrete bench outside the neo-Gothic hillside chapel of La Sallian University in Vancouver.

"How did you identify me?" Melvin asked.

"It's a long story."

Melvin looked over. "I could sue you for defamation or something and make you tell it."

"But you won't."

"No." Melvin sighed. "I won't."

Melvin then gazed out over the Canadian city, oblivious to the hushed rumble of traffic rising up from the freeways crossing the inlet below.

"I know the question in your mind," Melvin finally said, without looking over at Donnally, "so I'll answer it first even if I don't answer anything else: No. I didn't join the Christian Brothers in order to molest children. If this all becomes public, everyone who's important in my life outside of the church will think I did. But the truth is that celibacy was my life raft and I've never let go. Never." He looked over his shoulder toward the twenty-acre campus. "The tests of temptation were the students."

"Maybe you should've become a monk."

Melvin smiled for the first time since Donnally had knocked on his office door a half hour earlier.

"I didn't like the uniforms." Melvin's smile died. "Anyway, isolation wouldn't have solved the problem that Father Phil and the others left me with."

"What was that?"

"Sexual confusion. It's not as if a boy becomes gay because his first sexual experience is in the form of molestation by a man. It's that the act causes you to lose your bearings. It's a sudden exposure to unlimited possibility, like getting lost in the wilderness, or watching your mother murder your father, or seeing the World Trade Center collapse. The world seems to lose its natural order.

"If your first homosexual experience happens when you're older, in the army or in a seminary, you can place it into the context of the rest of your life. You know right away whether it's out of character or a turning point in your understanding of your sexuality—but not when you're a kid."

Melvin rubbed his forehead. "And when it's a priest, it's even worse. First it seems absurd, then like a betrayal." He lowered his hand and looked at Donnally. "But what's really weird is that you start to feel special, even privileged. After all, the priest picked you from all the rest of the boys for his attention. In time, of course, you discover there are others, and then it turns into a secret, exclusive society of the chosen."

He smiled again, this time with a hint of embarrassment.

"Isn't it strange that as adults we can be ashamed

of our naïveté as children? Delusions of imaginary friends, the mythic power of our blankies, games of hide-and-seek that seem as real as warfare. But for me and the other clients of Dr. Sherwyn—"

Donnally turned toward Brother Melvin. "Sherwyn? You were being treated by Sherwyn?"

He nodded. "Father Phil wasn't his patient. I was. He called it Reenactment Therapy."

Donnally stared at the young man, but his mind was seeing past him. "You mean . . ."

Brother Melvin closed his eyes and rocked back and forth. Tears formed and rolled down his cheeks.

"It seemed as real as the seven sacraments."

Reenactment Therapy.

Donnally took a sip of beer in the airport bar as he waited for his flight back to San Francisco.

That's what RT stood for.

He hadn't told Melvin, but it was his confessing it to Anna Keenan that had cost her her life. And it was that same knowledge that had plagued Trudy since the day of the murder and had sent her into hiding for more than twenty years, all that time twisting herself into a psychosomatic bundle of self-deception.

Trudy had overheard the arguments. RT wasn't Artie and it wasn't Robert Trueblood—and she knew that from the beginning, and pretended to herself that she didn't.

A pudgy seventy-year-old executive sat down on the next stool, his face soft and pink, his lips thin, his nails manicured. His tailored suit seemed to have been machined rather than sewn.

The man ignored Donnally as he ordered a martini, then stared into the mirror, tracking a blond-haired teenage boy in baggy pants strolling by behind them.

For a moment, Donnally wondered whether the man was one of the beneficiaries of Dr. Sherwyn's Reenactment Therapy and was a member of the secret society to which Melvin had told him its graduates had been introduced.

Maybe he had been one of those anonymous, elegant men who attended the parties that Melvin had told him about, who sat on the love seats with their arms around the shoulders of the youngsters or who scanned the boys playing in the pool, inspecting them with the eyes of casting directors searching for the exact one to play the required role in a burgeoning fantasy. And the boys glancing over to catch the eye of the one who would set them up in an apartment, give them an allowance, maybe even a credit card on which to charge their lives.

The paths of good intention.

That's what Brother Melvin had called the routes by which the boys arrived at Dr. Sherwyn's door: from the court, from Children's Protective Services, from probation, or, like Melvin, from the church.

And each walked through it thinking it was his escape from sexual abuse at the hands of his father or uncle or coach or priest.

Donnally cringed as he imagined little Melvin

sitting across from Dr. Sherwyn in his North Berkeley office, listening to a fantastical theory, one that he thought must be true because it had been sanctified by the monsignor and authenticated by science.

Then entering an almost hypnotic state of wonder and exhilaration in which everything—past, present, and future—made sense. And the warm pleasure of being invited into an esoteric world, whose integrity had to be defended by secrecy.

The image Brother Melvin had left Donnally with returned. Melvin on all fours on the carpet, Sherwyn kneeling behind, clothed, pantomiming the act, even down to the grunting and sweating and swearing. Boys like Melvin who had held still, even at the cost of shivering disassociation, passed the test. Then from one session to the next, hands began to reach and articles of clothing were removed.

Only too late did Brother Melvin come to understand that the purpose of Reenactment Therapy wasn't to get past the trauma, but to get accustomed to it.

On the flight back, Donnally figured out the kind of Reenactment Therapy he wanted to engage in: his hands around the throat of William Sherwyn.

CHAPTER 46

"That's absurd," William Sherwyn said to Donnally, standing on the landing of the doctor's Spanish Colonial in the Berkeley hills. "Completely absurd."

Sherwyn's hand still gripped the front door. He glanced past Donnally toward downtown San Francisco across the sunlit bay. He then locked his eyes on Donnally's and said, "And I'm not going to risk a lawsuit talking about someone who may, or may not, have been a patient of mine."

"Have it your way, but Charles Brown's lawyer is filing a motion to withdraw his plea, and it's all going to come out."

"There's no 'it,' other than the disturbed fantasies of a troubled man." Sherwyn smiled. "Did you ask this hypothetical patient where these so-called parties were? Who attended them? What about names? Did he have names?"

"He was a confused thirteen-year-old kid."

"And now he's a confused adult."

Sherwyn looked skyward and tapped his chin.

Donnally had the sense that the doctor was picturing himself framed by the mansion, his authority buttressed by its fortresslike solidity.

"Let me see who your witnesses would be." Sherwyn looked at Donnally again. "There's the bipolar Mr. Brown. There's Trudy who lost touch with reality sometime in the 1970s and who treated Anna like a lost dog she took in, rather than as a human being with a family who might have been anguished by her disappearance. It never even crossed dear Trudy's mind that Anna might have been a kidnap victim. And there is, of course, the delusional Melvin." He grinned. "I would pay to watch those three testify."

"They're not the only ones."

"New Sky? The ones who hid murderers, who conspired with Trudy, and who became drug dealers when their so-called dream died?"

"You were part of that dream for a while, until they threw you out for molesting a boy."

Sherwyn laughed. "Not only did that not happen, but everyone in New Sky knew it didn't happen. I was thrown out because they discovered what I was really doing there, observational research for my dissertation on counterculture sexuality." Sherwyn pointed inside his house. "You want to read it? I can loan you a copy."

"The way I heard the story, it was participant research."

"Let me guess, from somebody like Sonny the ex-con? The drugged-up dope fiend who saw the world through the windowpane of LSD and the brown haze of heroin."

Donnally felt the fragile web of Brown's and Melvin's half memories tear apart under Sherwyn's practiced hand, but the threads remained attached to something real, and Donnally fought back with that.

"I wouldn't be standing here if that's all I had," Donnally said. "Anna left a diary."

Sherwyn made his rabbit face for a moment, as if searching for an answer to a cross-examiner's unanticipated question.

One finally came: "The diary of a little girl written in the midst of the New Sky fantasy world is hardly evidence."

"That's not what I'm talking about. It's the diary of a schoolteacher that ended on the day she was murdered."

Sherwyn laughed again. "And the last entry says, 'Today I will be murdered by Father Phil Mc-Grath.'"

Donnally shook his head.

Sherwyn threw up his arms. "Is that what this is about? You're trying to say I killed her?" He jabbed a forefinger at Donnally's chest. "You're an idiot. Father Phil had the motive, not me. Anna couldn't do anything to me. She'd lose her house and her mother would go to jail for harboring Artie and Robert, and maybe even as an accessory to the murder of that cop in Berkeley. She was the first one to yell, 'Right on,' when they said, 'Let's kill the pig.' And then she went out and bought them guns. She was no different than those naïve Symbionese Liberation Army women for whom blood in the gutter was merely an abstraction."

That was it, Donnally thought. It had to be Sherwyn. Had to be. He hadn't argued back by giving reasons that he didn't do it, but only for why Trudy

would never turn him in. And Donnally understood why Trudy had kept her silence about who
had killed Anna: to save herself. A tug by detectives
on any of the threads that tied their lives together
would have led to her arrest.

Donnally felt nauseated. Every time he peeled
back a layer of Trudy's self-deception, she became
more and more disgusting.

"You know," Sherwyn continued, "this story of
yours doesn't work all that well as evidence. Perhaps
you should turn it into a screenplay and give it to
your father. He seems to have the same tenuous relationship with truth that you do."

With that, Sherwyn stepped back and closed the
door in Donnally's face.

Donnally reached into his pocket and turned off
his tape recorder as he walked down the steps, but
he was already replaying it in his head. No one so
far had known who his father was. All any of them
knew was that he was an ex-cop who flipped pancakes in a Mount Shasta café. Not even the press
had bothered to investigate his background.

But Sherwyn had.

Sherwyn knew that Donnally would become his
enemy long before Donnally did, which meant that
Sherwyn had something to fear.

Donnally paused at the bottom step and looked
back up at the house.

Sherwyn had inadvertently respun the web, no
matter how tenuous it might be.

CHAPTER 47

Donnally considered making a U-turn and heading back to the Burbank Airport for a return flight to San Francisco when he saw his father's porcelain white Bentley parked in the circular driveway of the Hollywood estate. But a wave from Julia arriving for her evening shift drew him in. It had been a call from her about his mother's weakening condition that had brought him there.

Julia looked at him with a cocked head and raised eyebrows as if to say she knew what he had been thinking.

He parked behind his father's car, then followed her up the front steps into the marble-floored foyer.

"Your father told me yesterday that he wanted to speak with you when you arrived." Julia pointed toward the stairway leading to the screening room. "He's probably down there."

It had been twenty years since his father had summoned him downstairs. He'd gone then because his mother was already in there, an object of both of their affection. Now, he suspected, she would be the subject.

Even back then, when his father was merely famous and long before he was referred to as the

Legendary Don Harlan, the screening room seemed to Donnally like a shrine his father had created to worship himself: Oscars and Golden Globes and Directors Guild awards lined up on shelves like religious icons. Low lighting like a chapel that forced visitors to lower their voices to a whisper when they entered, as though they had arrived in the presence of a divine mystery.

"Was it an invitation?" Donnally asked Julia.

"I wouldn't call it that."

Don Harlan looked back from where he sat in the first of the four rows of the theater as Donnally entered. The soft lights glowing from above had never made him seem more Hollywood, more statuesque, more artificial than he did at that moment.

At the same time, the room seemed hollow. The shelves were mostly bare. Donnally wondered whether the awards that had now sanctified him as a legend had outgrown the space and he'd moved the Church of Don Harlan to larger quarters.

In one motion he waved Donnally over and pointed at the seat next to him.

"I thought you were doing a reshoot in Vietnam," Donnally said in full voice as he sat down.

"Belize."

"Belize?"

"It was a jungle scene and Americans can't distinguish one from another." His father grinned. "So I've been shooting in Latin America."

"Your investors will be pleased."

"Not with this one. It's not what they thought they were buying." He pressed a button on the console before him, and the lights went down. "Let me show you a little."

"I'd really just like to check on Mother and then try to make the last flight back," Donnally said, leaning forward in the deep seat to rise. "I'm kind of in the middle of something up there."

"Humor your old man for a few minutes."

Donnally let an exhale be his answer and settled back.

Moments later he felt a surge of anger as he watched a fade-in to the pseudo-documentary beginning. He pushed himself to his feet and jabbed his finger at the grainy black and white image of the 1968 Saigon press briefing in which Captain Donald Harlan had blamed the North Vietnamese for the murder of the Buddhist monks.

"I don't have time for this bullshit."

His father answered, not from next to him, but from the screen. A voice-over:

> *The following is a story none of us had the courage to tell when it would've made a difference. None of the names have been changed to protect the guilty. None of the places have been changed to conceal the evidence . . . May God have mercy on our souls.*

Donnally felt his body slump. He reached for the armrests and lowered himself back down into the seat.

His father had slipped out sometime during the ninety-minute film. Donnally found him sitting alone at the kitchen table.

"What happened?" Donnally asked.

Donnally heard his voice, but his mind and heart were still filled with the final image on the screen, a frozen shot of the actor who had played his brother, his body lying in the grass outside the Vietnamese village where he had been killed.

"I realized that it was time to stop hiding behind the art," his father said, "and just tell the truth."

"That's not what I ever expected to hear from you. Even Janie has been trying to convince me that one was the means to the other."

His father's face reddened. Donnally knew why. It was his asking Janie to play the part of a prostitute.

"Sorry about that," his father said. "I keep playing the provocateur even when I don't want to anymore."

Donnally leaned back against the edge of the granite-topped island, wondering whether Janie had been right, that his father had been moving toward this moment and that Donnally hadn't been able to see it.

But the change, whether in himself or in his father or in both of them, was too sudden and he wasn't prepared for that kind of conversation, so he focused on the film itself.

"I think that's the first Vietnam War movie ever made about the Vietnamese," Donnally said.

"I thought it was time to raise the question of who we were fighting, why we were fighting them, and who we became while we were doing it. Understanding those things might have kept us out of Iraq."

Donnally felt his body tense, but he tried not to

show it. The question for him wasn't about Vietnam or Iraq, it was about who his father was when he'd lied to the world and deceived his own son into sacrificing himself for a cause that his father knew, even back then, could only be defended through lies.

"It looks to me," Donnally said, "like your answer was that we were fighting a fantasy of our own construction."

His father nodded, then leaned forward in his chair and folded his forearms on the table. He looked down at his hands for a long moment, and then back up at Donnally.

"I watched Clint Eastwood's *Letters from Iwo Jima* about a dozen times until I figured out why no one ever made a film like that about the Vietnamese peasants we were fighting. And the reason was guilt: It's easier to tell a story from the point of view of an enemy who attacks you than of someone you've wronged. That's when it hit me why all of my other war films were about us, and not about them."

His father took in a deep breath.

"And that's why I always made American soldiers and veterans out to be psychotic or psychically wounded or berserk supermen." He spread his hands and shrugged. "What else can they be when no one wants to admit that the people we wanted to save were also our enemies, and that they didn't want to be saved, at least by us."

His father paused and bit his lower lip. Finally he said, "It started out as idealism, but somehow it got corrupted—or we corrupted it—and we blinded ourselves to what we were doing." He sighed. "Finally, our lies became more real to us than the truth."

Donnally gazed at his father, seeing lines in his face and darkness under his eyes he'd never noticed before. He realized that his father had always appeared in his mind fixed at age fifty, prematurely gray and well-tanned. In fact, he'd become a pale old man with yellowing hair.

Donnally pointed at an aged-brown envelope on the table. "What's that?"

"It's the letter your mother and I received from Donnie's commanding officer after he died."

His father picked it up and handed it to Donnally.

"I've read it once a month for the last forty years."

Donnally's hands shook when he reached the section describing his brother's final firefight. The euphemism "he engaged the enemy on all sides" gouged into him, reopening the wound.

He pointed at the paragraph and looked up at his father.

"They made him into a hero when what happened was that he was ambushed," his father said, "set up by villagers anguished by the napalming of their children and the torching of their homes. It took me all of these years to let myself understand what really happened. And when I did, I realized why you became a cop. It's the same reason you were unwilling to let Charles Brown plead no contest to a manslaughter."

"You've been following that?"

"Every step. And it proved to me that you've always had the courage that I never had: to refuse to accommodate yourself to a convenient fiction."

His father stretched his arms out on the table, his palms open, turned upward, a gesture that seemed to Donnally to be a surrender to an elemental, existential exhaustion.

"I realized in making this movie that, in the end, my art has been basically juvenile, even when it claimed to be in the service of truth. I should've been more like you. Fuck the allegory and just say what is."

His father fell silent, his breathing labored, then he said, "I know this doesn't make up for everything . . . for me, for the way I've been . . ." He shrugged. "For the way I am."

Donnally didn't respond. They both knew what he was saying was true and that he wasn't expecting forgiveness.

His father glanced toward the floors above and said, "Maybe you should go sit with your mother for a while."

CHAPTER 48

"This is pointless." Brother Melvin said as Donnally drove his truck through the same intersection near the San Francisco Airport for the fifth time that afternoon. "I'm just getting confused."

Donnally felt like an archeologist of Melvin's memory, trying to reconstruct the past from fragments buried by time and by shame. It was the longest of long shots that Melvin would remember the route Sherwyn had taken on that night twenty-five years earlier, but it was the only path left that might lead to Sherwyn's exposure.

Melvin was certain that Sherwyn had gotten off the freeway and merged onto a wide commercial street. The wing and taillights of airplanes taking off had sparkled behind them. They turned right—or was it left?—along another busy street, then left—or was it right?—into a residential neighborhood.

It was a big house. A mansion. Spanish Colonial. Three stories. Stucco. Melvin was sure of that. Salmon-colored, at least back then, with a long driveway, or it seemed so to a scared kid facing the unknown in the distance.

Even after their repeated failures to find the

house, Donnally didn't want to give up, for he was running out of angles.

Sherwyn had anticipated the pretext call from Melvin that Donnally had staged the day before in an attempt to trick him into making an admission. Sherwyn expressed the false doubt that he was even talking to Melvin, claimed client confidentiality, refused to meet in person, and hung up.

It was, just like Sherwyn's background investigation of Donnally and his choice of the word "tenuous," a confession that only Donnally could hear and no court would accept.

Melvin pointed toward the evening fog rolling in from the Pacific and obscuring the western hills.

"It'll be dark pretty soon anyway," Melvin said.

"You willing to stay over and give it a try tomorrow?"

Donnally watched Melvin gaze at an airplane taking off, heading north.

"You can't keep running," Donnally said.

"It's less running than hiding," Melvin said. "I didn't realize until after we talked in Vancouver that prayer is a phenomenal form of repression, and I've spent the last decade praying like my sanity depended on it, which it did. I didn't understand until now why so many priests become alcoholics. It's prayer in a bottle."

Melvin paused in thought for a moment, and then returned his eyes to the road ahead.

"It was weird watching Father Phil and Sherwyn drink together. They sometimes acted like giddy children who'd broken into their parents' liquor cabinet."

"They were both alcoholics?" Donnally asked, turning toward the freeway on-ramp.

"As far as I could tell, but only Father Phil looked the part. His face had that windburned look and his eyes were always watery. Sherwyn was different. It didn't show. I think that alcohol was part of their seduction routine and they knew their parts, drunk or sober." Melvin emitted a disgusted laugh. "You should've seen those teenage boys standing around at the beginning of the parties with their glasses of Chardonnay, acting all sophisticated. And the men waiting for them to get drunk. Not leering. That would be too crude. Just waiting. Sweating with anticipation.

"There was one guy there. I think he owned the house. He kept a kind of regal distance from everything, like he was a producer taking in his Tony Award–winning play. Enjoying the perfection of it all. He was older than the other men, maybe midsixties. I never saw him doing it with anybody. Some of the boys believed he was impotent, but I wasn't so sure."

Melvin paused for a moment as he stared ahead.

"Some of those old guys seemed to get off just watching the show."

CHAPTER 49

When Donnally pulled into the driveway of Janie's unlit house at 8 P.M., he imagined the look on her face when she arrived home to find that he'd brought in another stray. But at least this one wouldn't be handcuffed in the basement.

Brother Melvin retrieved his small duffel bag from behind the seat, then followed Donnally up the front stairs and onto the landing, half shadowed by a streetlight.

As Donnally reached his key toward the lock, a Hispanic man dressed in black stepped out of the darkness. He pointed a semiautomatic at Donnally's face, then at Melvin's.

They raised their hands.

The man jerked his head toward the driveway.

Melvin drew back. "You can't make us—"

"Shut up," the man whispered. His accent was heavy, but his words were distinct.

"Take it easy," Donnally said to Melvin, then to the man. "What do you want?"

"We're going to take a ride."

Donnally flicked his keys toward the hedge on the side of the house. They jingled in flight, then rattled leaves as they dropped though the branches.

"Not in my truck," Donnally said.

The man shrugged. "We can walk."

Brother Melvin pointed down with his raised hand, "My wallet is in my back pocket. Take it. We won't call the police."

"This isn't a robbery," Donnally said.

"Then what the . . . ?"

"Sherwyn."

Donnally knew he was right, but it didn't make sense that Sherwyn would have the kind of connections that could put a contract killer on his doorstep.

In one motion Brother Melvin lowered himself to his knees and pressed his hands together in prayer.

Donnally tensed, fearing that the histrionic gesture would get them killed right then.

"Get up, *chingaso*," the man ordered, and then bashed Melvin in the side of the head with the gun barrel.

Melvin wobbled, but kept his balance. "Our Father, who art in Heaven, hallowed be Thy name. Thy kingdom come." Melvin's voice became louder. "Thy will be done—"

"Shut the fuck up."

"On earth as it is in heaven—"

"Fucking priests."

The gun butt crashed down on Melvin's head. He slumped toward Donnally, who stepped back and reached for the railing behind him, then jumped over. He hit the ground a fraction of a second sooner than he expected and slammed forward onto his hands.

A gunshot shattered the neighbor's window a foot above his head. He pulled his gun, waited for the shadowed figure to lean over the railing above him, then emptied it into his chest.

CHAPTER 50

Blood-soaked Brother Melvin was lying in the back of an ambulance when Lieutenant Ramon Navarro arrived. Neighbors crowded the sidewalk across the street. The crime scene techs had bagged the dead man's hands and had completed their gunshot residue swabs on Donnally and Melvin.

"You move anything?" Navarro asked Donnally, who was standing by the fireplace in the living room.

Janie had arrived home and was sitting on the couch, twisting a Kleenex in her hands.

"I rolled the dead guy off Brother Melvin, that's all."

Navarro glanced toward the front of the house.

"They're telling me that the guy didn't have any ID," Navarro said. "You find a driver's license?"

"I didn't look. Just flopped him over, then called 911."

"I don't know, man," Navarro said. "He didn't look like a robber to me. Pressed slacks. Slick haircut. New shoes. Helluva nice gun."

Donnally shrugged. "Times are weird."

An hour after the police had cleared the scene and Brother Melvin had been transported to SF General for stitches and observation, Donnally walked down to the basement. He reached into a box under the stairs, pulled out a paper bag, and dumped the contents onto the workbench.

"What's that?"

Donnally spun around, startled by the sound of Janie's voice. He turned toward her as she walked over.

"I thought you were asleep," Donnally said.

He tried to block her view, but she elbowed by him. Her eyes locked on the Mexican police badge.

Her voice rose. "He was a cop?"

She started to reach for it, but then pulled her hand back.

"Gregorio Cruz from Quintana Roo," Donnally said, turning toward her. "Cancun."

"What do you think you're doing? Why didn't you give this to—"

"You want your name in the news as part of an international incident? You want the FBI knocking on your door? You want diplomatic shadowboxing to block me from finding out what's going on?"

Janie didn't have an answer.

"I don't know how he did it," Donnally said, "but Sherwyn is behind this."

She pointed at the badge. "How do you know he wasn't sent to get even for the Mexican pot grower who got hurt?"

"Because they don't know who I am and I wouldn't be worth the trouble. Cartels view guys like him as expendable."

Donnally turned back toward the bench. "Somewhere in here is the connection to Sherwyn."

He separated out the items: wallet, cell phone, passport, scraps of paper, and a Budget car rental key.

Janie pointed at the phone. "Maybe Sherwyn's number is in there."

Donnally smiled. "That only happens on television."

She folded her arms across her chest. "I don't know what you're smiling about. I've haven't seen a dead person since I did my residency, and there was one lying on my porch tonight."

He reached around her shoulders. "Sorry. I didn't think Sherwyn had it in him to try something like this."

"It pisses me off."

He pulled his arm away. "I said I'm sorry. What else can I—"

"Not you. Sherwyn. When I think of the lives he's destroyed. And what he's willing to do now to protect himself."

Janie shuddered and looked up at Donnally. "Are you sure he won't try again?"

"I'm sure he will. I think it might be better if you stayed at a hotel for a couple of days."

Her face flushed. "I'm not going to let that man force me out of my house." She glanced at the Mexican cop's possessions, then turned and walked toward the stairway. "Do what you have to do."

After she returned upstairs, Donnally searched the called and received logs in Cruz's cell phone. All the calls were placed from within Mexico or from the U.S. back to Mexico. He made a list of the numbers and the dates and times, then used Janie's computer to run them through Internet telephone databases. All were unlisted.

He then checked for text messages and found only one. It showed his addresses in San Francisco and Mount Shasta, and Brother Melvin's in Vancouver. It, too, originated from a Mexican telephone.

How did Cruz communicate with Sherwyn? Donnally asked himself as he bagged up everything again except the car key. *It had to be through an intermediary.*

But who?

Donnally went out to his truck and cruised the midnight streets until he located the shooter's rented brown Taurus parked in the dark driveway of an empty house for sale a few blocks from Janie's. He searched it hoping to find a hotel room card key, but found nothing.

His cell phone vibrated as he locked up the car. It was Brother Melvin.

Melvin smiled up at Donnally from where he sat in a chair next to the hospital bed, then pointed at his bandage-ringed head.

"I know you were hoping I'd have it examined," Melvin said, "and it looks like I just did."

"That's not what I had in mind."

"I hope not." Melvin's smile faded. He gazed out of the third floor window toward the city lights, then looked back at Donnally. "I didn't like lying to police about what happened."

"What makes you think you lied?"

"I told them he was robbing us."

"How do you know he wasn't?"

"He said—"

"No. I'm the one who said he wasn't there to rob us." Donnally smiled. "He never actually addressed the issue." He handed Melvin his duffel bag he'd brought with him from Vancouver. "You want me out of here while you change?"

"It's okay, I'm used to the communal life."

Donnally sat down on the edge of the bed as Melvin slipped off the hospital gown.

"What was the idea with the praying?" Donnally asked.

Melvin shrugged, then grinned. "I thought I was supposed to. I'm not sure whether I read it somewhere or saw it in the movies."

"It sure ticked him off. Makes you wonder if maybe he had a problem with a priest when he was young."

Melvin slid into a pair of pants, then rose and buttoned them. He then pulled out a long-sleeve dress shirt from the duffel bag.

"I thought you guys had to wear the . . . uh . . ."

"It's called a clergy shirt, but not when we do detective work."

"Detective work? I figured you'd want to put this behind you and you'd be asking me to take you to the airport."

"I've spent a lot of years thinking about suicide," Melvin said, "but homicide I'm not so thrilled with, especially my own."

A nurse's aide entered, pushing a wheelchair.

She waited for Melvin to tie his shoes and collect the plastic bag containing his bloody clothes, then walked along with them as Donnally rolled him down the silent hallway toward the exit.

CHAPTER 51

At five in the morning, Donnally parked the Mexican cop's Taurus in front of William Sherwyn's house. He left the rear extending two feet into the driveway. The back half of the car was illuminated by a streetlight. The front was shadowed. He then climbed out and snatched Sherwyn's *San Francisco Chronicle* and brought it back to the car. He paged through it until he found the article about the shooting:

UNIDENTIFIED MAN KILLED IN ROBBERY ATTEMPT

Sherwyn emerged from his front door an hour later. He surveyed the landing, the front steps, and the grass for his newspaper, then looked up and spotted the Taurus. He glared at it as if annoyed by a negligent neighbor. The gesture satisfied Donnally that Sherwyn had never seen the car before.

Sherwyn reentered his house.

Donnally walked up the stairs thirty seconds later and tossed the newspaper against the front door. He then concealed himself in the shadow outside the range of the porch light.

Sherwyn stepped outside, picked up the *Chroni-*

cle, then skimmed through the pages until he found the story. His brow furrowed in puzzlement as he read. Donnally guessed that Sherwyn already knew that the killing hadn't turned out as planned, perhaps because Cruz hadn't called to confirm that he'd done it or come to collect his fee, but Sherwyn wouldn't have been able to figure out why Cruz hadn't been identified by the police.

Donnally stepped forward. Sherwyn lurched away from the shadow falling across his newspaper, then spun around. His eyes widened and his hand clenched the paper. Donnally pulled back his jacket to show his semiautomatic, then reached into the house and turned off the light.

They both glanced toward the street as a Berkeley Police patrol car cruised by.

"Don't even think it," Donnally said.

The officer turned left at the corner and drove down the hill toward the flatlands.

Donnally tilted his head toward the Taurus.

"What are you going to do?" Sherwyn asked. "Kidnap me and leave my dead body in the woods?"

"Seems only fair. You tried to do me in just the same way."

Donnally drew his gun and pointed it at Sherwyn.

Sherwyn hesitated, but then walked down the steps and across the grass. He looked up and down the sidewalk as he approached the car, as though hoping to spot a neighbor.

Donnally chambered a round.

"I'm just as happy to drop you right here," Donnally said. "I can have your body in the trunk before it even crosses anyone's mind that it was a gunshot and not a backfire."

Donnally stepped around Sherwyn and opened the passenger door. Sherwyn slid in, then Donnally climbed into the driver's seat and pointed the gun at Sherwyn.

"Put your hands where I can see them."

Sherwyn raised them.

"No," Donnally said, "against the dashboard."

Sherwyn complied.

"The problem is that we're sort of at a stalemate," Donnally said. "Even if the police identify the guy you sent to murder me, there'll be no way to connect him to you. You've spent enough years studying homicide files to figure out how to get away with one."

Sherwyn didn't respond.

"Don't worry," Donnally said. "I'm not taping this. I don't want to leave any evidence behind of what's going to happen next." He held up a gloved hand. "Not even any fingerprints."

Donnally started the engine.

"The guy looked to me like an LA gang type," Donnally lied. "I can't figure out how someone like you could get hooked up with somebody like that."

"I don't know what you're talking about."

"Yeah, just like you didn't know who Melvin was."

Donnally drove to the stop sign at the end of the block, then accelerated around the corner. Sherwyn pulled his hands away from the dashboard and braced himself against the console and the door.

"Put your hands back where they were," Donnally said, raising the gun.

Sherwyn again placed his hands on the dashboard.

Donnally took the next right, then pulled over. He didn't speak right away.

"Now that I think about it," Donnally finally said, "maybe you're worth more to me alive than dead."

"Blackmail?"

Donnally laughed. "That sounds like a confession. You should've said extortion. That would make you look like a victim."

"How much do you want?"

"Let me think . . . let me think . . . how about five hundred thousand for Melvin for what you did to him and five hundred thousand for trying to kill me."

"Where do you think I'm going to get a million dollars?"

Donnally looked over at Sherwyn, grinning. "So now we're negotiating?"

"Call it whatever you want." Sherwyn smirked. "I knew you had an angle. I just couldn't figure out what it was. If I had known it was only money we could've worked this out already and saved ourselves a lot of trouble."

"You mean like hiring a hit man?"

"Construe it any way you like."

"What's your counteroffer?" Donnally asked.

"Half a million divided between the two of you and a signed statement from Melvin that nothing ever happened."

"How about two hundred for Melvin and four hundred for me?"

Sherwyn nodded.

"But this all assumes you have the money," Donnally said. "Do you?"

"That's not your problem. I can get it."

Donnally put his gun back into his holster, then reached into his jacket pocket and pulled out a pad of paper and a pen.

"Write out an IOU. Make it out for services rendered. Due in two days."

Sherwyn wrote the sentence, signed below it, and handed it back to Donnally, who then shifted into drive and pulled back into the street. He took two more right turns and stopped in front of Sherwyn's house.

Sherwyn opened the car door and stepped out.

Donnally lowered the passenger window as the door closed, and said to Sherwyn, "Nice doing business with you."

Sherwyn looked up and down the street to make sure no neighbors were outside and leaned down.

"What makes you so sure I won't walk inside and call the police?"

"Because you know how tomorrow's headline will read. 'Priest Accuses Prominent Psychiatrist of Child Molesting, Sordid Tale of Abuse Poised to Destroy Careers.'"

Donnally drove down the hill and stopped at a phone booth to call Janie.

"How's my alibi?"

"You're drinking coffee in bed and watching the news. I'll have the recording for you to study when you get back. And twenty minutes ago you called your father from your cell phone. How'd it go with the doctor?"

"We'll see. He'll be trying to get some money together. Probably not as much as he agreed to, but who's counting?"

Donnally traveled back using the same route he'd come. Over the north bay, down through Marin County, across the Golden Gate Bridge, and to the house where he had found the Taurus. He sealed up the car, stuck his gloves into his jacket pocket, then walked back to Janie's.

She handed him his cell phone when he stepped into the kitchen. He punched in a telephone number.

"Ramon, this is Harlan. I found a rental car ignition key under the front steps. I thought you might be interested."

Navarro called twenty-four hours later as Donnally was replacing his neighbor's shot-out window.

"You were right, man," Navarro said. "We located the car a few blocks away from you. It had been rented with a forged credit card. We lifted fingerprints matching the shooter in the car. And guess what? We found William Sherwyn's all over the passenger side."

"Did you knock on his door yet?"

"Yeah. It was weird. I told him I was investigating the shooting at your place and were wondering about some fingerprints we found. His face just went white. In twenty years investigating homicides, I've never seen anything like it. Then he started babbling and saying that you kidnapped him and forced him to touch the inside of the car. When I asked him why you would do something like that he clammed up and said he wanted to speak to a lawyer."

"Did you arrest him?"

"No. He's not going anywhere and I want to get a warrant to search his house and office. And I need to check out a few things."

"Like what?"

"Like whether you've got an alibi."

"Alibi? Me? Man, talk about blaming the victim."

CHAPTER 52

Donnally didn't bother knocking. He just pushed open the door to Lieutenant Ramon Navarro's homicide unit office and charged inside.

"You told me he wasn't going anywhere," Donnally said.

"What do you mean?"

"I just found out from a neighbor that she saw Sherwyn loading suitcases into the back of his Mercedes last night."

Navarro reached for the telephone and called the Berkeley Police Department. He asked the dispatcher to send officers by Sherwyn's house and office.

"Did the neighbor have any idea where he was going?" Navarro asked after disconnecting.

"Not a clue. She said he travels about once a month, but never talks about it."

Navarro squinted up at Donnally. "And how did you happen to be talking to this neighbor?"

"I like to keep track of people who try to kill me." He glared down at Navarro. "And now it looks like I'm going to have to find him myself."

Donnally surveyed Navarro's desk. "Will I have to break into his house to find evidence of where he went or did you get the search warrants?"

Navarro tapped a manila folder. "I had planned to do his home and office this afternoon, but I think I'll do them right now." He rose from his chair and shook his head as he looked at Donnally. "Not a chance you're coming along."

Donnally pulled out his cell phone and scanned through the stored numbers.

"What are you doing?" Navarro asked.

"A reporter for the *Chronicle* called the café after Brown's competency hearing and left his number. Maybe he'd like to be there when you kick in Sherwyn's door."

Navarro waved off the threat. "Give me a break. How's it going to look if we allow you in there when Sherwyn's already accused you of manufacturing evidence?"

"How about you let me look through the stuff once you get it back here tonight?"

"Why? Chain of evidence. That's why."

"I won't touch anything. You turn the pages."

"What pages?" Navarro inspected Donnally's face. "What do you know that I don't know?"

"Nothing. Phone records, that's all I meant."

Navarro squinted up at Donnally. "Like maybe you want to compare them to some you already have?"

"Man, you've become a suspicious son of gun in the last few years. I just want to see if there are any leads to where he might have gone."

Navarro held his gaze, then shrugged. "Have it your way."

Donnally pointed at Navarro's phone. "You may

want to check with ICE to find out whether Sherwyn left the country."

Navarro glanced toward the hallway. "You see your nameplate hanging on an office out there with the rank of captain etched into it?"

Donnally smiled and shrugged. "Just a thought. I'll be here this evening when you get back."

CHAPTER 53 ━━━━━

"Sherwyn will be watching for me," Donnally had told Janie the day after he examined the evidence Ramon Navarro had seized, "not a Vietnamese woman."

And she'd said, "You're not that different from your father."

"I'm not asking you to play the part of a prostitute."

She laughed. "Only because William Sherwyn isn't interested in girls."

It was then that Donnally reached into his jacket pocket and removed two plane tickets to Cancun.

"Let's go get him."

"How? Where do we start when we get there?"

"With a trail of telephone calls."

Flying in, Donnally remembered the two Cancuns he'd observed when he made a trip down with other rookies the day after they graduated from the police academy. Despite having grown up a few miles from the Pacific Ocean, he hadn't been a beach kid, had never stood on a surfboard, never sat around a bonfire, nor passed out drunk on the sand.

He'd gone along to Cancun not because he

wanted to, but because solidarity required it, and what he found was fragmentation: separating him and his friends, the beach from the town, and the rowdy Americans from the better selves they'd left back home.

Rising at dawn the next day and leaving his hung-over friends still asleep, he'd caught a cab in front of their hotel, one of a dozen in the artificial district imposed on a sand spit along the Caribbean. The ride from the Zona Hotelera took him to Centro, the core of an expanding city that seemed to be wearing itself out as it grew.

He found it crowded with migrants who'd come to service the tourists. They lived in shacks built of cinder-block walls and corrugated aluminum roofs, and shopped in small markets after their bus rides home from work. He'd recognized their faces and their manner: They were the same as those who pop-ulated East LA, who suffered divided hearts and ate beans and rice and sent most of their earnings home.

The Cancun that he and Janie met when they flew in was a city the size of San Francisco, with the *mercados* of old replaced by big block Sears and Wal-Mart stores that he had been able to recognize from the air.

The one-story barrios had been replaced by stucco apartment blocks.

The beach was now covered with bunkerlike re-sorts.

And now Porsche and Cadillac dealerships had pushed aside the used car lots that once provided the hand-me-down vehicles for immigrants' dream rides into prosperity.

―――

"Dónde está el orphanage de las Arenas del Blanco?" Where is the White Sands Orphanage?

Janie did a double take as Donnally spoke to the fifteen-year-old Indian-looking boy selling flowers from a bucket on a corner near their downtown Cancun hotel.

William Sherwyn's telephone records showed regular calls to the orphanage and his credit card statements revealed monthly week-long visits to Cancun.

Donnally had been unable to find a listing for White Sands in the local directory, so they had walked around town for a couple of hours searching for a streetwise kid to help them out.

After watching the teenager make sale after sale by tuning his pitch to his customers' vibrations of greed or guilt or sympathy, Donnally decided that he matched the profile.

"I didn't know your high school Spanish was that good," Janie said.

Donnally glanced over at her and smiled. "Just because I don't say 'Chee-lay' for Chile?"

"Something like that."

The boy held out his small palm and said in English, "Two dollars and I show you."

Donnally reached into his pants pocket for his wallet. "How about five and you just tell me?"

He pointed at Donnally's green John Deere cap. "And the hat."

Donnally took it off and handed it to him, along with the money. "You're a helluva negotiator . . ."

"Eduardo, but you call me Lalo."

Lalo looked up at Janie. "No women allowed inside."

"In Arenas del Blanco?"

"No women. Not even maids."

Janie looked at Donnally. "So much for that plan."

"How do you know?" Donnally asked Lalo.

The teenager reddened.

"The man who runs it, Señor William, took me there once, like he does with all the boys who work on the street."

Lalo gestured with his chin toward a sixty-year-old Anglo in slacks and a loose shirt soliciting a boy at the corner.

"Like that man. He promised me money, but I ran away."

Lalo glanced around to make sure none of the tourists walking by was paying attention, then made a circle with his thumb and finger and poked the forefinger of his opposite hand through it.

"I wouldn't do that."

"Are there many who do?"

Lalo shrugged. "*La vida es dura.*" Life is hard. "*Y los hombres malos aprovechar de los muchachos.*" And evil men take advantage of boys.

"Who knows about this?" Donnally asked.

Lalo's eyebrow went up again. "*Suspechar o estar seguro?*" Only suspects or really knows?

"Someone who really knows."

"There is a lady."

"Maybe you can take us to her."

Lalo held up his bucket of flowers. "My boss says I have to sell all these."

Donnally withdrew his wallet and opened it. Lalo thumbed through the bills and pulled out two twenties.

"Gracias, señor."

CHAPTER 54

Corazon Camacho stood next to an armed guard inside the wrought-iron gate of the high-walled women's refuge on the eastern edge of Cancun, two blocks from the White Sands Orphanage. Her gray hair, pulled back tight against her head, reflected the stark Caribbean sun like burnished steel. Her sorrowful eyes surveyed Donnally, Janie, and Lalo on the other side. Donnally was wearing a hooded sweatshirt to conceal his face should Sherwyn happen to drive by behind them.

A soccer ball rolled to a stop next to her, but the young girls who'd been playing on the dirt patch behind her didn't approach them to retrieve it. The children seemed to Donnally like abused puppies that felt safe only when caged and out of reach.

"I already have one defamation lawsuit against me for naming the names of the predators and the people who protect them," Corazon said to Donnally. "I'm not sure I want to risk another."

Corazon's eyes moved from Donnally toward the distant rooftops as though she was scanning for snipers.

"At least I wasn't murdered like the reporter who

wrote the story, and the twenty other journalists killed for writing about other sex traffickers."

She then looked down at Lalo and pointed at a bus stop across the plaza behind them.

"*Espera allí, por favor*," she said to him. Please wait over there.

Lalo peered up at Donnally like a child who was left unchosen after the sides in a schoolyard game had been picked.

"We'll come get you when we're done," Donnally told him.

Lalo nodded and walked away.

"I think we know what goes on over at White Sands," Donnally said. "I'm just after the man who runs it."

"Señor William."

"Yes. Señor William."

"Is he at White Sands now?" Corazon asked.

"I believe he's in Mexico, and a number of calls were made from a cell phone in the United States to White Sands during the last week." Donnally pointed his thumb over his shoulder toward Lalo. "We drove by the place, then sent the kid back to take a look, but he couldn't spot Señor William."

"You won't get any help from the police in finding out," Corazon said. "Not even if you hold an Interpol warrant in your hand. It is them that protects him and those who back him."

"I know all about that."

"How?"

"You ever heard of a cop named Gregorio Cruz?"

Corazon clenched her teeth at the sound of the

name. A thin dust devil spun upward from the dirt ten yards behind her.

"The worst. Him and his twin brother, Jago. Snakes. Both snakes."

"They like molesting boys, too?"

"No." She glanced over her shoulder at the girls now collected together in the middle of the yard, huddled like ducklings in a storm. "Not boys."

Corazon gestured to the guard to unlock the gate.

Donnally followed Janie inside, then reached down and rolled the ball back to the girls. One came forward to intercept it, giving Donnally a hesitant smile as she gathered it into her arms.

Corazon led them across the playground toward the converted hacienda, then upstairs to her second-story office, her open window overlooking the yard and the city beyond.

Against the background of the laughs and squeals of the restarted soccer match, Corazon described Sherwyn's founding of White Sands ten years earlier, his contributions to local charities, his socializing with the head of the local child welfare agency, his payoffs to the police and the prosecutor, and his luring of boys with gifts of money and drugs and video games.

"Do the boys ever escape?" Janie asked.

"That's the wrong word," Corazon said. "They come and go as they wish. Since Señor William has all of the connections, the city itself is their prison. There is no escape."

"How does he pay for it all?" Donnally asked.

Corazon shrugged. "I don't know. He's not an *al-cahuete*—"

Janie looked over at Donnally.

"A pimp," he said.

"Men travel down from the States and pay the boys directly. I assume they also contribute to the cost of running the place." She smirked. "Maybe they even take charitable tax deductions back home." She thought for a moment. "There were rumors years ago that there was a very powerful man behind it all in the States, the one who bought the property that houses White Sands, but I've heard nothing of him for many years." She shook her head, her lips pursed. "Since then it's become like a timeshare for predators."

Corazon picked up the telephone and ordered coffee from the kitchen.

"And there've been no investigations?" Donnally asked.

"A year ago I made taped interviews with a couple of the boys and gave the transcripts to the newspaper. But Señor William's lawyer and the police paid or threatened the boys into recanting. That's why I was arrested for defamation." She smiled at Donnally's puzzled expression. "It's a criminal matter down here, not a civil one like in the States. The law was passed to protect drug dealers from exposure in the press. Even worse, they charged me in Chiapas because the prison sentences there are longer. I'm facing nine years."

Donnally doubted that Sherwyn would've sounded as matter-of-fact as Corazon about nearly a decade in custody, but Sherwyn also knew that it was something he'd never face, at least in Mexico.

"If there was a way to do it without exposing

yourself to jail time, would you help us put together some evidence that we could use to get Sherwyn indicted in the States? It's a federal crime to travel outside of the U.S. to engage in sex with minors. And the U.S. extradites in these cases."

Corazon thought for a moment, then said. "I'll need to know more about what you plan to do and whether you can really do it."

Donnally reached for his cell phone to call someone who could pitch the idea to the United States Attorney in San Francisco.

"This is Harlan—"

"Stop." Perkins's voice was edgy, almost to the point of panic. "Don't say anything else. I've been ordered not to talk to you anymore. We've been retained on behalf of William Sherwyn."

Donnally pushed himself to his feet and walked toward the office door. He waited until he was in the hallway before he said, "You can't represent that asshole."

"Not me, someone else in the firm. A name partner. Al Barton. He's practically dancing and shadowboxing in his office. The statute of limitations has long run on criminal charges for molesting Melvin and it's too late to file a civil suit."

"If Sherwyn has no exposure, then what does he need Barton for?"

Rattling cups and saucers caught Donnally's attention. A girl holding a tray stood feet away, mouth gaping, staring at his face, which he realized had darkened with rage. He turned away and walked to the end of the hallway, then glanced back and saw her flee into the office.

"Damage control," Perkins said. "Barton has already called the chief of police threatening a lawsuit if there are any leaks from the investigation and they sent someone to serve you with a letter saying the same thing."

"They're not going to find me."

"Why not?"

Donnally looked out through the slats of the shuttered window. He could see White Sands in the distance. He imagined Sherwyn holed up inside, orchestrating his defense, gazing over his stable of boys.

"Let's just say I've gone fishing."

He disconnected and called Navarro.

"I'm getting heat like never before," Navarro said. "The chief wants everything kept locked up in his office. Reports. Evidence. Everything. And nothing in the computer system."

"You mean he's trying to bury this thing?"

"Exactly the opposite. He wants to protect the investigation from outside manipulation. But there's a problem . . . hold on."

Donnally heard Navarro's office door close.

"The chief wants you put on a polygraph about how Sherwyn's fingerprints got into the shooter's car."

"He wants, or you want?"

"Let's say that I have my doubts, too."

"Sounds to me like an abuse of prosecutorial power," Donnally said. "Maybe I should contact the Albert Hale Foundation. Now that the Charles Brown case has gone bust, maybe they're looking for a new cause."

"This one would be as wrongheaded as the last."

"I don't think so. If Sherwyn wasn't behind the attempt to kill me, why'd he run?"

"Because it's possible to frame a guilty man."

"Hey, why didn't I think of that?"

"I think you may have. When can you come in?"

"As soon as I bring Sherwyn back from Mexico."

"Mexico? How do you know about Mexico? I never told you where ICE said he went."

"It was just a lucky guess."

"You search the rental car before you called me?"

This one Donnally answered truthfully. "The shooter's clothes and shoes were new and all had Mexican labels."

"ICE says Sherwyn flew from SFO to Mexico City," Navarro said. "You know where he went after that?"

Donnally looked again at White Sands. He could see a man dressed in a white shirt and slacks standing on a third-story balcony looking down into his walled courtyard: Sherwyn.

"No idea."

Donnally disconnected. He watched Sherwyn take a sip from a glass in his hand, then wave to someone below. He realized that the man wasn't holed up. He wasn't at all afraid of being seen. Didn't seem to care.

Only now did Donnally's gaze widen enough to take in the scope of White Sands. A nineteenth-century hacienda consuming half a block, three stories of stucco and stone and glazed ceramic tiles centered in courtyards and gardens, and framed with vine-covered walls.

A five-million-dollar velvet fortress.

Was it arrogance? Donnally asked himself. *Or just the fact of government protection?*

Immunity, Donnally answered. *That's what Sherwyn had. Immunity.*

But not in the States.

The question was what would scare him enough to make him run back, thinking the U.S. was safer? And make the Mexican police think it was wiser to send him packing, and wait for another foreigner to take his place?

Donnally knew it wouldn't be the Mexican press that would force Sherwyn to flee. Corazon had made that clear. And Donnally knew that no American newspaper or television network would take him seriously, not after he'd made a fool of himself in the courtroom just before Brown pleaded no contest. And, even worse, not after he acted like a lunatic when he pushed his way through the reporters on his way out of the courthouse. Cameras sure as hell wouldn't arrive at his request. It would take something more.

"We're going to need new interviews," Donnally said to Corazon, striding back into her office. "Pick three boys, the most articulate and sympathetic, and with no arrest history. And I want not only the facts of what happened, I want to hear how it affected each kid and their families." He looked at Corazon, but pointed at Janie. "She can formulate the questions in a way that can't be attacked for being suggestive."

Corazon propped her elbows on the desk and

rested her chin on her folded hands. She thought for a few moments, then said, "What happens to these children later, in the months or years it takes for your Justice Department to extradite and convict Sherwyn? If their parents had enough money to care for them in the first place, they wouldn't have ended up on the street. I don't doubt your intentions, Mr. Donnally, but you'll leave here in a few days and this will remain a children's prison."

"Isn't there someplace that will take them in?" Donnally asked. "Some kind of children's shelter."

"It's more complicated than that. These are teenage boys who have become accustomed to abuse. Not only do they need to be protected, but other children need to be protected from some of them."

Donnally realized that she was right. There was a tomorrow he hadn't thought about. He spread his arms and glanced around.

"How much does it cost to run a place like this?" he asked.

"Forty thousand pesos a month. About thirty-five hundred dollars."

He nodded. "I know somebody who'll cover it."

"That's over forty thousand a year," Janie said. "In ten years that's almost half a million dollars. I can contribute some and I know you will, but who's got the rest of the money?"

Donnally smiled to himself as he watched the circle close.

"Mauricio."

CHAPTER 55

"Harlan, this is Will." The voice coming through Donnally's cell phone was just a whisper. "A Mexican guy just came into the café looking for you."

His employees didn't know he was in Mexico. He'd led them to believe that he was steelhead fishing on the Trinity.

Donnally set down his just-purchased video camera on the hotel room table. Janie and Corazon would use it to tape the kids' statements about Sherwyn.

"What did he look like?"

"A pit bull. Heavyset. Dark skin. Strong accent."

Gregorio Cruz's brother, Jago.

"What did you tell him?"

"I didn't have a chance to say anything. Deputy Asshole was sitting at the counter waiting for his father. He told the guy that you weren't around. Then it was like a lightbulb went off in Pipkins's head. First the news article about the Hispanic guy you shot in San Francisco and then a Mexican shows up. I had some ham about to burn on the grill and by the time I looked again they were sitting in a booth, talking. Real friendly."

"Where are you now?"

"Still in the kitchen."

Janie interrupted her unpacking of the camera and cast Donnally a questioning look.

He mouthed the words "Will" and "Jago Cruz."

Her lips went tight.

"What should I tell him if he asks me again?" Will asked.

Donnally's cell phone beeped with an incoming call. He looked at the screen. A Mount Shasta telephone number.

"Is Pipkins making a call?" Donnally asked.

"Let me take a peek," Will said, followed a few moments later by "Yeah. He's got his phone to his ear."

Donnally let it go to voice mail.

"He just disconnected," Will said, "and now they're walking toward the door."

"The Mexican is probably the brother of the guy I killed." Donnally thought for a moment. "But Pipkins is so single-minded that he must think he showed up in Mount Shasta because of something to do with Mauricio."

"Hold on," Will said. "Let me get to the front window."

Donnally heard the whoosh of the swinging kitchen doors, then footsteps.

"Be careful," Donnally said. "If they see you on the telephone, they'll guess that you're talking to me."

"They're over looking at Mauricio's house. Got their backs to me." Will chuckled. "Deputy Asshole looks like a hog sniffing around a sty for a piece of corn. He seems to be trying to pry information out of the Mexican, but the guy is just standing there, real stiff."

"You got Harlan on the line, Will?" It was the voice of his waitress, Marian, in the background.

"Let me talk to her," Donnally said.

"You still up at the river chilling out?" Marian asked.

"Chill is right." Donnally forced a laugh. "The steelhead are coming up frozen right out of the river."

"What do you want us tell those guys about where you are?"

"The truth. I've got nothing to fear. But tell them that they won't be able to reach me by cell phone because there isn't service in some of the canyons I've been fishing."

Marian laughed. "It could take them a week to find you."

"That's what I'm thinking."

CHAPTER 56

Before breakfast the next morning, Donnally transferred to Corazon's office computer the video files of Corazon and Janie's new set of interviews with Sherwyn's victims. He cut out the names of the boys and dates that would allow Sherwyn to identify them, then copied the audio portion of the interviews onto a CD.

Donnally's cell phone rang as he pulled the disk out of the drive.

"Nothing happens in this place that I don't find out about," Sherwyn said, his words slurred, sounding like he had a hangover. "And not only will those kids recant, but their parents will say that you paid them to lie . . . in fact—"

Donnally heard muffled conversation in the background.

"In fact . . . the first ones have just come in." Sherwyn laughed. "You've been a bad, bad boy, Donnally. They're claiming you threatened them, and their children."

Sherwyn's voice hardened, like caffeine was kicking against the weight of last night's alcohol.

"You still don't have a clue about how things work around here, do you? This won't be any more successful than your gimmick to link me with Gregorio Cruz. The U.S. Attorney will have no use for recanting witnesses and the Mexican police will dismiss your little tapes as frauds. They may even charge you with witness tampering."

Sherwyn laughed again, but this time in a jittery way, as if he was an adolescent boy watching a horror movie and not comfortable in his desire to witness a horde of ax-wielding zombies disemboweling a victim.

"That's assuming, of course, that Gregorio's brother doesn't get to you first, and that could get quite messy."

Donnally sensed, underneath Sherwyn's arrogance, a racket of thoughts suppressed by techniques perfected while living a double, triple, and in the murder of Anna Keenan, a quadruple life.

He looked at his watch. Janie and Corazon were driving to Merida, the inland state capital, to hide the boys in a hotel.

"It doesn't make any difference what the parents claim," Donnally said, "you can't get to the kids."

"Eventually they'll come to me. They always do. They're part of my world now. They don't fit into yours anymore, and there's no going back."

For a moment Donnally thought Sherwyn had gone delusional, but then realized that Sherwyn's fantasy was just the distorted reflection of Corazon's prison analogy.

"It's out of their hands," Donnally said.

"Only if you intend to hold them as prisoners."

"If I have to, but it won't come to that."

Donnally decided to bring at least one of Sherwyn's fears to the surface.

"Aren't you wondering how I figured out you were down here?" Donnally asked.

Sherwyn didn't answer right away, almost as if the question hadn't crossed his mind because the answer would be too obvious. Donnally suspected that it was because Sherwyn had spent so many years expecting to be caught that he was no longer capable of surprise.

"And aren't you also wondering why SFPD hasn't released Cruz's name to the press? You think maybe it's to give the Justice Department time to negotiate a deal with the Mexican attorney general to cut out the local police and bring in the *federales* to haul your ass to jail?"

Donnally hoped he was applying pressure, but Sherwyn's "Get off it, Donnally" told him he'd pushed too hard.

"It's because you haven't told them," Sherwyn said. "You're not going to risk me getting caught up in the judicial system down here. This is the goddamn briar patch." Sherwyn laughed again, this time a rough, solid laugh. "Hey, I know what I'll do. You'll just love this. I'll surrender to the Mexicans and plead no contest. Get it? No contest. You know, Donnally, no harm, no foul."

"That's not going to happen."

"What are you going to do? Cut me up in little pieces and feed me to the barracudas out in the mangroves?"

"You're going back to the States. Alive and in one piece, and voluntarily."

"And why, exactly, would I want to spend the rest of my life in a U.S. prison?"

"Because it will be the lesser evil."

Sherwyn clucked. "Poor Donnally. How naïve. Eventually you'll learn that all of life is the lesser evil."

The line went dead, but seconds later it rang again. Donnally picked it up.

"I forgot something," Sherwyn said. "Slick move with the gone-fishing angle, Donnally, but you're the one who's not getting away. Even better was using that cop to convince Gregorio's brother that you were still in California. That is until Jago got pissed off. He wasn't so much interested in a two-day tour of the dirt roads along the Trinity River as in leaving you in a shallow grave next to it."

The line went dead again.

A shallow grave. A dark current flowed through Donnally as he repeated the words to himself.

He called the café. Marian answered.

"Have you seen Deputy Pipkins in the last twenty-four hours?" Donnally asked.

"No. And he didn't show up for his shift today. His father was in here looking for you, wanting to know what you did with him. Real angry. I'm not sure whether it was at you or his son. He wouldn't tell me what he thinks the kid did, but he's convinced that you've got him chained up somewhere."

Donnally thought back to the spot along the river where the deputy had intercepted him to serve him with the DA's subpoena for Charles Brown's hearing. He guessed that Pipkins would've started his search there, and then worked downstream toward the ocean.

But at some point during their search, Jago would have concluded that Pipkins's aim had been to divert him from Donnally or to cover Donnally's escape.

Jago would then either torture Pipkins for information that he didn't possess or kill him.

Or both.

"Describe the Mexican to the sheriff," Donnally said. "Tell him that he should start looking at Brush Creek Road along the Trinity and search the north side of the river down toward Salt Flat."

"Will you meet him there?"

"I'm too far away."

"Where's that?"

"It's better that you don't know."

CHAPTER 57

Lalo was flailing his arms at the hotel doorman when Donnally drove up in the rental car after mailing copies of the CDs to himself in Mount Shasta. Lalo's high-pitched voice pierced through the early morning traffic and Donnally's closed windows.

"*Déjeme adentro*," Lalo yelled. "*Déjeme adentro*." Let me in, let me in.

Donnally jumped out and pulled Lalo away. The boy fell into his arms, crying.

"The police kidnapped Janie. It was Jago Cruz."

"Where? Where'd they take her?"

Lalo pointed not in the direction of the Policía Municipal Building, but toward White Sands.

"Is she okay?"

Lalo nodded. "They didn't hurt her."

"How did it happen?"

Lalo pointed down the block. "They stopped her van right when she got back from Merida and they pulled her out."

Donnally led Lalo inside, and he called Corazon at the hotel where Janie had left her and the boys.

"Sherwyn and Jago have Janie," he said. He could

hear the sounds of cartoons coming from the television in the background.

Corazon gasped, then made a shushing sound and everything went quiet.

Donnally's cell phone beeped with an incoming call. He recognized the number that showed on the screen.

"Sherwyn is calling," Donnally told Corazon. "I want you to listen, but don't say anything."

Donnally connected the call and conferenced her in.

"*Usted tiene hasta el amanecer de mañana*," the voice said. You have until sunrise tomorrow.

It wasn't Sherwyn.

The man said the words with the calm inevitability of a train conductor in a country in which the trains always run on time.

"What do you want?" Donnally asked.

"Recantations. All three boys. And at the end, each will . . ."

The man's voice grew distant, as if he was talking to someone else. "*Cómo se dice, gratitud?*"

Sherwyn answered in the background, his tone tense and strained. "It's the same. Gratitude."

The Mexican spoke into the phone again.

"Each will express gratitude to the police for protecting him from the American predators."

"Let me speak to Janie."

"Then be at White Sands at first light tomorrow." The Mexican laughed. "Unless you're busy fishing."

"Let's make a trade right now. Me for her. And she'll return with the recordings."

There was a pause as the man on the other side seemed to consider the proposal, then he said:

"*No es una negociación.*" This is not a negotiation.

The phone went dead.

"I think it was Jago," Corazon said, after Donnally disconnected. "But I don't understand why he didn't want to make the trade. He wants revenge and that would've put you in his hands right away."

"Maybe he needs the tapes as much as Sherwyn does." Donnally accepted the inevitable, but didn't know whether that would include the release of Janie. "Tell the boys what we need them to do."

"Why don't I make two tapes," Corazon said. "One on which the boys say that they are recanting only because Sherwyn has kidnapped Janie. And then the other will contain the recant—"

"We can't take a chance. Sherwyn may want to talk to the boys before he releases her, and they'll be afraid to lie to him."

"How do you know he'll let her go?"

"I don't. But we have no choice but to act as if he will."

Donnally disconnected, then turned toward the hotel room door and signaled for Lalo to follow. He couldn't take a chance that the police had snuck in when he was at Corazon's office and bugged the room.

They took the elevator down to the lobby, then walked through the restaurant and out of the service entrance into the trash-littered alley. Donnally caught his breath when he was hit with the stench of rotting garbage and overused lard. He pointed at an open back door. They worked their way through the semidarkness of a locals' bar, then across the next street and down the sidewalk. They slipped between two fruit carts and into the recessed entry of an empty storefront.

"*Necesito una pistola*," Donnally whispered to Lalo.

Lalo rolled his eyes upward and rocked his head side to side as if imagining a route from where they were to where they needed to be.

"Nobody will sell to you."

"How about a go-between?"

Lalo frowned in puzzlement at the idiom.

"*Un intermediario*."

Lalo thought for a moment then smiled and said. "*Mi tío*." My uncle. He extended his hand, but shook his head when Donnally reached for his wallet, and said, "Telephone."

CHAPTER 58

Uncle Beto's hands rested on the mound of his belly as he inspected Donnally's face. They were sitting at the rough-hewn kitchen table in his adobe bungalow at the western edge of Cancun.

Lalo had just told him that Sherwyn had orchestrated Janie's kidnapping in order to prevent the release of the recordings.

Donnally felt Beto trying to read his character from his manner and through the loyalty of his nephew.

"*Quién es el oficial de policía que ayuda a Sherwyn?*" Beto asked. Who is the police officer helping Sherwyn?

Donnally answered. "Jago Cruz."

Beto's jaw clenched and his face darkened. He slammed the tabletop with this fist. "*Chingaso.*" Fucker. "A man with no shame. The only one worse than him is his brother, Gregorio."

"Not anymore."

Beto stared up at Donnally. "*Por qué?*"

"Sherwyn sent him to San Francisco to kill me," Donnally said, "but I got him first."

Beto's eyes widened, then he smiled. He held up

his hand to say that he'd heard enough, and then reached into the breast pocket of his bus driver's uniform and removed an address book. He opened the worn leather cover, then licked his forefinger and flicked through the pages. He squinted at an entry, frowned, then moved on. Finally he nodded and stood up.

"*Espere aquí*," he said. Wait here.

Donnally rose after Beto left and paced the small room, furious at Sherwyn, and at himself for bringing Janie with him. He felt Lalo's eyes tracking him, maybe even reading his thoughts.

His phone beeped with an incoming text message. It was from Margaret Perkins:

Press conference in a couple of hours. Barton knows you're in Mexico. He'll claim you fled the country when the police tried to question you about whether you framed Sherwyn. He'll demand they issue a warrant for your arrest.

Donnally looked at his watch. Twenty-one hours left.

But then he realized that the press conference was irrelevant and the police were irrelevant and a warrant was irrelevant.

Jago was aiming to kill him, or die trying.

The only relevant thing was whether he could get Janie out of White Sands first.

Donnally stopped pacing and looked out of the kitchen window. A birdcage hung from a porch rafter. The parrot, pressed against the bars, glanced over at Donnally, then down at the dirt floor below. The bird's unblinking eyes locked on a lizard standing poised to strike an ant crawling into its range.

"I need to know whether Janie is still inside White Sands," Donnally said, turning back toward Lalo. "And I need to know the layout of the place."

Lalo stared down for a moment, then rose and stuck out his hand. Donnally reached out with his phone. Lalo waved it away, then rubbed his thumb against his fingers.

"It is not for me," Lalo said. "I know a boy at White Sands."

"Tell him not to ask directly, but see if he can find out whether Janie is still there."

Donnally handed his wallet to Lalo, who took out the pesos, leaving the dollars behind. He returned it and ran out the door.

Turning again toward the parrot, Donnally imagined what the lizard saw, looking up at the caged bird watching him.

The parrot fluttered its wings and then grabbed the bars with its beak and claws and spun itself upside down as if preparing to dive. The lizard darted away.

Donnally reached for his phone and called the West Hollywood telephone number of someone who had connections he didn't have. His father's groggy voice answered on the third ring.

"I need your help."

Donnally described where things stood.

"What can I do?"

"The only way Janie is getting out alive is if we shine a spotlight on White Sands, but the Mexican press won't touch it. Can you get a U.S. news network down here?"

There was silence on the other end of the line. Finally his father said, "Hold on."

Donnally heard his father get out of bed, then the sounds of fumbling.

"I know somebody at NBC in New York," his father said. "Let me give you his number. You'd be better at explaining everything than I would."

"That won't work. The press already thinks I'm a lunatic, and Sherwyn's lawyer is about to go on the attack. Even if they sent someone down here, they'd yank him back as soon as they heard what the lawyer's got to say about me."

"I'll take care of it. I didn't spend my life becoming a legend for nothing. If they move fast, they might be able to get down there by late this afternoon."

CHAPTER 59

"**A**ny luck?" Donnally asked Lalo after he got back to Uncle Beto's house from White Sands.

Beto still hadn't returned with the gun, and Donnally was worried that he'd sold them out, either to Sherwyn for money or to Jago for a future favor.

Donnally glanced out the kitchen window toward the back gate, then looked at Lalo.

"Don't worry," Lalo said, pointing toward the yard. "*Mi tío* won't let you down. He hates men like Señor William and the police who protect them. The problem is that only the narco traffickers have good weapons, but to get to them he needs to use *un intermediario*, too. So it takes time."

Donnally nodded.

"I talked to a boy who lives at White Sands," Lalo said, handing Donnally a crude diagram of the hacienda. "There is tension. He heard a rumor that a woman is there, but he hasn't seen her. The foreign men have all left and moved into hotels along with the boys, but Jago has brought in more police. Señor William is still there, in his office on the top floor. Not eating. Just drinking. He stands at his window looking down at the front gate and street and out

over the city. A few times, he has telephoned someone the boys only know as El Mandamas."

Donnally knew the phrase from a Mexican gang
seminar he'd taken years earlier. It was a colloquial
expression meaning The Man with the Last Word.

A squeak of the gate drew their attention to
Uncle Beto striding toward them, carrying a backpack in his hand.

Beto laid it on the table and removed six items
wrapped in oily cloth. Two were small Smith &
Wesson revolvers. Two were large Beretta semi-
automatics. Two were boxes of ammunition, .32 cal
and 9mm.

Donnally picked up one of the pistols and asked
the price.

Beto grinned. *"Alquilar o comprar?"* Rent or buy?

Donnally knew that he meant, *Va a vivir o va a
morir?* Will you live or will you die?

"I think I had better buy," Donnally said. "I don't
want you getting into trouble with your source."

*"Trescientos cincuenta dólares para la Beretta, dos
cientos cincuenta para la Smith & Wesson."* Three
hundred fifty dollars for the Beretta and two-fifty
for the Smith & Wesson.

Beto smiled. *"Las balas son gratis. Una oración que
usted mata a Jago."* The bullets are free. A prayer
that you will kill Jago.

Donnally selected one of each type of gun,
loaded both, then wrapped them in separate cloths
with a box of bullets. He withdrew his wallet and
gave Beto six hundred dollars.

Beto took the money and then placed the two

weapons into a paper bag and handed it to Donnally.

"*Vaya con Dios.*"

"Tell me about the boy you talked to," Donnally asked Lalo as they walked the unpaved street toward the center of town.

"We were in school together. I think maybe he was molested by his father. That's why he went to White Sands." Lalo giggled. "He likes girls, but there's no money in it."

"Can he come and go as he pleases?"

Lalo nodded. "He's a *carterista*."

"A what?"

"A wallet boy. A pickpocket. He spends most of the day at the beach in the Zona Hotelera stealing from tourists."

Donnally stopped and withdrew the diagram from his back pocket and examined it. He pointed at the box marked office.

"Did he say how this room was laid out?"

"He said it was like a *biblioteca*. Shelves on all the walls. Señor William always warns the boys not to touch his books. Many are very old."

"Can you trust him to go into Sherwyn's office and steal something for me?" Donnally asked.

"Trust him? No. Can I buy him for a day? *Sí*. What do you need?"

"A book from Sherwyn's library. Any one, as long as it's this big." Donnally framed his hands in the size of a hardcover, then held a thumb and forefinger four inches apart.

Lalo nodded.

"And I'll need a more detailed drawing of his office."

"*No hay problema.*"

Donnally glanced back the way they'd come.

"Would your uncle be willing to help?"

The spot between Lalo's eyebrows wrinkled. Donnally couldn't tell whether it was caused by concern for his uncle or by some internal conflict.

"If he can't, that's fine," Donnally said. "He's done enough."

"He is a good man, *mi tío*, but he has to live here after this is over. So do his wife and their daughters. If he can help without looking like he's helping, then he will."

Donnally thought for a moment, his mind drifting over the deadly game of snakes and ladders that was about to begin, then nodded.

"That may be good enough."

CHAPTER 60

Donnally slid down in the driver's seat of his rental car as he watched Brother Melvin and a flak-jacketed immigration agent step out of the entrance to terminal one of the Cancun airport. The agent gripped Melvin's elbow and steered him to the edge of the sidewalk.

Melvin shielded his eyes from the glare of the sun setting behind wind-combed clouds and scanned the parking area. He looked dead-on at Donnally's car, then over at the agent, shaking his head, seeming to say, *He's not here.*

As they turned away, Donnally reached for his phone.

"What happened?"

"Bad luck," his father said. "I just talked to the producer. NBC screwed up and sent the *Dateline* reporter who did all of those predator investigations. An American tourist recognized him while he was waiting with the camera guy at baggage claim. She made a big deal about it. Next thing they knew, they were surrounded by immigration officers."

Donnally felt a rush of targetless anger, unable to lock on to an insubstantial coincidence.

"The producer told me that the White House

just announced that the U.S. and Mexican presidents are meeting next week. His guess is that they don't want a sex-trafficking story breaking just beforehand."

"Where's the crew now?" Donnally asked.

"In a room with a bunch of illegal Chinese immigrants. The producer introduced Brother Melvin and is trying to convince immigration that they're doing a story on the church, not on sex trafficking."

"Sometimes that's the same thing," Donnally said, "and they know it. He should have picked a better story."

"It's too late now." His father hesitated for a moment, then said, "Have you heard anything about, uh . . ."

"Nothing. No contact from her at all."

"Hold on a second," his father said. "They're calling again."

Donnally looked at his watch. The new tapes with the boys were done and Corazon was driving back from Merida to deliver them.

His father came back on the line.

"The producer is talking about catching a flight to Houston, filing a report that they were blocked by Mexican immigration from covering a story, then heading back down again."

"Too late. The element of surprise would be lost. They'll have to say what it's about and Sherwyn will move Janie somewhere I can't find her. There's a balance right now between Jago and Sherwyn that keeps her there. Sherwyn wants the tapes and Jago wants me. I don't want to tip it. Ask them to keep quiet for another twenty-four hours."

"I'll try, but they're pissed. They sense something big."

"If they'll just hold on, I'll give it to them."

Donnally paused, accepting his failure in his attempt to use the press to expose Sherwyn and the kidnapping and to force him to cave in.

"Unfortunately," Donnally finally said, "it'll be history by the time they find out about it."

"What time do they want to do the exchange?" his father asked.

"Seven A.M.. My time. Twelve hours from now."

Donnally called Brother Melvin and told him to go with the NBC crew back to the States, then drove from the airport parking lot. He checked for police surveillance by driving along the coast, then circled inland.

A light rain began as he turned south toward the beach town of Playa del Carmen. He parked in the Wal-Mart lot and followed some Hawaiian-shirted U.S. ex-pats inside. He overheard one warn of a storm from the Caribbean that was expected to hit land overnight. The other looked heavenward and said, "Good thing it's not hurricane season."

At least not for you, Donnally said to himself, then skirted around them and headed toward the electronics department, where he selected a sound-activated recorder and batteries. After paying for them, he drove to the Ace Hardware in Cancun and purchased fine wire, a soldering iron, a box cutter, and fast-drying paper glue.

Lalo was waiting for him on the sidewalk in front of the hotel when he arrived. He didn't wait for Donnally to ask whether he'd heard any news from his friend at White Sands about Janie before shaking his head. He handed Donnally an object wrapped in a paper bag. Donnally looked inside and nodded. The book was the right size and the new drawing had the details he needed.

Donnally brought Lalo up to the room and ordered dinner for him, then sat down at the table and spread out his purchases.

Lalo took the seat across from him. His eyes remained fixed on Donnally's hands as he opened the book and cut out an inside compartment. He then bored a tiny hole in the spine of the book.

As Donnally pried open the recorder, Lalo said, "I see. You want my friend to hide this in Señor William's office." He smiled. "Very smart."

Lalo thought for a moment and his smiled faded. "I don't understand why it's needed. You can tell the American police what happened." Then he understood why Donnally needed it recorded: He might not live to tell the tale. Lalo crossed himself. "I swear I will find a way to get it back and take it to Corazon."

Donnally reached for the diagram Lalo's friend had drawn and made an X where he wanted the book shelved, then pointed toward the door.

"Go find your pal while I finish this up and glue the pages together. It'll be ready in an hour."

Lalo nodded and headed toward the door.

CHAPTER 61

The burst of laughter from drunks leaving a cantina a block away sounded sharp against the low rumble of thunder as Donnally climbed Uncle Beto's hand-made ladder at 2 A.M. It was leaning against the bougainvillea-topped back wall of the White Sands compound.

Donnally worried about Lalo standing below, steadying the ladder. The worn pine sagged with each step and his shoes had uncertain purchase on rungs that were slick with wear and humidity.

The image of the satellite photograph of the property he had looked at on Corazon's computer remained fixed in his mind as he neared the top. Once he cut through the thorned branches intertwined into the heavy latticework, he'd drop down into a geometric garden surrounding a swimming pool.

A blast of low lightning lit up the alley and reflected off the stained glass windows of the church behind him. It gave him a moment of illumination, and just enough time to reach in with the saw toward the thickest branches. Uncle Beto's leather gloves protected his hands as he sawed, but the barbs tore at his forearms.

After he cut each branch, he hung it by a rope from the latticework. When he opened a large enough space, he gritted his teeth against the bite he'd feel in his hip, then climbed onto the top and grabbed the ropes. He waited for a round of thunder, then lowered himself to the ground in the space between the bougainvillea and the wall. As he did so, he pulled the branches back up and into place. He then slipped off his backpack and dug out the 9mm.

In the silence that followed, Donnally heard scraping as Lalo lowered the ladder to the ground and then his footsteps in the mud as he carried it away.

Moments later, thunder rolled again and the rain began.

Donnally heard drops ticking the canopy of leaves above him. Then the rhythmic squishing of rubber soles on wet concrete. They ceased and a flashlight swept the bushes concealing him. They moved on. A disciplined stop-and-go as the police officer worked the perimeter.

Donnally peeked through the branches, trying to locate the trellis Lalo's friend described as the easiest route to the roof, three floors up. It had borne the weight of kids using it as a jungle gym, but Donnally wasn't sure it would bear his.

For a moment he tried to imagine where Sherwyn was holding Janie, but put it out of his mind. If there were as many cops in the building as Lalo's friend had claimed, trying to rescue her now would be suicidal.

After waiting for the officer to make another circuit, Donnally skirted the courtyard. He reached through the ivy and pulled on the trellis. It held firm. He found a foothold and eased himself up, distributing his weight between his hands and feet. His damaged hip jabbed at him. He thought of Mauricio. Maybe his friend was right. Maybe he should've gotten it replaced years ago and broken the last link to his past, or at least not have relied on pain to maintain it.

As he reached the second floor, a flashlight beam swept the bougainvillea securing the perimeter. The light died. Donnally heard the rip of a zipper and the sound of the officer peeing into the bushes below him.

And Donnally let himself enjoy the fantasy of putting a slug into the top of the cop's head.

After the man moved on, Donnally continued upward and hoisted himself onto the roof. He removed a rope from his backpack, tied it around the air-conditioning unit, then lowered himself down the front of the building toward Sherwyn's office.

As he reached to pull the window open to climb in, he had a panicked moment, wondering whether Lalo's friend was still bought, or whether he'd sold them out to Jago Cruz, who'd be poised like an executioner on the other side.

CHAPTER 62 ====

Just after 6:50 A.M., Donnally alerted to thudding footsteps. The sound was deadened by the book-lined shelves of Sherwyn's office and the heavy closet door behind which he was hiding.

Then two male voices. Sherwyn and a Mexican.

The shadows of moving bodies skimmed the gap between the door and the floor.

"*Sientate.*" Sit. An order. Jago.

Lighter footfalls followed by scraping, maybe chair legs rubbing against the hardwood floor.

Janie?

Then a nervous drumming of fingers. Donnally guessed that Sherwyn was sitting or standing behind his desk a few feet away.

Jago spoke. "It's almost time."

"Let's get this over with," Sherwyn said. "I'll call him."

Donnally felt his cell phone vibrate. He let it go to voice mail, where Sherwyn would hear his recorded message:

Bring Janie to the front gate at 7 A.M.. I'll hand you a CD containing the recantations as she steps out.

"You need to hear this," Sherwyn said, presumably to Jago.

Donnally's phone vibrated again, and again he let it go to voice mail.

Thirty seconds later, Jago said, "Your boyfriend is not answering his phone." Then to Sherwyn, "Puzzling. Why didn't he try to force us to do it in a public place, a shopping center or at the beach? Doesn't he realize that my men will grab him before he even walks up to the gate?" Jago chuckled. "He must love you too much. It has scrambled his brain."

A crackle of Jago's police radio broke the silence, followed by his voice.

"*Está todo en posición?*" Is everyone in position?

Donnally guessed that Jago had sent his team out of the hacienda to set up along the streets bordering the property.

"*Sí.*"

Donnally lit up his cell phone screen: 6:55.

"*Andale.*" Jago again. Let's go.

"Aren't you coming with?" It was Janie's voice. "Or are you too much of a coward?"

"There's a better view from up here," Sherwyn said. "Anyway, I'll see him soon enough. Or should I say, he'll see me soon enough."

Janie and Jago's footsteps faded as they walked from the office and down the hallway toward the stairs.

Donnally heard Sherwyn take a couple of steps toward the bar next to the closet door. A quavering of glass on glass followed. Donnally imagined Sherwyn's hands shaking as he poured.

Sherwyn walked toward the window.

Donnally checked the time again: 6:58. Corazon should be parked down the block.

Sherwyn began pacing. A gulp. Then back to the bar. Another drink.

6:59.

Uncle Beto should be a few hundred yards away, driving toward White Sands in a rental car matching Donnally's.

7:00.

"Where is he?" It was Sherwyn speaking into his cell phone.

Donnally turned the door handle.

"No," Sherwyn said. "I don't see him—wait. I see his car. Get him." Now more urgently, yelling. "Get-him-get-him-get-him."

Donnally heard the whine of Beto accelerating, then the sirens of police vehicles chasing him down.

"What is Donnally doing?"

Donnally swung open the door. "Holding a gun to your head."

Sherwyn spun toward him.

"Put your hands up," Donnally said.

Sherwyn raised them, his phone in one and a glass in the other.

Donnally stepped next to Sherwyn. He then grabbed him by the back of his collar and pressed the barrel against the base of his neck. The glass fell from his hand and exploded on the floor.

Donnally glanced down toward the gate and took the phone from Sherwyn's hand.

"You hear that?" Donnally said to Jago. "Let her walk out into the street."

Jago drew his weapon and pointed it at Janie.

"You shoot, I shoot," Jago said.

Donnally covered the phone mic and said to

Sherwyn, "Let's go. We're going to fight this out in the courtyard."

Sherwyn struggled, now understanding Donnally's strategy and terrified of becoming a human shield.

Donnally braced Sherwyn against the window to control him.

The whump-whump of a helicopter rose up in the distance. Donnally guessed it was a tourist flight heading inland toward the Aztec ruins.

Jago lowered his gun to his side, waiting for it to pass over.

The helicopter slowed, then hovered above White Sands.

Donnally uncovered the mic and said, "Release her. You've got too many witnesses."

Jago looked up. Staring. Donnally saw his eyes widen. Jago licked his lips, then spoke into his radio. Donnally watched a cop standing across the street abandon his position and walk toward downtown. The officers surrounding Beto got into their cars and sped off.

Jago opened the gate. Janie walked through. Corazon climbed down from her van parked across the street, and Janie ran toward her.

Donnally looked up and saw what had spooked Jago.

CNN. The acronym painted on the side.

How did the old man get them to come here?

He looked down again. Janie was getting into Corazon's van. Jago was running toward the front door.

Why doesn't he make a run . . . ? Donnally asked

himself, but the answer arrived before he finished the question. *He wants a shot at avenging his brother before the world caves in.*

Donnally decided that it was better to battle him here than run for the rest of his life.

The helicopter rotated in place. Glare blocked his view. It rotated further. He saw a handheld video camera pointing down.

Something didn't look right.

Without showing himself, Jago yelled from the hallway:

"Throw out your weapon."

Sherwyn grabbed for the gun. Donnally pulled away. Sherwyn fell into him. They crashed against the bar. Sherwyn's grasping hands swept the bottles and glasses off the mirrored counter. The gun broke free of Donnally's hand and thunked to the floor next to the built-in bookcase. They both dived for it. Sherwyn grabbed first, but missed and sent it sliding across the floor toward the door ten feet away.

A gunshot shattered the bar mirror.

Donnally looked toward the doorway. Jago stood pointing a revolver at him.

Sherwyn crawled toward Donnally's gun.

"Freeze," Jago ordered.

Puzzlement consumed Sherwyn's face. "What are you . . . ?"

Donnally grasped Jago's plan, or what should be his plan if he was thinking clearly. Donnally decided to buy some time, even if it meant laying it out for him.

"He's going to kill you pretending that he was

trying to rescue me," Donnally said, standing up. "He's leaving no witnesses. That's the way El Mandamas would want it." He glanced at Sherwyn. "I suspect that at this point The Man with the Last Word, whoever he is, would conclude that you're expendable."

Jago smiled.

"But he'll need to do some staging first," Donnally said.

Jago shook his head, then pointed his barrel at Donnally's waist and jerked it up and down.

Donnally glanced down at Sherwyn. "Apparently he wants to count the weapons first." He then raised his shirt and jacket to show he was unarmed. Jago made a circling motion, and Donnally showed his back.

Jago nodded.

Sherwyn pushed himself onto all fours, as if testing to see how far Jago would let him rise. His breathing was heavy. His flesh red.

Donnally leaned back against the bookcase.

"What do you say, I'll stand here?" Donnally said. He extended his hand toward Sherwyn. "And you can be next to me."

Sherwyn stood and backed toward Donnally.

"Come on Jago," Sherwyn said. "I'll protect you. Everybody knows Donnally is crazy."

Jago shook his head.

Donnally pointed skyward. "He needs a story that matches the video, or at least close enough for the Mexican press. He has to make it look like he rescued Janie from you, then failed in rescuing me. He knows that once I'm dead, Janie will keep her mouth shut to protect Corazon." Donnally smiled. "But that means I need to be dead first."

Donnally glanced around the office.

"What do you say we make it look like even more of a fight?" Donnally asked. "Maybe throw some things around?"

He reached behind him and began pulling books off the shelf and spilling them to floor.

"You really are crazy." Sherwyn's voice turned desperate. "What are you doing?"

Donnally grabbed Sherwyn by his collar and shoulder and threw him toward Jago, then grabbed the book he'd hollowed out the day before.

He ripped it open and reached inside.

It wasn't the tape recorder Lalo's friend had thought he'd smuggled in, but the .32 cal revolver Donnally had bought from Beto.

Donnally fired once, hitting Jago in the shoulder. Jago fell backward, pulling Sherwyn with him.

The cop's gun discharged, the explosion muffled by Sherwyn's body.

Donnally ducked behind the desk. He raised his head in time to see Jago push Sherwyn away, then point his gun not at Donnally's forehead, but at the thin panel covering the leg space. Donnally dived to the side. Jago's shots punctured the desk and blew out the window behind it. Donnally rolled, fixed the gun in a double-handed grip, and kept firing until Jago stopped moving.

The helicopter's motor whined as it spun away.

Only then, in the silence that followed, did Donnally feel his hip joint raging. He clenched his teeth and pushed himself to his feet.

A groan came from Sherwyn.

Donnally limped over and kicked the gun out of Jago's hand.

Sherwyn looked up, his palm pressed against the wound in his chest. His face was pale, draining of blood.

"It's not as bad as it looks," Donnally lied. "Unless you bleed out."

Panic twisted Sherwyn's face.

Donnally poked at Sherwyn's ribs with his shoe.

"Maybe I'll keep you conscious for as long as I can so you can watch it happen."

Sherwyn grimaced, then squeezed out, "What do you want?"

Donnally retrieved the tape recorder from his backpack in the closet.

"I want a confession." He then pulled out his cell phone, punched in 066, the Mexican version of 911, and showed Sherwyn the screen. "As soon as I'm satisfied, I'll press 'send' and an ambulance will come to take you to the hospital."

Donnally thought for a moment. He needed a way for Sherwyn's words to live on in the world he would soon leave behind.

"How about you call it your dying declaration so you can't retract it later?"

He then kneeled down and switched on the recorder, knowing that the last sound on the tape wouldn't be the siren of a rescue, but Sherwyn's death rattle.

"After that, explain who El Mandamas is and how he fits in."

For the next three minutes, Donnally focused

more on his questions than on the content of Sherwyn's answers, for he'd already played his last card: He'd threatened the absolute.

At the same time, he knew from the terror in Sherwyn's eyes that he was a man who feared death more than shame, so Donnally knew he'd get at least some of the truth.

The whump-whump of the helicopter increased in volume as it once again approached the hacienda.

Donnally glanced toward the window, then looked back. Sherwyn had fallen silent. Dead. Donnally felt the satisfaction of knowing he'd called it right. Sherwyn wouldn't have lived long enough for an ambulance to have arrived anyway.

Donnally flicked off the tape recorder, then walked to the window and squinted into the rising sun to try to see into the cockpit.

He realized what was wrong. He'd never seen a CNN helicopter before. They always got their news feeds from local stations.

The machine rotated and the passenger side came into view. The camera operator lowered the video camera. Donnally recognized the flowing white hair before he recognized the face, then felt the thrill of weightless flight, as if the floor beneath his feet had fallen away, leaving him hovering, light-headed.

His father grinned and waved.

It was all an illusion, a substitute for a real world that wouldn't or couldn't act.

Donnally smiled back.

For the first time in both their lives, the old man really had shot the dawn.

CHAPTER 63

Janie ran toward Donnally when he arrived at the front gate. He embraced her, then pointed at Corazon crossing the street and held up his palm, telling her to keep the gathering crowd outside the hacienda.

He grabbed Janie's arm and they raced back up to Sherwyn's office.

Janie gasped and covered her mouth as she stood in the doorway staring at the bodies, the blood of the dead now intermingled in a dark pool between them.

Donnally retrieved his 9mm from the floor, then wiped off the .32 and put it into Sherwyn's hand. It was better to leave a confusing crime scene than one that pointed to Donnally.

He crouched down and rubbed Sherwyn's gun hand against Jago's to transfer some powder residue, then flopped it into the blood.

He straightened up and looked around the office.

"Let's grab whatever we can before the police get here."

They searched Sherwyn's desk, filling Donnally's backpack and a cardboard box he found in the closet with the doctor's laptop and every piece of paper they could find. Phone records. Bank records. Anything they thought might expose the network of men who sought the services of White Sands.

Janie picked up the hollowed-out book lying on the floor.

"What's this?" she asked.

"I had Lalo arrange to smuggle in an extra gun in case I got caught breaking in. It's got my fingerprints on it. Take it."

After they searched the file cabinet, Donnally called his father's cell phone. The helicopter rumbled in the background.

"Where are you?" Donnally asked.

"Are you okay?"

"I guess you could say that I'm healthy as a sunrise."

"A what?"

"I'll explain it later."

"We're on our way to land," his father said, "so we can strip the lettering off this thing before we return it to the rental company. And then we'll catch a charter flight back to the States before anyone figures out who we are."

Donnally heard the scream of police sirens, rising in volume like incoming mortar.

"How soon can you get back here?" Donnally asked.

"What do you need?"

"I'm going to leave my backpack and a box of documents on the roof, on top of the air conditioner. Can you get close enough to snag them?"

Donnally heard a quick interchange between his father and the pilot, then his father's voice.

"We'll figure it out. How soon?"

"Two minutes."

"I'll have them waiting for you when you get back to California."

CHAPTER 64 ═══════

But the twisted expression on the angular face of Captain Joaquin Felix sitting in his office an hour later told Donnally that their going home might not happen for a very long time.

Or it would happen by sunset.

Donnally had recognized the captain's name when he'd introduced himself in the doorway of Sherwyn's office at White Sands. He was one of the government officials whom Corazon had accused in the press of protecting sex traffickers.

Felix folded his arms on his desk and looked first at Janie, then at Donnally.

"Officer Cruz was not the self-sacrificing type. I can't imagine him risking his skin to rescue anyone." Felix's face relaxed. He leaned back in his chair and smiled. "Picking bodies clean of valuables afterwards, now that's something Cruz would do. It is not by chance that his nickname was La Buitre. The Vulture."

Donnally didn't smile back. "Sometimes true character is revealed in a time of crisis."

"Perhaps crisis is also the explanation for why his brother disappeared."

Donnally shrugged. "I wouldn't know."

The smile remained fixed on the captain's face. "Of course you would." He then removed a print-out of a *San Francisco Chronicle* article from his desk, spun it around, and slid it toward Donnally and Janie. It was the account of Donnally's shooting of an unidentified Hispanic male on Janie's doorstep. "What do you suppose we'll discover when we send the fingerprints of Jago's brother to San Francisco?"

"When you send them?"

Felix laughed. "Very shrewd. You're right. *If* we decide it's in our interest to send them."

Donnally fixed his eyes on the captain's. "My experience is that people usually find what they expect to find."

"You're just full of homilies, aren't you?"

"It's the wisdom of the ages. I'm merely its vehicle." Donnally glanced at the news article. "There's no way you'll send the prints to the U.S. The last thing you want to see in the media is a report that one of your officers was moonlighting as a hit man." He pointed upward. "You'll have enough trouble explaining to CNN what happened at White Sands this morning."

Felix rose from his chair and walked to the window, his narrowed eyes telling Donnally that he was imagining how the fiction of the rescue attempt would play in the Mexican and U.S. press.

Donnally became conscious of the traffic passing by on the street two floors below and thought of the U.S. president arriving in a few days. Perhaps what would've been a sex-trafficking exposé could be transformed into a victory of the police against the traffickers.

"I'll make a deal with you," Donnally said.

Felix turned back toward him. "You're not in a position to bargain."

"That depends on what I have to offer."

"Tell me what you want, and I'll decide whether there's anything you can do to pay for it."

Donnally pointed his thumb over his shoulder toward the door that led to the waiting room where Corazon and Lalo waited under guard.

"You drop the defamation charges against Corazon and I'll give a press conference describing Cruz as a hero who died rescuing Janie and me from Sherwyn."

Janie gripped his arm. "Don't do it."

Donnally laid his hand over hers, then looked from her to Felix and said, "We've got no choice. It's the only way."

"What did you mean it was the only way?" Janie said to Donnally as she walked into the Cancun airport terminal where he was waiting for her. It was less a question than an accusation, and it was the first time they had spoken since Donnally had gone with Captain Felix to the press conference and she had returned to the hotel to pack for the flight.

And the accusation tore at him.

Janie stopped and gazed through the windows at Corazon pulling away from the curb. She seemed lost amid the streams of passengers flowing past her toward the ticket counters, as though she was feeling submerged in the tide of events.

"She wanted the case dropped," Janie said, "but not by misleading the Mexican people about what's really happening here and who's responsible."

Donnally wanted to say, *No one was misled. Mexicans aren't stupid. They may not have understood why I told the lie, but they'll know that's what it was.*

But he didn't because he knew she was right, and in that moment understood where he'd gone wrong: He'd been swept away, caught in the updraft of his father's brilliant deception, and it had seduced him into committing another.

Corazon had deserved better. Just as Mauricio and Anna had deserved better—

And he cringed at his arrogance.

It wasn't up to him to take Corazon's life out of her hands. It was hers to decide what sacrifices to make and what risks to take.

"You're right. It wasn't my place."

Donnally paused as a fragment of an idea came to him to set things right, but it dissolved under the pressure of the countdown toward their flight's takeoff. He turned to her and said, "We'll find a way to fix it."

Janie looked up at him and nodded, then she smiled and said, "And maybe we can fix something else at the same time."

Donnally stared at her for a moment, until his mind caught up with her, and he smiled back. "That, too."

Then his smile died and he looked toward the check-in counter. "There's just one thing we need to do along the way."

"What's that?"

"Go after the man behind White Sands before he makes a run for it."

CHAPTER 65

But Albert Hale wasn't running.

Donnally found him wrapped in a wool blanket, sitting on the veranda of his Hillsborough mansion. He was gazing out at the cloistered garden, the high walls on either side covered by avalanches of vines and the far end cushioned by a private forest of oaks and eucalyptus. The Kaposi's sarcoma lesions on the old man's face and neck made it seem that AIDS was pummeling him to death, not draining the life out of him.

"How'd you get in?" Hale asked, after turning toward the sound of Donnally's footsteps behind him.

"Over the river and through the woods," Donnally said, using a children's rhyme to take a first jab at Hale. "How else?"

"Ah, yes." Hale half smiled and then added a line, "Spring over the ground like a hunting hound."

Donnally settled into a wrought-iron chair next to Hale's, then studied his withered hands holding a china teacup in his lap, and his eyes that had sunk into their gray sockets. From those alone Donnally understood that there would be no justice for Anna Keenan or Charles Brown, or even Deputy Pipkins, whose body had yet to be found. Hale had chosen a slow suicide years earlier by making his life an experiment in pathology.

Hale gazed at Donnally as if into a mirror.

"As you can see," Hale said, "you're too late. The cosmos has exacted its punishment. My HIV finally mutated into forms far outside what the drugs were designed to control."

They sat in silence for a few moments, then Hale set his cup on the table and reached for a silver bell.

Donnally grabbed his arm. "Don't even think it."

Hale laughed. "You need to relax. I merely thought you'd like some tea."

Donnally released his grip, then pulled aside his jacket, exposing his semiautomatic in a shoulder holster.

"You think I have goons lounging in my billiard room," Hale said, "waiting for the call to charge out here, guns blazing?"

"Your guns were blazing last week."

"Sherwyn was behind that. He still had something to fear."

"What about you?"

"Dead men don't have that problem."

Hale reached again for the bell.

This time, Donnally didn't stop him.

"How did you figure out it was me?" Hale asked after the butler had delivered Donnally's tea.

"The law firm representing Sherwyn inadvertently let on that there was someone behind him. It was in their phrasing. They said that they'd been hired *on behalf* of Sherwyn, not by Sherwyn himself."

"And you sensed an invisible hand."

"It dipped in, just like it did in the Brown case. But I couldn't figure out why it never seemed to form itself into a fist."

Hale extended his manicured fingers and examined them like they were instruments that had an additional use he hadn't considered.

Donnally swung past the unconvincing gesture. "Until Sherwyn told me."

Hale smirked at Donnally. "That's something that Sherwyn certainly would not do."

"The kids at White Sands referred to El Mandamas," Donnally said, "The Man with the Last Word, and a woman in Cancun talked about a wealthy man behind Sherwyn, and he confirmed it was you."

"That kind of confirmation is useless. A dead witness is no witness at all."

"There are witnesses. Some older Mexican boys who'd seen you down there years ago identified your photo, and Melvin Watson recognized this house as the one Sherwyn took him to."

Hale took a sip of tea. Donnally left his untouched.

"Having parties in my own home was a mistake," Hale said, "but I realized that too late."

Hale's eyes blurred as he gazed out at the garden as if he wasn't seeing the reality in front of him, but was reliving a distant memory, populated by beautiful boys on summer evenings.

"The men who came here. You would be surprised." Hale again looked at Donnally. "Maybe not you. I knew even then that it was a risk. Maybe that was part of the thrill. Eventually the balance shifted, and it seemed too dangerous."

"What changed?"

"One of our members was nominated to a high government position." Hale smiled as if enjoying a private joke, then said, "One might say that he became one of the knights at the round table. Fortunately the FBI was too busy chasing terrorists to delve too deeply into his past."

"And that's why you set up White Sands in Mexico."

"Of course. The problem is that sometimes the past is like a seeping wound that won't heal. Like Charles Brown."

"Why didn't you cauterize it and get rid of him?" Donnally asked. "Put an end to this when he was released from the Fresno Developmental Center?"

"You seem to think we are cold-blooded murderers. We're not."

"What could be more cold-blooded than the murder of Anna Keenan?"

"That was an act of desperation." Hale smiled. "I think Sherwyn surprised himself." He took another sip of tea. "You showing up threw a monkey wrench into things, but then we figured that we couldn't lose whether he got convicted or the case got thrown out on a technicality. Either way, the world would be convinced he killed her. The important thing was to make sure that the case never went to trial."

"And that's why the Albert Hale Foundation interceded and bought him the best defense money could buy."

"Exactly." Hale then dismissed the entire issue with a wave of his hand. "Anyway, that's all behind us now. The statute of limitations has run on everything I did and there's no way to connect me to the murder."

"What about public exposure?"

Hale snorted. "How terribly provincial. The hundred-million-dollar endowment of the Albert Hale Foundation will mitigate the minor inconvenience of some temporary bad press."

He turned toward Donnally. "Did you see *The Pianist*? I'm sure it must have played even in your little Mount Shasta."

Donnally pulled back. "You're not deluded enough to compare yourself to a Holocaust victim?"

"Not to the Jew, but to the director. Roman Polanski. He plea-bargained away charges that he drugged and raped a thirteen-year-old girl, and then escaped to France before sentencing. A few years later he received a standing ovation from the Hollywood crowd, probably including your father, when he was awarded the Oscar for Best Director. You see, the world is forgiving of those with enormous amounts of talent or money, and I neither drugged nor raped anyone. At worst I will be viewed as flawed, perhaps even weak, but not evil. And I can live with that."

"You mean die with that."

"That's implied, but until that happens I have time to spread my largesse around."

Donnally thought of the criminals who'd redeemed themselves in the public mind through power or artistic brilliance or payoffs to charity.

Hale paused in thought for a few moments, then asked, "Do you know the Goya etchings from the eighteenth century? I'm thinking of the one in which a woman averts her eyes in shame as she reaches to yank out the teeth of a hanged man because of their supposed magical power."

Donnally nodded.

"Expose me, if you will," Hale said, "but charities will soon become the alchemists of my rehabilitation. My penance will be their profit, and they'll find some way to justify it."

Hale gazed toward the rear of the property, his eyes pausing in the direction of his Labrador lying under a tree, now illuminated by the setting sun. The dog opened its eyes for a moment, blinked into the light, and then closed them again.

"And remember," Hale finally said. "Exposure goes two ways. You think little Melvin and the boys want to have their secrets displayed to the world? Can you imagine the looks he'll get from the parents of the kids at the college? They'll all wonder why the church assigned Brother Fox to the student chicken coop. I'm not sure he wants to live with that kind of humiliation. And even if he was willing, the church wouldn't let him."

Hale rested his cup and saucer on his lap.

"In the end, it's all about money, of which I have an enormous amount." Hale spread his arms to encompass the gardens and mansion behind him. "The only heaven is on earth, at least for those that can afford it. And my money is untouchable, should the boys sue me. Not only is it all under the control of the foundation, but the foundation itself is housed offshore. That way I can still control it. In this castle I'm immune, and from my throne I can distribute alms to those I choose, for the purposes I choose."

"But you won't be finishing out your days here, but in a hell on earth. A prison cell."

"Are you intellectually deaf or just not listening?"

"There's no statute of limitations on murder."

Hale snorted again. "Anyone who could tie me to any of the murders is dead. At most you have a circumstantial case. I may be the man with the last word, but there's no one alive who heard me speak it. The dead, my friend, are both deaf and mute. The most you could possibly have is hearsay."

Donnally extracted his tape recorder from his jacket pocket and set it on the table between them. He left his gun exposed.

"A confession?" Hale smiled. "You expect me to confess? You're insane." Hale reached for the bell. "I think I've had enough of this."

Donnally didn't interfere. Instead he turned on the recorder. The voice was a whisper:

This is the dying declaration of William Sherwyn.

Hale's eyes widened for just a second, then he looked at Donnally. "It doesn't make any difference what he said. It's all hearsay."

"You should've studied up for a day like this," Donnally said. "A dying declaration is the exception to the hearsay rule."

El Mandamas is Albert Hale. He established White Sands.

Hale glanced over his shoulder at the sound of the door opening behind him. He grabbed the recorder and fumbled with it, jabbing at buttons.

I was present in Hale's house when he gave Gregorio Cruz ten thousand dollars in cash and ordered him to kill Harlan Donnally.

Hale wrapped his hands around the device, muffling the sound, then thrust it toward Donnally.

"Turn this damn thing off."

Donnally took it from him.

When Anna Keenan threatened to expose us, I had no choice but to—

Donnally pressed the "off" button.

The butler came to a stop next to Hale, who looked up and waved him away.

Hale waited until the butler was out of hearing range. His face was flushed and sweating.

"What do you want? A payoff? Is that what this is, extortion?"

"It would more properly be called blackmail," Donnally said, smiling. "Extortion relies on a threat of violence. Blackmail on a threat of exposure or, in this case, of dying an excruciating death in a prison hospital." Donnally paused for a moment. "It's interesting. Sherwyn didn't make that mistake. He called it by its correct name when I offered him what he thought was a chance to buy his way out."

"So this was about money all along." Hale forced a smirk, attempting to conceal his vulnerability behind a wall of sarcasm. "So that maybe you can buy a new stove for your little café? Perhaps add some outdoor seating? Maybe a mosquito zapper?"

"Actually, I've decided on a new career."

Donnally extended his hands before him, mimicking Hale's earlier examination of his manicured nails.

"I think I've flipped enough burgers for a while," Donnally said. "I'm looking for something that would be more satisfying, something that will allow me to make a more substantial contribution to the world."

Hale swallowed and licked his dry lips. "And that would be?"

Donnally reached into his jacket and pulled out a power of attorney and held it up so Hale could read the title.

"I've decided to become the head of what used to be called the Albert Hale Foundation."

Hale shuddered as the implication of Donnally's demand blasted through the brick and mortar of his psychological defenses.

"Don't worry," Donnally said, handing him the two-page document and a pen. "I won't let you starve. I may even let you stay here."

Hale accepted it. His body hunched as though he thought the mansion was about to collapse over him. His hands vibrated too hard for him to focus on the words.

"I'll . . . I'll need to have my lawyer look at this."

"There are two problems with that," Donnally said. "First, your lawyer is the one that drafted it. And second, if you hire another one, you better make it a specialist in criminal defense."

Donnally pulled out his cell phone. He punched in a number, waited a few moments, then said, "This is Harlan Donnally, let me speak to Lieutenant Navarro."

"Give me a minute," Hale said, his face reddening around the crimson splotches of his disease. "You can't expect . . ."

Donnally reached for the recorder and held it up to the phone.

Hale threw up his palm. "Stop." He signed on the last page.

Donnally disconnected and took the pages back.

"You'll never get away with this," Hale said, intending the words to sound like a threat, but they came out like a whimper.

Donnally rose to his feet without answering, but before he could take a step, Hale reached out into the emptiness around him and asked, "What did you mean, 'used to be called the Albert Hale Foundation'?"

Donnally displayed the power of attorney toward Hale.

"Read the fine print."

Hale grabbed for it, but Donnally pulled it away. Hale bit on his knuckle as he skimmed down the text, then squinted at the last paragraph.

Donnally let him finish reading it, then turned toward the side gate leading to the driveway.

"Wait," Hale said. "I still don't understand. Who is Mauricio Quintero?"

Donnally stopped. Images of Mauricio clicked through his mind like falling dominoes, ending with the little man's lifeless body in the Mount Shasta hospital, his sad brown face framed by the starched pillow, his handwritten confession lying in a drawer next to him.

Who Mauricio Quintero had been was the question that started Donnally on the trail that had brought him to this spot. And in understanding Anna's life and death he'd found an answer, but it wasn't one Hale had the right to hear, much less one he'd understand.

Donnally started walking toward the street and the declining sun that would soon abandon Hale to an empty twilight, and then said over his shoulder:

"Let's just say he was a friend who asked me to deliver a letter."

The idea for the story told in *Act of Deceit* arose out of a number of events.

In 1986 an individual I will identify as X walked into a furniture store in California and stabbed a clerk. He fled, leaving the broken blade in her body. X was arrested, charged with attempted murder, and sent for psychiatric treatment. After X completed counseling, the district attorney moved the Superior Court to dismiss the charges, which it did.

A year later he slashed his next-door neighbor to death.

On the motion of the public defender, X was sent under 1368 of the California Penal Code for an evaluation of his competence to stand trial for the homicide. He was found to be both mentally ill and developmentally disabled. He was returned to court a year later and was again found to be incompetent.

Since that time, no court has made a determination on whether X has recovered his competence to stand trial. Indeed, for more than a decade the Superior Court had not received a report of his mental condition. The most recent report I found in his court file concerned another defendant altogether.

This all came to light a couple of years ago when a friend of mine, who had spent his career working in the mental health field, reminded me of the concerns he had back in 1988 that X was pretending to be mentally ill, malingering, in order to avoid trial for the homicide. Indeed, the head psychiatrist at the out-patient facility that X was attending at the time of the crime had warned the staff prior to the murder that X was not mentally ill, but was a sociopath who was a danger to others at the facility.

My friend's more general complaint was that since so many sociopaths claim mental illness to excuse their crimes, the public has come to believe that the mentally ill are more dangerous than everyone else. And this is not, in fact, the case.

After this conversation with my friend, I decided to find out what happened to X.

Because of medical and psychiatric confidentiality rules, this was not an easy task. The details of my investigation are unimportant, but in the end, I discovered that X was housed in a developmental center in a county far from the one in which he was arrested and being detained solely under a California civil code that allows developmentally disabled violent individuals to be held until a civil court determines that they no longer represent a danger to the community.

Based on information from those I interviewed in the course of looking for X, it seemed unlikely that X was developmentally disabled, since the symptoms first appeared, not when he was a child, but when he was in his twenties. And based on the fact of his transfer from a psychiatric to a developmental center, it was clear that state psychiatrists had already determined that the mental problems that had otherwise justified his detention had been resolved.

I interviewed X, who acknowledged to me that he had killed his neighbor. Although he referred to the crime as a "murder," he offered a manslaughter defense: that he hadn't taken his medications, that he was under the influence of drugs and alcohol, and that he had "blacked out."

More likely than not, he went to his neighbor's house to rob her of money to buy drugs. A felony murder and a capital crime.

X also told me that he had been advised by his attorney on the morning of our conversation that there was a good chance that the civil court judge hearing his case on the following day would grant her motion to set a date for his release.

I made sure that didn't happen.

At X's next hearing, I understand, the positions taken by the state and by his attorney reversed: the state arguing for his release from the center and his return to the county of his arrest for trial, and his attorney arguing for his continued detention.

As of this writing, no court has yet been asked to rule on whether X is currently competent to stand trial. I don't know whether he is or he isn't, but the integrity of the justice system requires an answer.

It then crossed my mind: What if one of the many criminal defendants in civil detention around the country was, unlike X, factually innocent of the crime with which he or she was charged?

As always, when the innocent have been wrongly prosecuted, the guilty escape punishment.

This suggested the idea of using the civil commitment of a mentally ill but innocent person as part of a cover-up.

At the same time as I had these thoughts, my wife was engaged in one of her numerous investigations on behalf of victims of Catholic-priest child molestations. Many of her investigations required her to locate witnesses and documents relating to incidents that happened as long as forty years ago. In the course of her work, and with the help of Catholics disturbed by the church's defensive and immoral response to the allegations, she was able to develop contemporaneous evidence of the crimes.

In a separate context, and unrelated to the molestation cases, I was asked to investigate whether, and to what extent, there existed corporate and financial links between the Vatican and the church's operations in various countries. I learned that the Vatican had structured itself in a manner to insulate it from liability for acts committed in the church's name and had employed banks and private bankers in the main money laundering and tax evasion centers around the world in an attempt to do so.

In a very few instances, the church has accepted responsibility for not turning the guilty over to the criminal courts for prosecution and for reassigning molesters from one parish to another.

In many cases, however, representatives of the church destroyed personnel records containing complaints of abuse and the names of the victims and witnesses; spent tens of millions of dollars on teams of lawyers (it once sent five law firms up against a single plaintiff's lawyer, and still could not prevent an adverse judgment); attempted to mislead judges, juries, and the public about the facts of the cases; and while building in Northern California the most expensive cathedral in the nation at a cost of nearly two hundred million dollars, complained that the plaintiffs were financially ruining the church.

There were, of course, many more victims of abuse than have come forward. Some declined out of embarrassment, some because they didn't want to have their suffering reduced to a matter of cash value, and some because they didn't want their lives flayed open by church lawyers.

And until the church begins to treat the abuse of parishioners as a matter of moral inclusion, rather than of legal combat, and fulfills the duty of confession that it imposes on its members, the number of victims will never be counted and justice will never be done, either in the United States or abroad.

At the same time, the church has no monopoly on the abuse of children. In the course of my work, which took me to many parts of the world, I interviewed victims of sex trafficking—Thai, Chinese, Indian, Mexican—and met those who were complicit in their abuse—business leaders, parents, smugglers, government officials, police officers—and I wanted to display the roles of at least some of these coconspirators in this story.

In particular, I made Sherwyn a medical professional not only because I knew of a molested child who was again molested by the psychiatrist to whom he was sent for treatment, but also because, like doctors who keep prisoners healthy enough to be tortured, there are doctors, particularly in the Third World, who assist sex traffickers by keeping children healthy enough to be abused.

ACKNOWLEDGMENTS

An investigator's task ends when the facts have been discovered. A writer, on the other hand, can't leave well enough alone. It was during my migration from one to the other that I conceived this novel.

Helping me in doing so were: fishing and environmental writer Seth Norman, a master of character and meander. Rick Monge, a master investigator and barbecuer. Bruce Kaplan, whose "What about . . ." has made me a better writer. David Agretelis, whose keen hands are as deft with an editorial pen as they are on the keys of a saxophone and the grapes on the vine. Denise Fleming, who understands that the first fifty pages are a lifetime. Melissa Buron, European Art Curatorial Assistant at the Legion of Honor Museum in San Francisco, for help in locating the particulars of Goya's "Hunting for Teeth" in the *Los Caprichos* etching series.

Special thanks to my editor, Gabe Robinson, whose insights helped me weave together the sometimes disconnected threads of my story; to Pamela Spengler-Jaffe and Wendy Ho, who have done such a magnificent job of introducing my books to readers; to Eileen DeWald, who guides their production; and to Eleanor Mikucki, whose last, careful reading of the manuscripts has been invaluable.

Thanks also to those whose good selves, great work, and useful lives have brought light first to an investigator's life, then to a writer's, spent too long in the shadow of evil: Gail Monge, Margie Schmidt, Judy Barley, Gary Cox, Jean Rogers, Julie Quater, John Beuttler, Barbara Marinoff, and Kristi Bradford.

I borrowed from my mother-in-law, Alice Litov, her use of spreadsheets to keep track of elderly or homebound members of her church for whom she organizes visits.

As always, I borrowed from my wife, Liz, her good judgment.

5848

ELECTRIFYING SUSPENSE FROM #1
NEW YORK TIMES **BESTSELLING AUTHOR**

ANDREW
GROSS

THE BLUE ZONE // 978-0-06-114341-0

The Blue Zone: The state most feared, when there is a suspicion that a subject's new identity has been penetrated or blown. When he or she is unaccounted for, is out of contact with the case agent, or has fled the safety of the program.
—from the Witness Protection Program manual

THE DARK TIDE // 978-0-06-114343-4

On the morning Karen Friedman learns that her husband, a hedge fund manager, has been killed, Detective Ty Hauck begins his investigation of another man's death in a suspicious hit-and-run. The two seemingly unrelated tragedies are about to plunge Karen and Ty into a maelstrom of murder, money, and unthinkable conspiracy.

DON'T LOOK TWICE // 978-0-06-114345-8

The truth behind a drive-by shooting is a gathering storm of secrets and corruption that could tear through the mansions of the town's most powerful—ravaging a family . . . and pitting Ty Hauck against his own brother.

RECKLESS // 978-0-06-165601-9

A close friend from Ty Hauck's past is murdered along with her family. Now Ty will risk everything to avenge her death.